DEATH'S DOOR

Small Mountain Publishing

Other books by Dannie C Hill

IN SEARCH OF A SOUL

TYLER HILL'S DECISION

OUTER WORLD PRAIRIE

DEATH'S DOOR

By

Dannie C Hill

Author: Dannie C Hill

Published by
Small Mountain Publishing

Houston, Texas
http://smallmoutainpub.com

ISBN-13: **978-0-9826924-6-2**
ISBN-10: **0-9826924-6-3**

Cover Design by **Amanda Matthews**
http://amdesignstudios.net/

Copy Editor, **A Mauren**
http://amdesignstudios.net/

Proof Editor, **Sherry Ruschell**

Interior Design, Small Mountain
Publishing

First printing in
The United States of America

Note from the author:

Writing a novel isn't a one person effort. The author writes a manuscript and it is his/her feelings, mind and heart that come to the pages. Then the hard work to make a manuscript a novel begins. Without supporters, readers and editors a novel would not reach the stage of being ready to present to readers.

Terry Patterson- First Reader

A Mauren- Copy Editor

Sherry Ruschell- Proof Editor

Amanda Matthews- Book Cover Designer

All of these people, and more, work behind the scene to help make Death's Door a good and professional read that people like you will enjoy.

Dedication:

I want to thank my friends and family for their support
and understanding during my writing process. The love
of my life, my wife, always gives me the time I need
and kind touches when I ignore everything around me
while my muse takes control of my life.

Death's Door

Chapter 1

"Dell, snap out of it! We've got business to take care of."

Dell Sharpton's mind was a black cloud—a place he lived in more and more these days. He was nothing—a part of the void—and it suited him fine. He felt the nudge of his consciousness but didn't respond. Darkness had followed him all his life but it seemed to grow stronger as the years passed by.

Bill Anders, Dell's longtime partner, whispered, "Come on, Dell."

"What's the matter with him? We can't have this wacko here right now. Wilson, take him downstairs and get him out of the way. Then get your butt back here. I have a bad feeling about this one."

"Hang on, Captain. You know he gets these feelings and it's saved my life more than once." Bill turned his attention back to his partner. "Dell, come on back. We're going to need you on this one." Bill slapped Dell lightly on the cheek a few times and he heard the now familiar groan. "Here he comes. Just give me a minute to wake him up."

"We don't have all day, Anders. If these suspects run on us, it will take years to find them again. Besides, this tip is real.

If they've got that bomb-making material in there, we may all be joining them in paradise. You've got three minutes!"

Light was breaking up the darkness and in Dell's vision he saw two men standing behind a plain brown door with shotguns ready. There was death in their fevered eyes. They glanced at one another and each in his turn touched his heart and kissed his lips with his right hand. They were ready to die and receive the bounty of paradise.

"Come on, Dell. It's time to get back in the game. Don't leave me hanging."

"Yeah, yeah. Give me a minute," Dell said as he wiped his face with his hands. "Help me up. What's going on?"

The captain blurted out softly, "What's going on? Oh, man. We don't need this clown. Take him downstairs, Wilson."

Wilson moved to Dell's side and lifted him to a standing position. Dell was six feet one inch tall with wide shoulders and Wilson had to take a good grip while Dell got his balance.

Dell's vision cleared and he looked down the long hallway and saw the plain brown door. He shook his arm loose from Wilson's grip and felt for his pistol. It was there in his underarm holster.

"Okay. Bill, hold these... these people back and let me take a quick look." He started down the hallway and the captain whispered, "Where the hell are you going?"

"Take it easy, Captain. Give him a minute to take a look."

"Wilson, you and Herman get down there with him. If things go bad, I'll send in the army." Wilson and the other officer moved down the hallway about ten steps behind Dell.

Dell never hesitated. When he reached the doorway, he pulled his weapon and emptied his clip into either side of the doorway and the last two rounds into the center of the door.

As he fired, shotgun blasts from the other side of the wall tore away the doorframe sending chards of wood and lead pellets flying past Dell. Hearing a grunt, he turned to see both Wilson and the other man lying on the floor. Dell looked back at the brown door hanging by one hinge and put his left foot into it sending it flying into the room and then he stepped through. He had already put a fresh clip in his .45 cal. pistol. Two men were lying in pools of blood. One had part of his face torn off and the other had a pink froth bubbling from his chest. His hand reached for something in his pocket and Dell put two more rounds into him, one in the head and one in the chest. He stepped past the bodies, avoiding the pooling blood, and entered the *crime scene.*

Dell added two rounds to his clip and as he holstered his weapon he heard a rush of people coming at him. He never looked back.

The captain pulled his radio out and called wildly, "Get me EMS up here, pronto! We got two good guys down and two bad guys." He looked at the bodies lying inside the room and screamed at Dell, "What the hell was that? We have a search warrant, not a shoot the hell out of everything warrant. What do you think you're doing, buster?"

"Captain. Don't bust a blood vessel over this. Let's see what we've got," said Bill.

Dell returned from the main room and after a deadpan look at the captain he gently opened the jacket pocket of the man he finished off and pulled out a tiny device with a red LED light on. He carefully opened the back and removed a green wire and the light went dead. Then he tossed it to the captain. "You can push the button now and we probably won't die."

Bill Anders had slipped past Dell and called out, "Captain. Get in here!"

Captain Phil Teasdale walked into the room after he told the others to set up a crime scene and let no one else enter. Bill was standing beside a table laden with what looked like bricks of plastic explosives, all neatly stacked, and a green flag with a crescent moon and morning star draped over one corner.

"If it was me, I wouldn't push any buttons on that thing. Or if you do, give me about a five-minute warning," said Bill Anders.

Captain Teasdale lifted the flag off the corner of the carefully arranged stack of explosives and saw another red LED with wires running to the explosives. He bent over to look at the wiring. Dell came up behind him and slapped the tabletop, making Teasdale jump up and hit his head on the bottom of the table. "Oow! What the...?"

"Move out of the way and I'll deal with this," said Dell. And before Teasdale could respond—actually he was trying to make sure his heart was still beating—Dell stooped down and yanked the wire lead with the detonators out from the stack of plastic explosives. Dell turned and said, "Okay, now you can push it." He walked out of the apartment.

Captain Teasdale, still holding his chest, muttered, "I hate that guy. He's going to get us all killed one of these days."

Bill said, "He might at that, but today he saved our asses. Let me deal with him, Captain. He's had a pretty rough time of it lately." Bill hurried out to catch up with Dell.

A member of the bomb squad checked the explosives and gave the okay to bring in the crime scene team to gather any information they could find.

Captain Teasdale's cell phone rang and he jumped and then looked around sheepishly. No one laughed but several men and women held tight to their smiles.

Captain Teasdale answered the phone with a gruff, "Teasdale. This better be good. I'm investigating an important case and don't have... Yes, Commissioner... sorry. We've just finished off two terrorists that had a large bomb ready to go... Yes, Commissioner. I'm ready to listen." The others could hear the buzz of a loud voice that didn't sound happy. The captain said, "Yes, sir. The NSA wants Dell Sharpton to report to Washington ASAP. I hope they know what they're getting into. He's a nutcase and... Yes sir, he did kill both terrorists and defuse the bomb, but he could have gotten us all... Yes, sir. I am glad to be alive... Yes, sir. I think that's a great idea. I will put a lid on my mouth. I'll have him report to your office as soon as I find him... He just took off and I sent Bill Anders to make sure he wasn't going to... Yes, sir. I remember what you said. He'll be there in thirty minutes. Thank you, Commissioner, and I would just like to say... Commissioner?"

Teasdale closed his cell and muttered to himself, "How does he always know what just happened?" He looked around at everyone looking at him. "What is this? It's not break time! Get back to work! I've got a list of your names and if any of that last conversation gets out I'll have all your asses up..." A lamp fell with a loud crash just behind Captain Teasdale and he jumped, screamed and then grabbed his heart again. He left the room as a few muffled chuckles broke out.

Bill Anders found Dell in a local pub just a few blocks away from the crime scene. He was downing a *Jameson*—neat—with a disgruntled bartender looking on. Bill never said a word but just walked in, sat next to Dell and pointed at the bar in front of him. The bartender started to open his mouth but the look Dell gave him made him reconsider. He served the drink and then refilled Dell's glass. Dell already had three unfiltered cigarettes stubbed out in an ashtray in front of him.

"I wish you'd learn how to drink a good Scotch. This Irish stuff tastes like warm..."

"If I wanted bog dirt in my whiskey I'd get my own dirt. This *Irish wine* is the only thing I can drink without getting sick."

"You keep smoking those camel turds and they're going to kill you."

"I can only hope."

"Are you okay, Dell? That stunt back there took five years off my life. And the captain is going to have to change his shorts. I'm surprised he didn't break that table with his head. You sure know how to influence the boss."

"Teasdale's okay. He just needs to back off. I'm thinking about putting in for a transfer, but who else will have me? How are Wilson and Herman doing?"

"Their vests caught most of it and Herman took a few pelts in the left arm. Wilson was nicked in the leg."

"They shouldn't have followed me. I had it under control."

"Under control? You went in there like John Wayne blazing away. What if you'd hit those explosives?"

"One round did. That stuff is like *Play-Doh* as long as our friendly neighborhood Hajji doesn't push the switch."

"Well, he won't be pushing anything but daisies now. Do you think they're enjoying the seventy-two virgins?"

"Those martyrs are dead and gone. There ain't nothing but a black void waiting for them and us."

Bill looked at Dell for a moment trying to judge how far their friendship really went. Bill took to Dell as soon as they were made partners. He was a big guy with dark brown hair that always seemed to need combing and Dell had deep brown eyes that either looked inside you or through you. Right away Bill knew this was the kind of partner that would watch his back.

He asked, "I know you don't like to talk about your past but you are getting crazier every week."

"What do you want, Bill?" Bill was right. Dell could feel his mind wanting to stay under and it was the perfect place for him.

"Why are your blackouts getting worse? How do you get these visions?"

Dell looked at Bill. He was the closest thing to a friend Dell had had in years and the truth was he kept Dell alive. Dell didn't blame him for that. "There are two answers to that; the one I used to give the shrinks, or the one I've never told anyone. Which do you want?"

"If you're going to tell me anything, I'd like the truth," Bill said as he downed the Jameson with a grimace.

"I was in Sudan as a kid living with a Bedouin tribe and I was bitten by a desert spider. The wound got infected and I should have died, but the people wouldn't let me.

"Ever since then I've had vivid dreams—every night. Now I get little glimpses of bad things about to happen. These... dreams are coming more often and at any time of the day or night, but I don't know why."

Bill said, "Never mind. If you don't want to tell me... Where is Sudan?"

Bill's cell chirped out *You Drive Me Crazy*. "That's either my ex-wife or the captain—either way it can only be trouble," he said as he touched his phone. "Anders... Oh, hi, Captain... Yeah, we're just enjoying a cup of tea... Just down the street. What can I do for you...? The Commissioner...? Okay. I'll get him there pronto. Oh, Captain. Dell says he's sorry for startling you... Well, no. He didn't actually say that but I know how he thinks."

Bill ended the call and dropped his head before he spoke. "The Commissioner wants to see you right away."

Dell motioned for a refill, turned it up, stood and paid the tab. "Let's get this over with." He started for the door.

"Maybe you're going to get a medal."

Commissioner Pat O'Hara sat in his office wondering how he was going to convince Dell Sharpton that seeing NSA people was a good thing. He had worked with Dell his entire career. He actually liked the dark-minded SOB. Even at the academy he was a magnet for trouble but he always came out the other end—without a smile. He had never met anyone so determined to die but never succeeding. He had been on the streets with him in the old days when Dell would walk right in the middle of a shootout or a gang-fight and never get a scratch. As the years went by, Dell became the resident expert on Mid-Eastern and Asian troublemakers and later when they turned into terrorists he was right on top of them. He knew Arabic—several dialects—and Farsi from his youth. Dell's dad had been a *spook* and included his entire family in his travels in the Middle East. Dell was a fast learner.

The Commissioner in those days sent him to a number of top seminars on terrorist activities until the Feds refused to allow him to attend after he made them look like asses. They tried to recruit him but he would have nothing to do with their rules. Dell was a nutcase, but he was good.

The next Commissioner refused to waste money on someone determined to die, so Dell was put on Cold Case files. When Pat O'Hara took over the position he brought Dell back into the action and never received a word of thanks from Dell, but that was just the way it was with him.

Dell walked into the Commissioner's office without knocking and Bill hurriedly stepped in to close the door.

"Hold on, Anders. I want you in here with my favorite black cloud. A partner ought to share the benefits since you'll get half the credit."

"If there are any benefits for working with Dell... well, I'd just as soon be left out."

"Did that sound like a request?"

"No, sir." Bill closed the door and took a seat. Dell had already taken a seat and reached into the Commissioner's cigar box. He was snipping the end of a twenty dollar Cohiba.

"Just help yourself, detective. Mi casa es su casa," the Commissioner said in a condescending tone.

Dell reached over and plucked two more cigars, tossed one to Bill and put the other one in his jacket pocket. "Thanks, Pattie."

Bill said, "Now, Commissioner, don't listen to everything Captain Teasdale has to say about what happened..."

"You mean the part where you and Dell saved a squad of men and a bunch of civilians from getting blown to bits? Is that the part?"

"No, I was thinking of the other part, and Dell's the one that saved us. I didn't have much to do with it."

"All right. Let's cut the crap. I've known you both for a long time and I also know that if it wasn't for you, Dell would be dead and buried by now."

"Thanks a lot, Bill."

"Dell, I'd give a hundred dollars to know what went on inside your head... well, maybe ten. That was a good job out there today. I'd say brave but in your case bravery's got nothing to do with it. Now for your reward. The NSA wants you down in Washington as soon as I can get you there. And Bill, you're going to see that he gets there."

"What's the NSA want with me?"

"Damn, I knew I should have brought my crystal ball with me today. How the hell am I supposed to know? I can tell you this: it doesn't have anything to do with your charm. The Vice President called me and told me what they want and it's you, Dell."

"I don't go anywhere without Anders."

"Didn't I just say he was to get you there?"

"What I mean is he's in or I'm out. Call the VP and tell him that. By the way, who is the VP now?"

"Johnston Barley. He's so right wing the leftist media won't even attend his press conferences."

"Sounds like my kind of man. Too bad I don't vote."

"I'll do what I can to get Bill in there with you, but I can't promise anything with the Feds."

Chapter 2

Bill was driving north to I-195 to cross the Garden State and head south to D.C. Their state task force headquarters was in Brick Township and it was a bit over two hundred miles to Washington. "Do you think I should use the lights and siren?"

"If you do I might be forced to shoot you. Just drive and let me rest. We're going to hit traffic no matter how fast you go so take it easy."

Dell eased into the black void and the two men he had killed a few hours before were waiting. Their bodies were shredded but their eyes blazed red in the darkness. Dell smiled and he wondered how they were enjoying paradise. He wanted to join them full time and be done with his miserable life.

Even from childhood he could count on one hand the times he had actually been happy. It always involved a woman or the desert. The rest of the time he felt like a ninety pound weakling on a football team: worthless. But here in the void he was exactly what and where he wanted to be. No decisions, no hurting, no heartache, just nothing. He could spend forever here but there was always something calling him back.

He used to think it was his partner but these last few months he would catch the outline of someone small. He fought to escape this form that followed him and usually it only lasted for a moment, but other times he could feel it stalking him, waiting for him. He turned to confront it but it slipped into the black mist and never let him get a good look.

There was someone else in Dell's dreams and he came more and more often these past few months. Dell's twin brother. It had been a hot summer afternoon in the woods three miles from the family farm in South Carolina. Dell and Peter were five years old and they were chasing a flying squirrel. It had run up a spindly tulip poplar tree and Dell sent Peter up to make it jump. Dell had the cardboard box ready to catch it when it leaped for the ground. They were getting good at catching them. Their papa made cages out of dried kudzu vines and chicken wire. They would sell the squirrels in town. It was considered good luck to have a caged squirrel. Dell and Peter even had one of their own they called Melvin. Melvin the flying squirrel was a real prize.

Dell had taunted Peter to move faster and not to let it climb too high. The squirrel ran out a long thin limb and sat there watching the show. Dell wanted a new Schwinn Phantom and if Dell wanted it then Peter wanted it too. That's the way it was with the twins. Dell thought up what they wanted and Peter automatically wanted it as well.

Peter never hesitated as he moved out onto the thin, brittle, smooth gray limb. He was halfway out when it cracked, causing the squirrel to leap into flight. Dell ran as fast as he could and the squirrel flew right into the box. Dell let out a whoop and excitedly ran back to where Peter lay on the ground. Dell was yelling to Peter that they finally had their bike but when he saw the blood he stopped ten feet away. Peter's eyes were open, looking at Dell, but Dell knew he was dead.

Dell turned and ran to his father's workshop. He never opened the box with the squirrel inside. He just picked up a big hammer and crushed the box until he saw the blood seeping out.

"Dell... Dell. Come on, buddy. We're here." Bill got out of the car after rolling down the windows and reached in to slip Dell's weapon from its holster. Then he shook Dell and slapped his face. "Rise and shine."

Dell reached for his weapon and opened his eyes with a wild crazy stare.

"It's me. No need to go off on anybody. Snap out of it."

Dell's mind finally caught up with him and he looked around at the tree-lined street and then turned his head to look at Bill standing a few feet away from the car.

Bill said, "It's me. Man, that was some dream you were having. Are you okay? We're two hundred yards from the address the Commish gave us."

"Don't ever take my weapon."

"I'll take it every time when I see you stiff as steel and your knuckles white from the fist you are making. Remember the time I didn't take it? You almost blew my head off. You okay, Dell?"

"Yeah. I need a drink."

"Not 'til we see these people. Here, put this monster away," he said as he handed the weapon back. "You're getting worse all the time and it's even starting to scare me."

Dell looked around at the tree-lined street with neat manicured lawns and smallish middle-class houses. "Where are we?"

"Somewhere in Arlington Forest. Doesn't seem like the place the NSA would hang out."

"Let's get this over with. These *spooks* really like to play it up. I guess if I were a terrorist this isn't the place I would look for them."

Bill got back in the car and drove to First Street north to an older two-story redbrick house with a front yard in need of work and a paved driveway that went around to the back of the house. He pulled in the drive and approached a steel gate that offered no view of the back of the house. There was no callbox, but as he approached the double gate swung open and he drove through. There was a black Suburban SUV parked in front of a two-car garage. The garage doors were open and Bill pulled in. As soon as the car cleared the doors, they shut automatically and bright lights filled the room. He could see cameras sweeping his car and a number of lights blinked on other equipment.

A voice said, "Exit the automobile to the left and arrange your weapons on the bonnet. Then take two steps back."

"The bonnet?"

Dell said, "The hood."

They got out, with Dell sliding over to the driver's side.

Bill said, "I'm not giving up my pistol until I see who's doing the talking."

"Just do it," said Dell as he placed his weapon on the hood and took two steps back. Bill did the same.

The LEDs blinked several times and the voice said, "Mr. Anders. The backup piece as well." Bill pulled a small .32 revolver from its ankle holster and placed it on the hood. Then a door opened that led into an enclosed walkway.

"Follow the green array." Small green lights flashed in sequence and they followed them into the hallway. The door slammed shut behind them.

"What the hell is going on?" Bill asked.

"I guess we're getting ready to take off."

"What?"

Dell said, "Don't worry. It's just *spook* stuff."

At the end of the hallway another door opened and they followed the stairway down to a lavishly appointed foyer with an office beyond. They stepped through the doorway and it slammed shut.

"Hey, Dell. I got a bad feeling about this."

A young man came through a hidden door on the other side of the room. He wore what looked to be Armani and he practically pranced over to Bill and Dell.

"Spot on time. I am William and I will assist you on your visit. Can I offer you a cuppa tea?"

Dell said, "Jameson for me and he'll have water."

"I do apologize, but we only offer tea. I think Earl Grey with cream will hit the spot. Please have a seat."

As he left the room Bill leaned over and whispered, "That one might not be gay but I bet he sits when he pees." Dell didn't reply. The young man returned and gave Bill a scathing look but then smiled at Dell and served them tea.

Dell downed his tea in one gulp and said, "Let's get on with this. I've got better things to do than sit around drinking tea. And where are the crumpets?"

"Oh, my. I've abandoned my manners. I'm afraid that one," pointing at Bill, "well, he isn't very polite, is he?" Without waiting for an answer he swished from the room and quickly returned with a tray of cookies, giving Bill another condescending glance. After they wolfed down a couple of crumpets William said, "I will introduce you to Madame Loretta Smithe in a twinkling but I must elucidate the proper social deportment and, of course, the necessity of secrecy with any and all things that may or may not transpire while under her invitation. Am I making myself decipherable?"

"What the hell did he just say?" asked Bill.

Dell answered, with a near smile touching his eyes, "Mind your manners and get ready to get shot if you tell anyone about this. Be nice to Loretta."

"Oh..."

"This way, gentlemen." He looked down his nose at Bill as he spoke.

Bill said, "What did I do? You're the one that people usually hate right off the bat. I don't think this *Twinkie* likes me."

"Maybe you should take him out for dinner and dancing when we get through here."

William ignored the remarks as best he could but at the mention of dinner and dancing he gave Bill a bright, soulful smile. Bill muttered, "Don't get your hopes up, Willie."

William led them to a paneled wall and went through a process of touching paintings on the wall and adjusting a figurine and finally the panel slid aside to elevator doors that stood open. He stood to the side as first Dell and then Bill entered. His hand caressed Bill's as he passed by and Bill jerked his hand so fast it hit the door frame with a bang. Before he could say anything, the doors slid shut and they began to descend.

"I'm going to pop that guy in the mouth if he comes on to me again!"

"You should be flattered. I think he likes you."

"Well, he can kiss my..."

The door opened before Bill could finish. They stepped out into a bright airy room that gave the feeling of being down in the South Carolina low country on a backwater bayou near Charleston. The smell of the ocean mixed with saltwater marsh and magnolias filled the air. The scene outside the window was a beautiful open lawn with giant water oaks lining the wide driveway. Men and women on horseback trotted through the yard dressed in light riding outfits. The southern heat was there as well.

"You think they have one of those transporters like in *Star Trek*?"

"Bill. We're at least fifty feet below ground and we're still in D.C. Remember this is the NSA and don't go getting friendly with the natives. I need a drink."

Loretta Smithe watched the two men as they gazed out at the scene in front of them. Dell looked just as she knew he would. Dark, brooding and strong. She wanted to get closer to him.

This was her first look at Bill. He hadn't been part of her plans until she read Dell's file. Bill was six feet tall with dark red hair and sky blue eyes. Looking twenty-five, he was actually thirty years old. He had a thin frame but it denoted strength. It was his face that she admired the most. Bill had an open face and smiled most of the time. He had one of those faces that couldn't hide what he was thinking. The kind of face that made people automatically like him. Loretta knew that Dell would do nothing for them if Bill wasn't included.

"Please. Won't you join me?"

The men turned around and looked at a beautiful woman standing with a bright smile on her face. "Mr. Anders, Mr. Sharpton, please come in and have a seat. Can I get you anything to drink?" She hugged and kissed them and waited for their answers.

Dell said, "If it's tea, I'll pass."

Her laugh was so sweet Bill just stared. She had a soft southern accent that would put anyone at ease. "I see you've met William. Don't let his... ways put you off. He's a darling— really. Let's see. May I call you by your given names? Bill, I believe you are a Scotch man and I know for a fact Dell only drinks Jameson. I prefer the Irish myself. Please, follow me."

"Close your mouth, Bill. You look like you're hunting flies."

"Dell, did you get a look at that one? I'd like to take her home and..."

"Keep in mind they can hear everything you say and we don't know the way out."

"Okay, okay, but she's a beauty!"

"If you like that type."

Loretta Smithe walked towards a sideboard to prepare the drinks. She was wearing a light yellow sundress that hugged her tall slim figure. Long blonde hair cascaded down her back and bounced in rhythm to her swaying hips. A scent of jasmine trailed in her wake. When she got to the sideboard, she turned to rest her hip against it and gave them a good view of her tight athletic figure.

"If that's not your type then you need to see a shrink. She's hotter than a two-dollar pistol. I've never seen lips that red before."

"Okay. She's pretty. Just keep in mind where we are. Wipe your mouth. You're drooling." Bill hurriedly wiped his hand across his mouth but his eyes never left Loretta.

"When you boys are through gossiping and admiring the view, come and have a seat. Your drinks are ready."

They sat down on a dark leather couch and she stood across the coffee table and bent to serve them. Despite Dell's supposed lack of interest, his eyes locked on the creamy cocoa-tanned breasts that threatened to leap out at them. She gathered her drink and moved to stand in front of them and clinked her glass with theirs. Bill sat staring at her breasts and when he realized she was watching him he blushed and started to put his drink down on the table.

"Now, Bill, you know it's bad luck not to take at least a little sip after you touch glasses. See, Dell knows what to do." Bill looked over at Dell who was finishing his off. He glanced back at Loretta's big blue eyes looking at him and quickly gulped down a big swallow and nearly choked.

"There now, that's better." She took a small sip of hers and then handed it to Dell. "Take this one, Dell, but go slow. I like a man that goes slow. I'll mix another." She turned and returned to the sideboard.

Bill leaned over but before he could say anything Dell held up his index finger to shut him up. Loretta came back and took a seat next to Dell. Their hips were touching.

"Miss Smithe. What are we doing here?"

"Please now, Dell, call me Loretta." She leaned over him to touch Bill's arm, pressing her breasts into Dell. "And that goes for you too, Bill." She turned her head and looked into Dell's brown eyes. She could see the green flecks and a spark of interest in them. She sat back and then decided to move to the leather chair across from them. She crossed her legs and smiled at Bill until his eyes finally looked up into hers.

"William's going to be disappointed that he's not your type."

"My type! Hey, I'm not a..." He gave it a second to change what he was going to say and then, "I mean, I'm only interested in women."

"I've noticed," she said with that angelic laugh. "You know you're not even supposed to be here. I could get in real trouble if this gets out, but I knew Dell wouldn't come unless you came with him. I was wondering if maybe you two had something going on, but I can see by your looks that's not the case."

Dell was warming to this woman. He could feel himself rising up out of his hole and wondered what kind of mayhem would follow. A woman was the only thing that could take his need to die away—if only for a little while. These people were good and he'd have to be on his toes. "Loretta, as Bill said, you're hotter than a two-dollar pistol but I wasn't asked to come down here to admire your figure. Why am I here?"

"Bill, did you really say that? That's so sweet." Bill continued doing his impression of the sunset but said nothing. "And, Dell, you're right. We need your help and it seems to me if we're going to get it then Bill is in this as well. I'll have to make a call but I do have a way of getting what I want. Finish your drinks and then I want to show you something."

She led them to another hidden door—it seemed the place was full of secret passages. They entered a darkened, rough rock tunnel that immediately took away the good feelings produced by the sunny southern room. The smell of stale, damp air and the crumbling rocks had its effect as Bill moved closer to Dell's side and he reached for his missing pistol.

Dell's mood dropped and he continued to have bad feelings about what they were getting into. It was a long passageway, perhaps one hundred and fifty yards in length. Dell had the sense that they were going in a large circle, but because the tunnel bent left and right it was hard to tell.

Ahead a single bare bulb attempted to push back the gloom but did a poor job of it. Loretta stopped in front of a battered metal door and touched a thumb pad beside the door frame and the door swung open. They entered an office that reminded Dell of a prisoner of war movie he had once seen. There were chains hanging from the wall and the ceiling. A single unfinished wooden desk and three bare wood chairs sat in the center of the room. There was also a smell of sweat, fear and other body odors that Loretta's jasmine scent couldn't blanket.

"Bill, please have a seat. I need to change so I don't muss my dress and I have something that I want to show Dell. We'll be back in a jiffy. Come along, Dell." She led Dell to another doorway and closed the door behind them.

Bill heard a loud clunk as a heavy lock barred the door. He looked around at the bare room and noticed what looked like blood stains on the floor near the wall where the chains hung. A chill ran down his spine and he looked to the door where Dell had gone, wishing they would return. His ears picked up sounds of groaning and then a muffled scream. He reached for his missing gun and swore he would not give it up again—if he got out of there alive.

Loretta led Dell to another room filled with the soft lighting of a well-appointed boudoir with plush carpet and a large four-poster bed. She turned and pressed herself to him, smiled and then she kissed him softly on the lips. "I've wanted to kiss you ever since I first read your report."

"Is that all you want to do?" He started to wrap his arms around her but she slipped from his grasp.

"We'll see. I need to change. Please have a seat." She went to an armoire and opened it to reveal a concoction of outer wear; from slinky dresses to heavy fatigues. With her back to him she reached up and slid the strings off her shoulders. She moved in slow motion as she let her dress fall to her hips. Her bare tan back revealed strong muscles that flowed down the lines of her back to two soft dimples. As she slipped the material off her hips, Dell watched the muscle play of her back and then his eyes locked on red string panties that covered nothing of her firm rear. She slipped out of her *hooker heels* and then her panties. She bent at the waist to open a drawer at the bottom of the armoire and she smiled as she heard Dell's intake of breath.

Dell forced himself to remain seated when what he really wanted to do was rush over and throw her on the bed. She was good and he knew in the back of his mind that she was playing him like a fish. He had taken the bait. She selected a pair of black panties and turned to face him before she slipped into them. Her flower was covered with a short crop of blonde hair.

Loretta knew Dell preferred that style to the bikini wax that most women had now. She liked the heat in his eyes. She watched his eyes move to her large pink nipples that came to a point. They were swollen and stiff as they moved with her body.

She turned again and selected a sports bra, pulled it over her head and then turned and moved to him, letting him take it all in. She sat in his lap and said, "You know this is all planned and it's part of my job to... entice you, but I just want you to know that I enjoyed letting you look at me. Maybe when this is over we can get together."

"That was quite a show and I enjoyed it but I have at least ten years on you and I know I'm not the kind of man you're used to. Why all the buildup?"

"First, you are the kind of man I am interested in. You may find this hard to believe but I don't troll the streets looking for men."

"Baby, you don't need to troll anywhere with your looks. Forget what I said. If you want to get together all you have to do is bend a finger." He took her in his arms and kissed her. She tasted of peaches. He moved his hand across her breasts and then slid it all the way up and took her small head and tenderly cupped it. He finished the kiss and looked into her eyes. He could see the heat and need there. "Now, what's this all about?"

She stood and as she moved back to finish dressing she said, "I know about your special talent. You know, the one where you get your visions. Like the one you had today about the suspects standing behind the door with shotguns and explosives. We have need of that talent."

"I can't control that. It just happens once in a while. Besides, I have a job that keeps me busy. The NSA has plenty of gee-whiz secret stuff. You don't need me."

"My small group is within the NSA but outside the loop. We're pretty low-tech when it comes to gathering info, but we get real creative when it's time to take action. Let's just say we don't have any letters or even a name."

"Black Ops?"

"They're a bunch of pussies."

"Who do you answer to?"

"That's classified, but we aren't some rogue group running amok doing whatever we want. We're given simple assignments and then we do whatever we have to to get the job done."

"What if I say no?"

"You won't. This is exactly the kind of job you've been wanting for years. Dell, I know all about what happened to your brother and you didn't crumble; you got back up, even if your sole purpose is getting yourself killed. What I admire most is the fact you go at it making sure no one around you dies."

Dell said, "You seem to know a lot about me."

"I know I'd like to screw you silly when this is over but what I would like more than that is to help make that need to die go away. I have my own issues. Maybe we'll compare notes one of these days."

"You are a nutcase. I'm guessing I don't have a lot of choice in this?"

"You no longer work for the New Jersey State Police."

"What about Bill? I don't want him getting into this and I don't want him losing his job."

Loretta stood by the armoire and finished dressing. She was now wearing outdoor work clothes— blue jeans and heavy cotton shirt-- still looking good. "Bill is your trigger. I'm not sure why but he's the one that controls you when you get your... visions. If it were just me doing this, I would agree with you, but you know how the government works. It's usually 100% without thinking who gets hurt. I will tell you this: I will take care of you both and keep Bill as safe as I can. I'll be out there with you and you're going to have to trust me."

Dell noticed that her cute little southern accent lost a lot when she was talking business. It was still nice to listen to but her words... penetrated. He was screwed no matter which way he turned and that's how he liked it. He'd been slipping from near death to near death for years waiting for the end but there was always something that got in the way.

Bill was divorced, had no kids and was still young. He lived for the job almost as much as Dell did. He didn't have a death wish but he never left Dell's side until Dell told him to and then he was only a few steps away. The truth was that Bill Anders had kept Dell alive for a long time and he probably wouldn't stop now.

"How is it a hot young thing like you is running this... whatever it is? What kind of background do you have? And what I really want to know is was this performance just to get me to join this venture you've got going?"

"So many questions. Can't you just enjoy the moment?"

"You've already said you're not going to screw me until I do what you ask and I have my doubts that you will even if I don't die doing whatever it is you want me to do. And I haven't enjoyed-the-moment for three years."

"First, I would ask you to trust me... a little. If I give my word then death is the only thing that will keep me from doing what I say. This *performance* is all on me... my idea. There are no hidden cameras or listening devices in this room. I made the sweep myself.

"I'm not as young as I look, but I am young for an operations chief. My background is something we may discuss at a later time, but I..." She switched to Arabic and said, "I see the warmth of your heart and the pain. You are like the hot wind of the desert that flows over ice from the White Mountain. Your soul chills me with heat so join my need to see death brought to all who would destroy goodness. You will be my sword and I will be your sheath."

Her Arabic was perfect. Dell's parents had traveled and lived in the Middle East for many years. His dad worked for the State Department as a liaison between oil rich Saudi Arabia, Egypt, Iraq, Arab Emirates, Iran and the U.S. Later Dell came to understand his father was a spy, but growing up all he knew

27

was that he was dragged all over the desert and rocks of the Middle East.

At the age of three he and his brother were sent to princes and tribal Bedouins for months at a time to learn their ways and their dialects.

After his brother's death, Dell was sent back to the desert to live with the Bedouins in Sudan.

By the age of twelve he was fluent in ten dialects of the region. He was not only fluent but spoke with the accent of a native. He was *adopted* by a Bedouin Chief who despised the oil rich kingdom of Saudi Arabia. Dell lived the hard life of the desert and rocky plains off and on until he was seventeen when his father was killed.

Before his father's death, he would return to the U.S. from time to time but only for short periods. Dell spent most of his time in the desert and that gave him little time to dwell on his brother's death.

His mother returned him to the U.S. and he entered college at the age of seventeen. University gave Dell a way to submerge himself to stop the hurt he felt for his brother's death. This was one of the many secrets Dell kept from others.

Dell answered Loretta in a dialect that most westerners would not know. "I will pierce you with my golden horn and you will fall at my feet and never dream of the cool winds of the oasis. Offer me a sweet date but place your lips on mine before I taste its nectar. This will be your proof to me."

Loretta's eyes glistened with heat as she turned and went to the nightstand beside the bed. She returned and knelt at Dell's feet, opened her shirt to reveal those perfect breasts and removed an undried date from between them. She slid up into his lap and kissed him softly and then placed the fruit in his mouth.

Dell said, "This is going to be some ride."

"I hope so."

"What do you want me to do?"

"I need you to find some people for me. We have to question them so killing is not an option at this time."

"You played this game just for that? You could have had me when you gave me the Jameson."

Chapter 3

Loretta's southern accent came back with a flourish, "If I can't play with someone that interests me then what's the point? This may even turn out to be lots of fun. Now, darlin', let's go get Bill and I'll show you what I need your help with."

They entered the *prison* office and William had Bill pressed into one of the chairs with his legs encapsulating Bill's left leg and was whispering away at Bill. Bill sat stiff-backed with a hard, frightened look in his eyes. Those eyes turned to Dell and shouted, HELP ME!

A real smile creased Dell's face as he said, "I knew William was your type."

Bill jumped out of his chair nearly knocking William over, but William was as agile as a cat as he sprang away, looking sheepishly toward Loretta.

"Now, William. I have asked you not to play with our guest. Have you explained the situation to Bill?"

"Madame, I assure you I was merely pointing out the operational procedures to Mr. Anders. I think he has a grasp of our requirements."

Loretta asked, "Bill. Do you agree with what William has explained to you?"

"Even if I don't know the way out of here, if this guy comes on to me again I'm going to pop him! Dell, let's roll. I need a cigarette and fresh air. This is some kind of nuthouse."

"Sorry, buddy, but looks like we're in this for the long haul whether we like it or not. Did you understand everything William said?"

"Said? All I was doing was trying to keep him from grabbing my... No. I didn't understand." Bill's eyes were jerking from William to Dell to Loretta and his hands had a tremor Dell had never seen before.

Loretta said, "William, leave us alone for now. We'll talk later."

"As you wish, Madame." He turned to Bill and Bill jumped back. "I'm sorry if my actions were inappropriate, Bill. I certainly did not mean to aggravate you. I was merely trying to..."

"I know what you were trying to do."

William heaved a sigh, turned, and just before he left the room he turned a dazzling smile to Bill.

"What do you mean, it's too late now?"

Dell looked at Loretta, nodded, and she said, "Bill, I have some good news and some bad news. The good news is you will be Dell's partner in this new venture. All expenses paid—up to a point—and it includes travel to exotic places. The bad news is you no longer work for the New Jersey State Police. The other bad news is everything you are hearing is classified and there would be jail time if you let any of this out. That's what William was trying to tell you."

"I know what he was doing but I didn't hear anything about a new job or jail! Dell, is this for real?"

"It's real. I only know a little more than you. That's what we've been discussing in the other room."

"I know what you were doing in there. Why do you get to be with a pretty woman and I get... William?"

"Don't worry, Bill. She told me you're next in line with her."

"Really?" Bill looked at Loretta and she winked at him. "Are we really fired?"

Loretta said, "Don't think of it as fired. Think of it as a positive move in keeping our country safe. We'll go into details

30

later and I'll personally make sure you are... satisfied. How does that sound? You and Dell wait here for a moment while I make sure everything is ready." She left them alone.

"Dell. What the hell is going on? I like my job. Just because you finally get laid, well, that's no reason to quit your job and take me down with you."

"I didn't get laid or quit. This was done as soon as we left Brick Township. Let's see what she's got for us. I didn't want them to bring you into this but that wasn't an option. It's my fault you're in. They think I can't do whatever it is I'm going to do without you."

"At least they're smart enough to know that. You can't do anything without me. I've been carrying you for eight years—except for the times you've saved my life. Hey, am I really going to get a shot at Loretta? That's enough to make my day!"

"Don't get your hopes up but I'm sure there's going to be some exciting times ahead that include her. Heck, maybe you'll hook up with William."

"They'll have to drug me to get something like that to happen."

William came into the room and gave Bill a big smile. He had a cup of tea on a tray and said, "Mr. Anders, may I offer you an exotic tea? I think it will hit the spot. I have personally prepared a room for you to relax in."

Bill's anger flared but he got ahold of it before he said, "Listen, William. I'm sure you're a nice guy. You and me isn't going to happen. I like women, not men. And I don't want to relax. I want to know what is going on. You help me with that and I'll try to be a little nicer to you."

"You are so sweet. Very well. Madame Smithe is ready for you both now. If you'll walk this way, I'll take you to her." He set the tray down, turned and pranced out of the room.

Dell looked at Bill and Bill smiled and said, "I'm not going to say it." They followed William. "Dell. How was it? Was it worth getting fired over?"

"Oh, yeah. And you're next. I just hope William hasn't spoiled you."

"So how does she look naked?"

"You've got a slow, one-track mind. You know they can still hear every word."

"Hey, they sicced a flamer on me and a hot piece of..." Bill looked around the darkened tunnel and decided he didn't want to get stuck down there. "Do you have any idea of how to get out of this funhouse?"

"Do what they say and put a lid on that mouth. Let's see what she wants."

William led them to another door and stood aside as they entered the room. He closed in behind Bill but didn't touch him.

The room was a part of a modern interrogation room with a two-way mirror, recording equipment, and an array of sensors blinking red and green. William indicated they should take a seat and then touched a switch on the wall. The mirror was a large LCD and it cleared to show a brightly lit room where a Middle Eastern man sat at a table. Loretta was there offering him a drink of water.

"Here drink this, Hamid. It's only water."

The man took the cup and drank the contents down. "I have nothing to tell you. Kill me now and save us both a lot of time."

"Now, Hamid, I'm not going to kill you. What makes you think that?"

"You Yankees kill everyone you think is a terrorist. Just because I am Muslim and from Jordan you think I must be a terrorist. I have lived in the U.S. for many years and I fled Jordan to escape just this kind of torture."

Loretta slammed her small fist down on the metal table and Hamid jumped in fear. "If you've lived here for years then you should know that calling me a Yankee is offensive to me. I'm a Southerner. Find another word when you talk about me or I might just cut off that big Arab nose! And how have I tortured you? I just want you to answer my questions."

"You want me to betray my people."

"Are your people terrorists?"

"The Palestinians—the ones you call terrorists—thought I was an informer because I did business with Americans. That's why I fled Jordan with my family. We are Americans now."

"Not for long, if you don't help us. Here, take a look at this." She opened a laptop and set it so Dell and Bill could see the screen. It showed a pretty Arab woman and three young children sitting in an airport. The woman looked worried but the children were excited to see the airplanes parked out on the tarmac. A voice over a speaker system said, "Boarding for today's flight to Amman, Jordan will begin in twenty minutes. Please make sure you have proper ID to receive a boarding pass."

Hamid looked up at Loretta in alarm. "If you send my family back to Jordan they will be tortured and killed by those fanatics!"

"And to stop this all you have to do is answer a few questions."

"Why are you doing this? I love America."

"Hamid, we tried it the easy way several times and you refused to help us."

"If I am seen talking to agents of the U.S. my family will be killed."

"By whom?"

Hamid only looked down at the tabletop and refused to answer. "Last chance, Hamid. Help us and you can return to your life with your family. Refuse and you will be on the next plane to Jordan but your family will arrive ten hours before you do."

"You can't do this. I am an American."

"You are not a citizen."

"Next month I will be a citizen."

"Next month you will be in Jordan unless you cooperate."

"And if I do, what will you do for me?"

"You get your family and life in the States back."

"And you will leave me alone?"

"An American citizen is expected to help his country stay safe."

"I must think."

"Ten minutes. That's all you have before your family boards that aircraft." Loretta left the room and came to where Dell and Bill sat watching. "What do you think?"

Dell said, "That guy is no terrorist."

"He's Muslim. They're all terrorists."

For the first time Dell's anger surfaced. It had been a long time since he'd felt the kind of heat that threatened to boil over and spew out his mouth. He said in Arabic, "You are a fool to believe that! A terrorist takes tactics like threatening a man's family with death. There are terrorists on both sides of the fence. What do you want from us?"

"Your help in finding a group that intends to kill and put fear in thousands of Americans. If you don't like my methods, what would you suggest?"

Dell switched to English. "What do you need to know?"

Loretta looked at William and nodded. He produced a thin file and placed it in front of Dell. Dell looked through it and Bill could see—just for a moment—Dell's face go white and fear in his eyes. And then it was gone; replaced by his normal insensitive look of not caring about anything. Dell looked up at Loretta and said, "Tell me the truth. Are you really going to put his family on that airplane?"

"Of course we are. They are returning from a trip to Disney World. We are sending them home to Kentucky. We added the soundtrack for Hamid to hear."

"Is this real?" Dell asked looking at the open file.

"Yes. Do you want to see the supporting documents?"

"Not right now, but let me talk to this man."

"He's all yours. But Dell, we have to have the information on the man in the photo. Make any kind of deal you want but he won't leave here until we have the info."

"I need a strong, sweet Arabica coffee and two cups."

William gave Dell two plain porcelain cups with no handles and a small coffeepot on a tray. Dell entered the room where Hamid sat despondently. He set the tray down and said, "Salaam Alaaikum." He held out his right hand. Automatically Hamid responded and took Dell's hand. Dell released Hamid's hand and touched his heart. He then sat next to Hamid and began the traditional Arab formalities. When that was out of the way he said in his perfect Arabic, "I regret that we must continue in English but I will tell you this; I am not here to threaten you or your family. I will make you my guest in this... this place and I will consider your family as mine."

"Why would you do this? You do not know me."

Dell switched to English. "How could you be my guest if you were a longtime friend? I don't expect you to believe me but if I give my word I will tell you I have never failed and I take you as my guest in the Arab way." This meant that he would give his life in protecting Hamid.

"Why am I here?"

Dell spoke for ten minutes telling Hamid all he knew about what was going on. He knew in the back of his mind that if he failed to get the information then Hamid's life was over. He would not be allowed to leave without giving the information.

Dell had spent long, happy times with the Arab people all over the Middle East. His happiest times were with the Bedouins learning the hard life of the desert and seeing the beauty of the land and the strong hearts of the people. He also knew of the hatred many Muslims had for the west. A number were so caught up with the past that they only saw blood in their future. These were the ones that must be stopped in any way possible. He knew that few Muslims in the Middle East and other parts of the world could express their views if they were against these fanatics.

Dell told Hamid a little of his childhood but made it clear he was intent on stopping terror.

"Are you a true believer in the one true God?"

"I am a Christian."

This seemed to satisfy Hamid and he said in Arabic, "It is enough that you know the true God. The Christians of today are not the ones who slaughtered my ancestors. I will help if I can."

Dell glanced at the mirror and then said, "We are looking for your cousin Abdul Baari." The name meant "servant of the creator."

A few minutes later Loretta entered the room wearing a conservative dress and shawl over her head. She made the proper greetings in Arabic and then said, "Perhaps we have much to learn from this teacher." She indicated Dell. "He has the heart of a lion and the voice of a peacekeeper. Please accept my apology for my discourtesy. Shall we start again? But I must warn you that I am under obligation to obtain this information."

Hamid said, "This man has told me much. I fear my family and I are in great danger if I am allowed to leave. I don't think my words will be enough to keep you from my door."

In English, Loretta said, "That's very true except that I too take my word as my life. Help us and we will offer you and your family accommodations and protection."

"You would place us in prison?"

"No. I will see that you are in a safe, open place and free to enjoy where you are. Your family will think it is a wonderland and you will tell them it is a new job you've accepted. The one restriction is that you will not be allowed to leave the area until this is over. You will also be required to cooperate with us during this time, but your name will never be spoken or written in any way that will point to you as someone who has helped us in the war on terror. I say all of this in faith that you will provide the information we need to find Abdul Baari. If you do not, we will not take revenge, but you and your family will be kept in a facility until this is over. It is for you to decide."

Hamid turned to Dell and asked, "Do you believe this woman who hates the word Yankee?"

Dell almost smiled as he said, "I am under the same obligation as you and, yes, I do believe her."

"Very well. Ask and I will answer."

Loretta opened her laptop and turned the screen so Hamid could see. Hamid's children were waving goodbye to Mickey Mouse as they walked to the boarding gate. "You will soon be with your family. They are safe." Hamid nodded.

Hamid took their word that he was now a guest, a word that means much more in the Arab Muslim world than in the west.

Loretta laid out enough information about the activities of Abdul to show there was no doubt that he intended to kill and disrupt the lives of many westerners—specifically Americans.

Hamid again said he loved America and that these acts, if they were carried out, were in no way the teachings of Mohammad or the will of Allah. He told all he knew of his cousin and offered to be a go-between in order to stop him. He was horrified to hear that his cousin and other fanatics were planning to set off at least one huge *dirty* bomb in a city in the U.S. and may already have the materials needed.

After the first productive meeting with Hamid, Loretta, Bill and Dell met in the living room of the house at Arlington Heights. William was serving tea and giving Bill seductive looks.

"William, what is with you? I'm not gay, never been gay and don't want to be gay, so back off." Bill looked at Dell and said, "I can't work under these conditions."

Loretta said, "Okay, William. Turn it off."

William's entire demeanor changed abruptly. Looking at Bill with the intense look of a killer, William put the tray down and moved to sit across from Bill. He moved like a fighter and one that would do whatever it took to win.

William said, "Be careful what you wish for. Few people get a good look at me and live." He spoke to Loretta without taking his eyes off Bill. "Does he live or die?"

"Live or die? What the hell is he talking about? All I wanted was for him to stop giving me those looks, but I really don't like this new look either," said Bill. "Help me out here, Dell!"

"Hey, this wasn't my idea."

"It wasn't mine either. Loretta, what is going on?"

"William is our top agent. He's not called in unless things get dramatic and he never fails. He might be gay but I don't know. In fact, I'm not sure if he even has sex. I've learned not to ask too many questions about him. Let's just say it's much better if he doesn't think about you at all."

"Well, ask him to stop looking at me. I feel like a mouse in a snake pit."

"William, leave Bill alone. He's on our side. I think I'll have you spend some time with Bill and give him a few pointers. He's going to be in the middle of this operation and it's going to be on him to protect Dell and help him get what we need. I have a feeling that he's going to be an important part of destroying these jihadists."

William said, "I work alone. You know that."

"This is not a request, sweetie."

The intensity in William's eyes flared for a moment and then he relaxed and death left his face. He glanced at Loretta and then nodded.

Bill said, "I am very confused."

Loretta smiled and said, "That's the way I like it—in your case. Just look at Dell. He's the picture of don't-give-a-damn. That's how I need him."

"The reason he looks like that is because he always looks like that. He's been trying to get himself killed for as long as I've known him. This is sounding more and more like the perfect job for him."

They all looked at Dell and he was in his little black world: eyes unfocused, completely relaxed and not-at-home.

"See what I mean."

"He's the only reason you're here, Bill. You're his minder and keeping him from getting killed is what you do. Why don't you bring him back so I can set the stage."

Bill walked over to Dell and raised his hand, then stopped. He checked to make sure Dell's hog-leg was still missing and then he gently slapped his face a few times. "Com' on, buddy. Time to join the living. Come on back. Look, Loretta is naked and I think it's for your benefit."

Dell was musing about staying where he was. He didn't care if Loretta was naked. Well, maybe a little. At that thought his vision cleared and he saw four men in casual clothes hovering over a large steel drum. One was holding a device and the meter was pegged. Dell looked around and saw a small, well-lit room. A door behind the men was labeled WAREHOUSE ENTRANCE.

He blinked several times and looked into Bill's face. "You're not the first thing I wanted to see." He looked at Loretta and she was smiling and fully clothed. He gave Bill a hard look.

Loretta said as she smiled, "Maybe next time, sugar."

Dell said, "They have the radioactive stuff packed in a 55 gallon drum."

She said, "What? How do you know that?"

"That's why you hired us isn't it?"

Bill said, "Hey. That's right! How much are we getting paid anyway?"

"How much do you want?" she responded.

Bill smiled and gave her a thoughtful look and then said, "We want to live the rest of our lives on a tropical island, all expenses paid."

Loretta gave Bill a hard look and said, "How 'bout six feet under on that tropical island?"

Even William laughed at that. Bill gave him a hard look but went back to his chair and sat without a word. He did mutter a few things but no one understood him.

Loretta laughed and then jumped up and leaped into Bill's lap. She kissed him hard and with a big smile said, "You just might get a turn after all. Don't worry, honey. Loretta will take good care of you both."

Dell caught himself in a smile and quickly let it drop.

William reached over and slapped Bill on the back.

Loretta returned to her seat and asked Dell, "Do you know where the material is?"

"Somewhere in a warehouse."

"In the States?"

"I don't know but the sign was in English."" Before Loretta could ask he finished, "All it said was *Warehouse Entrance*. There were four Arab or Iranian men and one of them was Abdul Baari."

"Can't you go back into your trance or whatever it is and find out where?"

Bill answered, "That's not how it works. Checking out is not a problem for him but having a *vision* is hit or miss and mostly miss. Maybe you should get naked. That seemed to do it this time." Loretta only smiled. "So what do we do now?"

"You're going back to work and acting as if nothing unusual happened today. You'll both get a new phone on your way out and I'll be able to contact you no matter where you are."

Dell said, "I thought we were fired."

"You are but you and Bill are the only ones in New Jersey that know it. Do your job and don't make trouble. I don't want anyone getting suspicious. And don't get killed."

Bill said, "If Dell doesn't make trouble, everyone will be suspicious."

Chapter 4

It was an odd place for a meeting of political point men and women but they were taking no chances that what they were doing might get out.

The concrete room had only two entrances. One was a long underground tunnel that led from the basement of the Washington Hilton in Dupont Circle and the other a heavy reinforced double steel door that opened to a side street. Both were guarded by hand-picked armed men. The head of security, Leo Jeffers, stood near the bottom of the stairs that led down to the tunnel. He knew everyone attending the meeting but also used a facial recognition program hooked into a small laptop that one of his men held. The man stood just forward and slightly to the left.

The room had been a storage area at one time but a wealthy Saudi prince had purchased it from the Hilton Group and turned it into a pleasure room. The prince was dead and an arrangement had been made by Sundial, Inc. to purchase the facility as a meeting room for its board members and to conduct very specific trials of some R&D programs. In reality, it was only used by one man to hold private meetings. That man was Derik Bartholomew, Senator from Wyoming.

Senator Bartholomew had personally greeted each of the five well-dressed people who now sat in easy comfort. He looked over each person, gauging their potential commitment to what they were about to hear. All were hand selected, watched over a several month period and each was enticed to watch their reaction and behavior. Then each was privately approached and parts of a plan were discussed—not enough to endanger the operation but enough to let them know it was highly illegal and a matter of possible treason.

The senator had begun with eight candidates but three proved to be a possible risk. Accidents befell all three and each as a member of Congress was buried with the honor they deserved.

Senator Bartholomew said, "I think it's time we begin." His baritone voice stopped the others and they placed their glasses on the nearby side tables and almost as one turned to face the senator.

Congressman Liam Coy from Texas said, "Derik, before we begin, I would like to know if there is an exit strategy if this plan of yours falls apart." Liam was a junior representative, having been elected the year before. He was known for his business acumen and his fervent patriotism. He had made millions in 'Green Technology' and his dislike for the oil rich Arabs and oil barons of his home state was well known. He had won a hard fought political campaign with the help of wealthy liberal backers.

Congressman Wilbur Hatcher from Ohio said, "Liam. We've been over this before. There are plans but the fact of the matter is it's impossible to get any stink on us. Let Derik lay out what we have so far and where we're going with this."

Liam nodded and settled back into his chair.

Senator Ottilie Weber from Tennessee sat with a knowing smile. She didn't need to say anything to draw attention. She was statuesque, with strawberry blonde hair and blues eyes that could look right through you. Her charm could get most any man or woman to go along with whatever she wanted. She was also known on the Hill for her sexual appetite. It was a mere rumor to most of the members and staff, but to the lucky few who had tasted it she was dubbed *Wonder Woman*. She was a third-term senator and chairperson of the powerful Senate Appropriations Committee. Senator Bartholomew considered her his most important acquisition to the team. She might very well become the next President after his plan was put into effect.

Derik said, "Our plan is taking shape right on schedule. I have made clandestine arrangements for three groups to go forward with our mission. I want you to meet the—"

Homeland Security Director Hornealius Hapholte said, "You know, Derik, there is a small team from the NSA sniffing around already. I've kept it away from the other agencies but NSA has some free runners that I can't control." Hornealius—known to his friends as Horny—was not only Director of Homeland Security but headed the new Omnibus Security Committee. He had his fingers on every security issue, open and clandestine, that the federal government was involved in. He was essential to Senator Bartholomew's plan to restore the might of the United States. He was also the only black member of Derik's team.

Derik said, "Well, Horny, tell us about that." He knew everything about it but wanted the others to see how he was controlling the situation.

"The NSA has a few small teams that take no direct instructions from, well, anyone, including my people. Even their director has only minimal control over them. The President is the only person who is able to get a direct report and he's turned over most of those duties to the VP.

"One team headed by a Loretta Smithe has brought in outside help."

Omar Shalze asked, "What kind of help and do we have anything to worry about?" Omar was the last member to join this secret group and one of the richest men in America. He also loved America so much that he would do whatever he could to see it remain the most powerful country in the world—including sacrificing the Middle East and parts of the U.S. He was the money-man and his presence was proof to the fanatics that this was not a ploy by the Americans. Little did they know that Omar detested everything about the Arab world except the beautiful women.

Hornealius said, "I'm keeping an eye on this team and it seems they are stupid enough to rely on psychic powers." He chuckled as he continued, "They've brought in a New Jersey State Trooper to *read* the situation. And he's brought in his partner to keep him from killing himself."

Ottilie asked, "What's the trooper's name?"

"Dell Sharpton. He's a guy that seems to stay in trouble with his superiors, but he has actually resolved a few cases of terrorism in the great state of New Jersey." This brought laughter from everyone except Senator Bartholomew.

Derik said, "Actually, this man has been involved in a number of incidents and he is well liked in the Arab community. He speaks several dialects of Arabic and does seem to have a sixth sense. He's also very hard to kill. We've tried twice. Now that he's come to the NSA we'll have to back off but if all else fails and he gets too close I'll use my secret weapon." He turned his head and looked at Ottilie. Her eyes focused on him and he felt his body stir. She gave him a small smile and nod. "For now we'll let them run but I have found a solution to this NSA problem if it becomes... difficult. When you want to control the body, you must control the head.

"Let me introduce someone who will handle our Arab allies and Loretta Smithe." He looked up to the ceiling in the back corner of the room and nodded.

The door opened and a person stepped through but before Derik could continue Wilbur Hatcher jumped up and in a loud voice said, "Are you recording these meetings, Derik? You know I won't stand for this!"

Derik said in a calm voice, "Settle down, Will. There are no recording devices of any kind at any of our meetings. You of all people should know the danger in that. I have a narrow beam video feed that shows only my face. It is being monitored by Jeffers for our safety and in this instance to allow this lady to enter on my signal. No voice recording—that's why I nodded. Satisfied?"

"Sorry, Derik. I'm just a bit nervous after that last bit of recording got out and nearly ruined me." Wilbur had gone with his oldest son to a meeting to help him out of some large debts. Wilbur had no idea they were meeting with a Mafia Don until he sat at the table. Then Tony Conte tried to use a recording of the meeting to get the FBI to back off an investigation into some of his dealings. If not for Derik and the men he sent in to eliminate the problem, it could have meant Hatcher's career in politics.

"Now, can we get to the business at hand?" Derik looked to the others and saw they were ready. "I would like to introduce this beautiful lady. Let's call her Aisha for the sake of a name. She is the head of the Arab part of this plan. Don't let her small size and beauty fool you. She is deadly and probably the most powerful woman in the Middle East. She will also control this NSA team if they get too close."

Aisha stood before them and gave each a defiant stare. Her look lingered on Ottilie. Then she took a seat Derik had just provided.

Horny took an immediate interest. She truly was beautiful and petite. Her silky black hair fell past her shoulders and her face was a classic Arab setting of beauty. She had a pronounced slender nose, big dark eyes and a body men dream about. As she sat, she crossed her legs and Horny caught a glimpse of white panties that stirred him even more.

Omar stared in open contempt and spoke Arabic. "You come in here dressed like a whore and we are to believe you are of the true faith and a leader of men. I say you let them hump you like a goat but you do not lead Arab men."

Aisha said, also in Arabic. "I was asked to wear this by the senator. I will, as a true believer, do whatever is required to destroy the West and let the world see the power of the Arab people. Speak to me in this manner again and you will be dead before I leave this room, you son of a pig."

Omar jumped to his feet but before he could get a word out Aisha was in front of him with a knife at his neck and a handful of hairy balls. She squeezed and beads of sweat jumped to Omar's face. He looked in her eyes and saw death.

Derik said, "Release him, Aisha. I don't know what he said but I'm sure he won't say it again. Am I right, Omar?"

Omar could only nod. Aisha released him and returned to her seat.

Omar straightened himself and then with his right hand touched his heart and kissed his lips and said, "Forgive me, Lady. I spoke in haste."

Aisha merely touched her heart and brought her hand away from her body.

Derik said, "Now that that's settled let's hear from Aisha. She's going to give us an update on several items. And please, no interruptions."

Aisha uncrossed her legs, flashing a patch of white, and stood. "I have been brought into this plan by Senator Bartholomew. I will be honest with you by saying your country will never defeat the Arab world. We have suffered for hundreds of years and are ready to exact vengeance. What will happen if this goes forward is that we will come to terms, the Arabs and Americans, and there may come a day of peace in the future." She looked at Derik and smiled.

"I have three cells of fighters ready to carry out this plan of yours. We wait on the material to be delivered. We will pick the site of the explosion a week before we set it off. There are three or four optional cities. You will be advised to stay away from all of these places.

"As for the NSA and Loretta Smithe, it may interest you to know that she has a few secrets that only two other people know about. I am one of them." She looked to Derik and he nodded. "This American operative is under control. She will follow my orders to the letter." Aisha sat back down and gazed at the faces watching her. She crossed her legs and saw that all but Derik lowered their gaze. She thought, *these western pigs are all the same. They want money, power and sex. It's no wonder they would have no problem killing their own people to keep this power and wealth. Pigs.*

Derik said, "Thank you, Aisha. My driver will return you to your home. I'll be in touch later." Aisha rose, gave Horny a direct look and left.

Hornealius said, "Now, that's my kind of terrorist." He looked at Omar and said, "I don't know what you said to her but damn she's quick. I thought you were a dead man."

Omar said, "I still find it hard to believe that she leads Arab men. Is she being watched?"

Derik said, "While she is here, yes. Once she goes to Jordan or Lebanon it's very hard to keep track of her. Perhaps Ottilie will go see her tonight and smooth some of her ruffled feathers."

Ottilie smiled and said, "I was just thinking that myself. I'll take care of her."

Liam Coy said, "Now about this explosion. Are you actually intending on setting off a nuclear bomb? I thought we were only going to put the fear of God in the American people."

Derik walked over to Liam and put his hand on his shoulder. "It's a conventional bomb with nuclear material in it. It is not meant to level the city, just make it uninhabitable for a few years. There will be some deaths from the bomb but that will be minimal."

Wilbur said, "Don't you listen to what's being said? We've been over this. Now, Derik, does this Aisha think we're going to give her the high-grade stuff?"

"That is what she thinks and it will be impossible to tell the difference with the equipment we provide her with. None of us here want long-term destruction. We only want to wake the people up and demand action. Using our influence, we will step in and retaliate against parts of the Middle East. Not only will it end the terrorist threat but we will have our own people in the White House and leading Congress. We will lead this country back to its greatness and control it for many years to come."

Derik moved over to Ottilie, offered his hand and she stood. He kissed her cheeks and then turned back to the others. "I present you with the first woman President of the United States of America!"

Chapter 5

A few weeks after returning to work Dell and Bill entered a halal-Muslim restaurant in Hoboken looking for three suspects in an armed robbery of a Jewish diamond merchant.

The owner rushed to them speaking Arabic. "Welcome, *Desert Rider*"—Dell's nickname from his days living with the Bedouin. "I am honored you visit again. Please have a seat and bring Abyad Uf'Uwan, *White Snake*, with you." *White Snake* was Bill's nickname because of rumors about his endowment. Dell never told Bill.

Dell and Bill were led to a small table near the back and Dell gave the quick friendly greetings. Bill muttered something about needing to learn the language as he sat quietly. He had learned a few of the formalities of Arab traditions but he was getting tired of being the butt of all the jokes.

In English, Dell said, "We're looking for the three who robbed and beat Ephraim the jeweler."

"I heard the Jew was nearly killed. Of course, we do not condone these kinds of actions in this great land. Who do you look for?"

"We have video of four Arabs. One is named Ghalib and another is Hamzah." Dell saw the spark of recognition. "I will have them one way or another."

"You know I cannot help you. I would suffer for it."

"If you aid the robbers I will charge you as well."

"Why do you threaten me in my house? You who know the ways of the Arabs and have never treated us as if we are all fanatics. Even *White Snake* has always treated us well and not attacked our women with his weapon."

Dell almost smiled as he said, "Hamdi, no one has threatened you. And I didn't come to cause you trouble or to turn the *Snake* loose. We are looking for these men and I am hungry. You know that this kind of crime is viewed as a hate crime by many. I'm trying to save your community trouble and embarrassment. Now, Bill and I would like your famous brazen chicken."

"Forgive my outburst, Mr. Dell. You are a true friend to the law-abiding people here. I do not know the men you have mentioned but..." he lowered his voice, "If I were to seek them then there is a gambling house at 561 21st Street that may have promise." He clapped his hands and shouted to a server to attend the lawmen.

Bill asked, "Why is it every time Hamdi looks at me he says, 'Abyad Uf'Uwan'? Is that my nickname and is it something I should get mad about?"

"Don't worry about it."

"It is something bad. I knew it! I'm going to learn Arabic. I guess I should have been raised by a Hajji and then..." He looked around as everyone stopped eating and stared at him.

Dell spoke a quick phrase and the people began to eat their meals again but they were still glancing at Bill. Dell said, "I'm going to start your lesson right now. Don't say that word unless you're ready to fight. Now look around at everyone and touch your heart with your right hand. Do it, Bill. These people actually like you but that could change if you don't learn to watch your mouth." Bill looked around and did as Dell told him. The patrons smiled and turned back to their conversations.

Dell went to the kitchen to talk to Hamid. While they spoke a loud shriek came from the dining area. Hamid and Dell rushed out to find a pretty young waitress with her head covered in a hijab, shawl, crying out and pointing at Bill. Hamdi asked her what was happening and she told him the *White Snake* had spoken improperly to her.

Dell stepped in and asked Bill, "What did you do now?"

"I just asked her what that word meant and then she went crazy. I didn't do anything!"

Dell spoke in Arabic and explained to the girl that Bill was uneducated in the holy language and he meant no disrespect. She calmed down and then asked if Bill's intentions were to be engaged to her. This time an actual smile passed Dell's face and he turned to Bill. "She thinks you are asking to marry her."

Bill jumped up and stared at the young woman. She had lowered her hijab exposing her beautiful big dark eyes and gave Bill a direct look. Bill moved closer to Dell and said, "Dell, get me out of this. All I did was ask her what that word meant. I'm not looking for a wife."

"She is a pretty little thing. She might be just what you need."

Bill blushed deep red and the patrons all laughed at his color. A few made comments about the *Red Snake*. "Please, Dell, this isn't funny. Get me out of this."

Dell spoke to the young woman and she accepted his answer. She looked at Bill, touched her heart and kissed her lips. Dell told Bill to return the salutation with a smile. Bill did and she turned away but gave him a soulful look as she returned to her duties.

Dell said, "Her name is Jamila and she likes you. She also said she would be glad to teach you her language."

"I'll want to talk to Hamid," Bill said.

The SWAT team was in position around the corner from the gambling house on 21st Street. Captain Teasdale was giving a speech on how the operation would go. Dell stood quietly off to the side and Bill had ear buds in his ears listening to an Arabic language tape.

"Anders... Anders, did you hear what just I said?"

Bill looked up, yanked the buds from his ears and said, "Roger, Captain! Every word. The *White Snake* is ready." He looked at Dell with a smile. Dell gave him a sour look.

Bill had taken Hamid to the kitchen and forced him to explain the term. He walked out of the restaurant with his shoulders back and a smile on his face. He stopped at a local bookstore and bought a cassette player and tapes to learn Arabic.

Dell walked over to the SWAT commander, spoke and then walked away.

Captain Teasdale shouted, "What's going on? Where is he going?"

Bill spoke to Teasdale and told him that Dell and he would be at the back exit. Captain Teasdale's shoulders slumped and he just nodded to the SWAT commander. He watched Bill follow Dell down the alleyway that led to the back of the house.

SWAT hit the door at 10:30, used a flask-bang in the hallway and entered *en masse*. Dell had jammed the rear exit with a steel pole and the people inside were ramming the door trying to escape. The banging slowed and he could hear the operations team grabbing people and taking them into custody.

Captain Teasdale rounded the corner at the back of the house and huffed his way to the blocked door. "How are we going to catch anyone with this door blocked? This here is a violation of the fire code." He grabbed the steel pole as Bill touched Dell's arm. Dell just shook his head and waited. As Teasdale pulled the pole loose, men rushed the door. It slammed open knocking the captain to the ground and six men trampled over Captain Teasdale.

Dell clubbed two men and Bill was grappling with another when Teasdale jumped up yelling, "There's going to be jail time for you people!" The fourth man of the group pulled a pistol and aimed at Captain Teasdale. Dell reached out and hit his arm just as the weapon went off. The bullet clipped Captain Teasdale's left ear and he let out a howl. Dell brought his big pistol over hand and clubbed the man. The suspect crumpled to the ground.

Teasdale, holding his ear as blood poured out, turned on Dell, but before the yell left his lips Dell shouted, "Look out!"

Captain Teasdale hit the ground and rolled over with a wild look in his eyes. His pistol was out and he aimed wildly but Dell stepped on his arm and removed the weapon from his grip and then helped the captain to his feet. Bill ran over to the captain and said, "It's all right, Captain. We got the ones we're looking for but I think three suspects got away. Are you okay?"

Captain Teasdale stood up, blood running down the side of his face, and tried to brush himself off. Something dark stained his hand and he lifted his hand to his nose.

Dell said, "That's dog shit."

Captain Teasdale flung his hand away from his nose and desperately looked around for somewhere to wipe it. Bill offered him his handkerchief.

The SWAT commander came out the back door and said, "That was text-book. I can see another commendation in your file, Captain. Good job." He offered his hand to Captain Teasdale who shook the other's hand while still trying to hold his left ear. The commander looked down at his stained hand and took a tentative sniff. He gave the captain a withering glare.

An ambulance roared up and the medics jumped out to attend to the captain's wound. The SWAT commander yelled, "Give me a handy-wipe! And give one to this... to the captain."

Bill asked Dell, "Wasn't one of those three that got away the guy we're looking for? Loretta said.... Ohoof."

Dell pulled his elbow out of Bill's midsection and gave him a hard look. "Shut up, fool." He looked around but the captain and commander of the SWAT team were busy cleaning their hands and didn't hear anything.

A few hours later Captain Teasdale stood in the Commissioner's office. His head was wrapped up like he had taken a head-shot. He was not happy. "I want those two idiots off my team!"

"Is that a command, Captain?"

"Well, what I mean to say is, well, Sharpton and Anders are loose cannons. They won't listen to anything I tell them. I want... I mean, I would like them moved to another squad, sir. Sharpton is undermining my authority."

"Let me tell you. Sit down. Now!" Captain Teasdale jumped and hurriedly took a seat. Commissioner O'Hara took a deep breath and settled back in his cushioned chair.

"Colin," Captain Teasdale's full name was Colin Phillip Teasdale, but most everyone that knew it pronounced it as Colon. "You wouldn't be standing here right now if it weren't for Detective Sharpton. He saved your life—again. All-in-all you wouldn't be a captain if it weren't for men like Dell and Bill." Captain Teasdale shifted in the seat but didn't say a word. "The fact is, you are the best administrator I have. Your unit is the best run and organized division I have and your men respect you. Let's admit it, you're high-strung and a bit unpredictable in the field. I also know that Dell and Bill are two of the best men you have for solving cases. I know Dell is a pain in the butt, but he is someone you need." O'Hara took another deep breath.

"Now, Colin. That was a great piece of work today. You caught the four men we wanted and I've already had calls from the Governor and the Jewish community congratulating you for your fine work. I'm recommending you for a heroism award. There just aren't many division commanders who take a bullet fighting right alongside his men.

"I also received a call from the Feds telling me... telling me to give Dell and Bill open reins on anything they're working on. It wasn't a request. I'm smart enough not to ask any questions. Are you?"

Teasdale said, "I'll tell you one thing right now. The Feds can take a flying leap! I'm not working with Sharpton, and that's all I got to say about that!"

"You know, Sergeant Teasdale, I like a man that speaks his mind even when he's ordered not to." He pushed the intercom switch on his desk. "Gina, I'm assigning Sergeant Teasdale to traffic in Morristown. Let the post commander know he'll be there in two hours.

"Now, Teasdale, get your ass out of my office and my advice is not, I repeat, not to say a word."

Teasdale was up and out when it dawned on him what just took place.

Pretty, dark-haired, tight, pink fuzzy sweater, big-breasted, big-bodied Gina was holding a folder for him by the exit to the office.

"Did the Commissioner just call me sergeant? Why would he make a mistake like that?"

Gina pressed those big pink fuzzy breasts against Teasdale's chest and said, "That wasn't a mistake, honey."

Teasdale said, "That's got to be wrong. I'm going in to talk to him."

Gina pressed even tighter, let her hand brush the front of Teasdale's trousers and whispered in his ear. "That envelope on my desk is for you if you don't leave. It's labeled Corporal Teasdale. Phil, I got something you can take it out on this evening but right now you better get out of here. I'll find out what's going on."

Sergeant Teasdale started to open his mouth when from out of the office came, "Gina. Is he still in my office?" The Commissioner jumped up and looked into the reception area and only Gina stood there looking good. "In three days, tell Teasdale to report to my office."

Chapter 6

Dell was in his favorite spot. Sitting on his broken-down couch, TV on, a half bottle of Jameson in his left hand and the other half coursing through his veins. He was in his world with a load of Irish wine warming him up. He had no intentions of leaving. He was so tired of all the crap he had to go through. He needed to find a way to move on so he would be free of his life.

Dell came back to the real world and reached for his pistol but it wasn't there. His eyes cleared and he looked into the beautiful, blue eyes of Loretta. They had a black ring around the irises and the pupils were small and piercing. "Welcome back, darlin'. Did you miss me?" She pressed against him and kissed him softly. He reached for her and she slipped from his grasp. "Not until this is over. Then you're going on the ride of your life."

"Why wait?"

"Anticipation. Like a good wine. It's even better when you wait. Now, tell me about the men you saw on 21st Street."

"They were the men I saw with Abdul."

"Are you sure?"

"Yes."

"I've already started a sweep but we haven't come up with anything, except maybe a sighting near Morristown. Do you think the material is in the States?"

Dell said, "I have no idea."

"I want you and Bill-baby to go down there and take a look around. Bill will be here in ten minutes and you'll leave right away. I have an unregistered car outside for you to use."

"What is it we're supposed to do?"

"Have one of your visions and try to find them."

"You know I can't turn that on and off."

"That's where Bill comes in. I've already had a talk with him and he seems willing but he insisted I call him *White Snake*," Loretta said with a laugh.

"That's the worst thing that could have happened: him finding out what that meant."

"Is it true?"

"Find out for yourself. It would make him happy." He turned to look at her and she just smiled.

"We'll talk later, *Desert Rider*." She walked out of the apartment.

Bill came through the door a few minutes later with a big smile on his face. "I think the *White Snake* is making progress with Loretta. I'll try to hold back until you have a shot at it. I'd hate to spoil things for you, *Desert Rider*." Bill started laughing and had to sit down. In rudimentary Arabic, he said, "I am learning this new language so the *White Snake* will impress with more than his weapon."

"Shut up, Bill. Let's get going."

They parked and were walking to a nearby Halal-restaurant in Morristown. Bill said, "Look over there. Isn't that the captain directing traffic? I bet that hat hurts his head."

Phil Teasdale, in uniform, stood in the middle of an intersection with traffic swirling around him. He was blowing furiously on his whistle but no one was paying any attention to him. Bill called out to him and he turned, gave them a sour look and then turned away.

The two men they were looking for exited the restaurant about 70 yards down the street and disappeared into an alleyway next to the restaurant. Bill and Dell hurried to catch up. Just before they rounded the corner Dell heard two spurts from a silenced weapon. Throwing his arm out to stop Bill, he then peered down the alleyway. Two bodies were lying on the ground and a small, dark-haired woman was walking away. She reached the other block and turned onto the main street. Dell told Bill to check the men and he ran after the woman.

When he reached the street, she was nowhere to be seen. He walked down to the intersection where Captain—now Sergeant—Teasdale was trying to take control of the traffic. It was flowing well without his help. Dell stepped between traffic and came up behind Teasdale. Dell yelled, "Hey, Teasdale!"

Teasdale blew his whistle so hard it flew from his lips and he hit the ground covering his head. A red Ford pickup had to dodge to the right and missed his head by inches. Dell helped him stand as Teasdale held his hand over his heart. His whistle hung from the lanyard around his neck.

Dell asked, "Did you see a dark-haired woman wearing a scarf and a green dress pass by here?"

Recognizing the voice, Teasdale spun and his hand dropped to his pistol. "What the hell do you want?"

"I just told you, Sergeant. There was a shooting just a minute ago and I think the woman was involved."

"Get away from me, Sharpton. You're nothing but trouble."

"Sorry, Sergeant. I need you to cordon off that alleyway until the crime scene people get here and I'm going to question the people in that restaurant. I'll go and keep anyone from leaving."

"Sharpton..."

"That's Detective Sharpton, Sergeant. We don't have time for a pissing contest right now. Get moving." Dell turned and headed for the restaurant and Teasdale let out the longest word Dell had ever heard. He thought that if he separated the word a little it would turn out to be something very rude. He didn't bother trying.

The two men were shot in the front of the head at pointblank range and no clues were found at the scene. No one in the restaurant knew anything about the men or the woman. An hour later Dell stepped out into the growing darkness and saw a black Suburban SUV parked a block down the street. It flashed its lights once and he walked to it. The rear passenger door opened and he entered. Loretta was there dressed in a bright red pantsuit. "Hi, Sweetie. What happened?"

"Two of the men we are looking for were taken out, but you already knew that."

"Was it a robbery?"

"It was a hit. No question about it. A woman did the... What do you people call it...? Wet work."

"It's so cute when you talk like that." Her southern accent was in full force as she smiled brightly at Dell. "Why don't we go get something to eat and talk about where we go from here?"

"You need to find the other two before we lose track of that material."

"No, honey. You need to find the other two before something happens. If they set the bomb off in the U.S., we're all in big trouble." She nodded to the driver and he pulled away heading for the interstate. She called Bill to let him know where to pick Dell up and told him to turn the scene over to the State Police.

The next day Bill and Dell walked into the Commissioner's office and took a seat. Gina followed them in wearing a fuzzy green low cut sweater and yellow skirt that covered just about everything that should be kept private. She had a tray with two cups and coffeepot. She fussed over Bill and made sure he got a good look at her ample breasts that were just this side of popping out. Then she turned to Dell and nearly stuck her rear in Bill's face. She turned her head and smiled back at Bill.

As she left Bill leaned over and whispered, "Do you think she's heard about my nickname?"

Dell ignored him.

The Commissioner said, "I don't know what you two are up to, and I don't want to know. I had to give Teasdale three days off to recuperate. He's a nervous wreck."

Dell said, "He's just a little high-strung. I don't think he was made to be a traffic cop."

"That's just a lesson in who's the boss around here. He'll be back at division next week. Try and take it easy on him, Dell."

"I'll try, Pat, but he's such an easy target."

"He's your boss and does a good job. Cut him some slack. It's all I can do to keep you on the job.

"I've been told that you two are on special assignment and I'm to release you for as long as you're needed with whoever it is that needs you. Do you need any help?"

"Pat, when I find out what it is we're doing I'll try and let you know but there may come a time when we do need help, and if we do, it needs to be hard and fast. We're pretty much in the dark on this but you know the old saying, 'If I told you I'd have to kill you'? That's pretty much what we're running on and under the same rule. Right now we don't need to know."

The Commissioner asked, "Bill? What is that in your ears?"

Bill sat dreaming about Gina's fuzzy breasts and listening to his Arabic tapes. He looked up and saw the hard look coming from the Commissioner, jerked the ear-buds from his ears and said, "Sorry, Commissioner. Are you talking to me?"

The Commissioner looked at Dell and said, "I hope you two don't get killed."

Dell smiled and said, "There's always that chance."

"Get out of here and report back to me whenever you're finished doing whatever it is you're doing. Don't blow up the world."

Chapter 7

Dell and Bill sat in their undercover car waiting for a contact from Loretta's outfit. Dell was in his dark world but the ghouls seemed irritated with him. Things were different: darker and the mist swirled at times as if it was a turbulent storm. Dell couldn't feel the wind but he could tell it was affecting his host. The wraiths were an older bunch, dressed in desert robes of the Bedouins. This was new but it really didn't matter to Dell. He even made out women this time.

Dell felt the now familiar nudge and resisted but the mist began to fade quickly. He was looking at a street filled with people. Women wore hijabs covering their faces and the men wore dishdasha, robes, or western clothing. A man passed close to him and he recognized Abdul Baari hurrying away. Dell followed him into a shop and saw him pass through a curtained doorway in the back of the store. Abdul met five men and a woman wearing a dark blue burka. One of the men had a briefcase and possessed a map.

The man with the case laid out the map on the table and pointed to a city. Dell couldn't tell what city it was but it was clear that this was part of the plan for the dirty bomb. The woman was giving instructions to the men. Her covered face turned to look at Dell and then she hurried from the room.

"Dell. Come on back. Our contact should be here any time now. Come on. Snap out of it."

Dell's vision cleared and Bill was looking at him with some concern. "Man, you were out for a long time and muttering the whole time. That's the first time I've ever heard you try to talk when you are... wherever you go. Are you okay?"

"Where are we?"

"We're in Levittown, just outside Philadelphia. You were out almost the whole way. You know if you only got paid for the time you are awake you would be a poor man. We're meeting one of Loretta's agents but I don't have a clue why. Do you?"

"She didn't tell me anything. The terrorists are still in business and they have the plans ready for the bomb. I saw the map but they're not in this country."

"Is it just the two that are left?"

"They have a new crew and one of them is a woman."

The car door opened and a man dressed in jeans and a red plaid shirt sat down in the back seat. Bill reached for his pistol but the man grabbed his shoulder and held a government badge up.

Dell said, "Take it easy, Bill. I think this is our contact."

Bill turned in the seat and said, "He looks like he just fell off a mountain. Who the hell are you?"

"Lissen, purty boy. I'll kick yor ass and then turn you over a log and make you squeal. I'll bet you could call in a passle of critters. You shore got a purty mouth." The man sounded like he had just walked out of the mountains of West Virginia and smelled like it too.

Bill grabbed for his pistol again but this time Dell stopped him. "Bill, take a good look at our friendly hillbilly. I think he likes you."

"Why am I always attracting these crazies? I thought we were here to make contact with an agent—not a... a... whatever he is."

"Take a closer look."

Bill looked the scruffy-looking hillbilly over and there was something about his eyes... "William? Is that you?"

"It shore is!" William gave him a sweet smile and said in a normal American accent, "Loretta told me your nickname, *White Snake*, and I asked to be your follow-up contact. Is it true?"

"Is what true?"

"Your nickname."

"You'll never find out! What are we doing here?"

William laughed and said, "Like I said, I'm your contact. We think that the cell with the bomb is in a house two blocks from here."

Dell said, "You're wrong about that. They are in the Middle East and they are making preparations to set the bomb off somewhere in the U.S."

"How do you know?"

"Where is Loretta?"

"Something you should know about her. She doesn't tell anyone where she goes but I know this case is high priority. Wherever she is, it concerns this cell. Now, tell me what you know."

Dell turned in the seat and gave him a long, hard look. "Apparently Loretta trusts you and I know you're more than a... sensitive assistant. But I keep what I know to myself until it's time for others to know."

Bill said, "That's the truth! He doesn't tell me anything until just before the bullets start flying. The good news is he's always right and I'm still alive."

"Bill. You and I are going to get along fine."

"Don't get your hopes up. I don't think I work well with a... uhm... someone of your persuasion."

William switched back to his English accent. "You will be quite intrigued when you become more acquainted with me, my good man. I think that one day you shall kiss me on the lips in gratitude, actually."

"If you hold your breath for that, you'll die."

"And I will most certainly discover the truth about your nickname."

Bill looked at Dell and said, "I'm not working with him," shoving a thumb in William's direction.

Dell said, "I don't think you'll have much say-so in that, partner."

Dell told William what he had seen in his vision and William said he would report to Loretta.

Before William left Bill said, "I'm going to ask a dumb question but if I'm up to my neck in this then I better get some facts straight. What exactly is a dirty bomb?"

William said, "You're so right, Bill. You better understand what you and Dell are getting into. A dirty bomb is the next *best* thing to a nuclear weapon. It isn't as destructive but psychologically it can devastate a population; demoralizing and causing them to live in constant fear."

"Where do they get something like that?"

"Bombs are something the terrorists are well versed in making. The bigger the better. Its destructive power doesn't have to be tremendous, but they will want to use a shaped type charge to launch the nuclear material upward and then the wind will carry it across a city."

"Okay, I can see how it would cause a lot of problems but how bad could it be? I mean, we go in and clean it up and in a few months everything is back to normal."

"Have you ever heard of Chernobyl?"

"The nuclear power plant in Russia?

"It's in the Ukraine but near the Russian border. It was a much bigger incident with much more nuclear material than we are talking about but it's a good example of what could happen. A very large area around the plant is still restricted. Almost all of Europe was and still is affected and that was over twenty years ago. Hundreds of thousands of people are still feeling the effects and many thousands died. Can you imagine what would happen if even a small event forced residents of an American city to evacuate and never return in their lifetimes? And just add the fear of it happening again. Chernobyl was an accident and people can grasp that, but if it were deliberately done by terrorists, how could they feel safe? How could the government assure the population that it couldn't happen again?

"One consequence of an act like this is the population would probably turn on the Muslims of America. We know that most of the Muslim people in America and around the world are good people. They may disagree with the way the west is fighting in Afghanistan and Iraq but they also disagree with the way fanatics are killing people to terrorize the west and their own people. Most are afraid to help because they will be viewed as against Islam and they might be killed by the bad fellows."

Bill said, "Dell has taught me a lot about the Arabs in Jersey and I like them. I'm in this no matter what because Dell's in it and someone has to look after him." Bill looked over at Dell and saw he was in his own little world. Bill then turned to look at William and said, "I'll tell you this. You people better be straight up with us because Dell will know and then shit will happen."

William smiled and in an American accent said, "Sweetie, I am on your side. I've always worked alone but for you I'm making an exception."

"Com' on, Dell. Don't do this when he's around. Wake up and let's get out of here."

Dell felt the tug and resisted for a moment but then the darkness turned a lighter shade of gray and he saw a white house trimmed in dark green. Inside the house were four men sitting at a table gambling. On a couch were six young Asian girls wearing only panties and shackles around their ankles. They looked terrified.

Bill got William to exit the car with him and then he reached in and slapped Dell two times. Dell jerked and reached for his weapon, which Bill had in his hand.

"One of these days you're going to take my gun when I need it. Stop doing that!"

"Buddy, I'm here protecting you until you come around so don't worry about needing this monster. And I don't like looking at it from the wrong end when you wake up."

Dell wiped his face with his hand and looked around. Four houses down on the other side of the street was a white house with dark green trim. He looked at William and asked, "Are you carrying?"

"Always."

"Bill. Go around back of that white house and bust in when you get the signal. William. You come with me. There are four men with six girls in chains inside."

William said, "This isn't what we're... In chains?"

"Yes."

"Count me in."

William had started out working against slave trading in Asia and he was still haunted by things he had seen.

William and Dell approached the front door and William whispered, "How will Bill know what the signal is?"

Dell took three long strides and put his left foot into the door near the handle. With a tremendous crash that shook the entire house, the door slammed open and Dell continued into the house with his pistol ready.

William followed close behind and said to himself, "Oh."

As they entered the room to the left of the hallway William heard a crash at the back of the house.

Three men jumped up from the table reaching for weapons, but Dell bowled into them and clubbed one while William punched one and back-fisted the other one.

Dell said, "There's one more. "

Bill came in through the kitchen door with a man bleeding badly from his nose. "This one was jackrabbiting until he met the *White Snake*."

They cuffed the four men and found the key to the shackles. William was talking to the girls in Laotian and had them smiling within a few minutes.

Before the FBI and Philadelphia Police Department showed up William made his exit. He had made a call and told Dell and Bill that no one would ask them anything except to send their report that night to the FBI. Then they could leave as soon as the PPD showed up. He instructed, "Don't show your badges or give your names to anyone."

Dell was just getting a good start on his fresh bottle of Jameson when Loretta let herself into his apartment. "Mind if I join you?" she asked in her seductive southern accent.

"Do I have a choice?"

"There is always a choice, Dell. Do you want me to leave?"

"Have a seat." He poured her a drink and looked her over as she moved around his apartment. He had seen all of her but he was thinking he wanted more. Her long, tan legs moved in concert with her tight, firm ass and it was obvious she wasn't wearing a bra or panties. She left a trail of cherry blossom fragrance as she checked out the place.

"No photos, no music... This place looks like a motel. Dell, you need to brighten it up. I think I'm going to help you."

"Get naked. That'll brighten it up."

Loretta moved to his lap and kissed him hard. "I'm afraid if I do it will mess things up... for now. I do want you, baby." Dell reached up and lightly squeezed her breast and she let out a soft moan, pressing her body to him. "Dell... Don't."

Dell kissed her and she opened her mouth to him. His hands continued to explore her. He touched her knees, and her legs, as if spring-loaded, opened and he could feel her wiggle in excitement. "Don't what?" he asked.

"Don't... don't stop, darlin."

"I thought you said we weren't going to do this until this was over."

"Shut up." Those blue eyes were filled with heat as she removed her blouse. Her hands cupped her breasts and one at a time she offered them to his mouth.

Dell suckled each nipple until it was firm and swollen.

Loretta whispered, "I lied. I want you now. We'll get back on track later." She stood and removed her skirt and then reached out and pulled Dell's shirt over his head. Kneeling between his legs and kissing his nipples, she ran her hands through the soft dark hair of his chest. Reaching out she unbuckled his pants and pulled them down with urgency. "Oh, my," she said. "You are happy to see me."

As Dell stood he lifted her into his arms. "Very happy." He carried her into his bedroom.

Later that night as she lay in Dell's arms, Loretta said, "Dell, we can't do this again until our job is done." He started to protest but she stayed his words with a finger to his lips. "I've wanted this ever since I was given your file and I want more but this isn't the way I work. I don't run around screwing everyone I need for a job. It's just... we have so much in common and..." She switched to Arabic, "I feel your ice melting and I want to bathe in your cool waters. We must see this through and bring the justice of the desert to the ones who bring our world so much pain. Let us return to the water of life once more, *Desert Rider*. It will let me live until I drink from your oasis again."

"I can't believe it. I think you are actually smiling," Bill said as Dell got in the car. "You got laid last night. Didn't you?"

"Drive."

"You did! Was it Loretta? Oh, man. I hope it was. Did you take any pictures?"

Dell turned in his seat as he reached for his pistol but stopped when he saw the pure joy on Bill's face. He was happy that Dell got laid—and laid good, by the way. "What are you so happy about? And drive." Dell asked.

"It was Loretta!"

Bill pulled out in traffic and romped down on the Dodge Charger the Feds let him use. He burned rubber and did a power-slide into the outside lane.

"Here's the deal, Dell. When you smile, I have a good day. Do you know how many good days I've had? Never mind. We're going to have a good day and it's all because you put it to Loretta. She's got a body to dream about..."

"Shut up before I shoot you."

"Okay, buddy. But man, tapping..." Bill picked up his ear buds and jammed them in his ears. He hummed softly as he drove to meet William in Millville.

Bill pulled off Interstate 55 and stopped across from a *Denny's* in a strip mall parking lot. A dapper looking William walked up to the car and slid into the back seat.

"My, my, Bill. You're looking well today." He never said a word to Dell.

"Don't get your hopes up, Willie. What are we doing in Millville? I thought the only thing going on here was sand." Millville was famous for the quality of sand in the area used for making glass.

"Oh, it is. I've purchased several beautiful glass sculptured pieces here. It's also known for its Arab population. I've never figured out why the Arabs enjoy New Jersey so much."

Dell said, "It's the sand."

"And what did you do to Loretta? She called me a few hours ago and she sounded... inebriated. I've never known her to take more than a tiny sip of liquor or wine. She seemed very distraught."

"I knew it! So you and Loretta..." Bill closed his mouth when he saw the deadly look Dell gave him.

"Come now. Loretta doesn't mix business with..."

Dell asked, "Why are we here?"

William took a moment to compose himself and then said, "We have reliable information that at least one of the men we are looking for is situated on F Street. We need to confirm this and then a team will watch the house. Let's take a drive around the area and then I'll go to the house and speak to the occupants."

Bill drove a circuit four blocks away from the house in question. He then moved in a block and saw nothing out of the ordinary.

"Drive down the damn street," ordered Dell.

Just before turning on F Street Dell said, "Stop."

Bill pulled to the curb as Dell was staring out the window. He was looking at a billboard with a picture of the street he had seen in his vision. It looked hot, dusty and many people crammed the street as they went about shopping. The marquee read, *Come Home to Lebanon*. As Dell looked at the billboard memories of a recent vision came to him. The vision was blurred and he knew it was Loretta's fault. He was almost happy, and that could only come from a woman.

Bill said, "Dell?"

Dell held up his hand as he concentrated on the vision. Dell saw a group of men armed with automatic weapons looking out the window of a blue lap-sided house. They were agitated and more men rushed into the room pointing towards the rear of the house. There were ten men all together and one of them was one of the men they were looking for.

"Dell. Com' on back, buddy. Man, you are getting worse. I was watching you this time and you just checked out. Wake up! What's going on?"

Dell said, "One of the men we want is in the house but something's going on. They are armed to the teeth and ready for something. Don't drive down F Street. Go down the alleyway."

Bill spun the car around and entered the garbage truck alley. A SWAT truck and three other vehicles were blocking the alley and a full squad was suited up.

As Bill pulled in behind the last car Dell said, "William, make your way to the front of the house but stay out of sight. They have AK's at every window. Be ready if our guy makes a break."

Bill asked, "Do you need a vest?"

"I'm wearing one." William got out of the car and moved out of the alley.

Bill and Dell got out and started toward a group of men. They could hear Captain Teasdale saying, "Now, I want to get one thing straight. We're not going to shoot up this town! We're here on a tip and all I want is to search the premises. This ain't Dodge City."

Dell stopped just behind the captain and said in a normal voice, "Hey, Captain." Teasdale spun and tried to grab his gun but his holster had slipped around to his back. Dell grabbed him by the back of his vest and said, "Sergeant, You've got to get a grip on yourself."

Captain Teasdale spun around looking at Bill and Dell. "What the hell are you two doing here?"

Bill said, "Captain, keep it down. That house is full of bad guys."

"I don't give a... It is?"

"That's what Dell says."

Teasdale looked around while massaging his heart and saw Dell talking to the SWAT commander. He limped over to Dell, spun him around and said, "I'm a captain!"

"Well, of course you are. I'm glad to see you away from traffic duty. Hold on a sec, Captain." Dell turned back to the SWAT team and started dialing on his cell phone.

Teasdale looked like he had swallowed a chili pepper and it was trying to escape. Bill pulled him back out of the way and said, "Settle down, Captain. We've been through this before. Remember?"

Dell was speaking in Arabic, "Flee the house! The infidel police are coming. Go out the front and flee. Leave your weapons or they will kill you before you can complete your mission." Dell listened and then he said, "I speak the truth of Allah." He closed his cell phone and nodded to the commander. The team left two men to watch the rear and the rest rushed into the backyard and down both sides of the house.

"What the hell is going on?" cried Captain Teasdale. He watched Bill and Dell running towards the front of the house.

He looked around and he was alone. His shoulders slumped and he muttered to himself as he walked around the house. Men were laying all over F Street while the SWAT team handcuffed them. As Teasdale reached the scene, he saw a man talking to Dell that he didn't know.

Before he reached Dell, Bill turned to the captain and shook his hand. "Great job, Captain! You'll probably get another medal."

"Who is that talking to Sharpton?"

"What, Captain? There's no one talking to him."

Teasdale spun around and Dell stood off by himself looking back at the house. He marched over to him and demanded, "Who were you talking to, Sharpton?"

"A Spook. And try and remember what the Commissioner told you the last time you went to see him." Dell turned and walked toward the back of the house.

Teasdale was bright red again as he watched Anders hurrying after Dell. "I hate that guy."

William was in the car when they arrived. "That wasn't the fellow we are looking for. I recognized several of the men. They're just local hoodlums. No need to worry."

Bill asked, "Where to now?"

"I'm done here. You two just go about your normal business. I'm sure Loretta will be in contact. If she sobers up. Dell, you should be ashamed of yourself." Dell said nothing and William exited the car and walked away.

Bill and Dell sat in the NSA house in Arlington Heights. Loretta looked sad and bleary-eyed. Dell spoke first. "We need to go to Lebanon."

Loretta asked, "Why Lebanon?"

"I saw a billboard and it was the place I saw the terrorists with the map."

Bill blurted out, "Do they speak Arabic in Lebanon? That's in the Middle East, right?"

Dell gave him one of his sour looks.

Loretta said, "Yes, Bill. It's in The Middle East but I don't think it's a good idea to send both of you there."

"I don't travel without Bill."

"And I want to practice my Arabic," said Bill.

Loretta said in Arabic, "You may find more than you want in the land of the sacred cedar. Your name may be listed on the scroll of the lost." Bill smiled, only catching a few of the words. She switched to English and said, "I have good information that the one who has planned this attack is in Egypt. If you need to go then that's where you are going. This is not open for discussion."

Dell could see the anger in her eyes and didn't know how to respond. Was she mad at him? She started all the sexual stuff. Dell's good mood had left him on the car ride to Washington, so if that was how she wanted to play, then that's how it would be. He stood and started for the door.

"Dell." She turned to Bill and asked, "Would you give us a moment?"

"Sure."

Loretta led Dell into an adjacent room and closed the door.

Dell said, "You can make the ticket out to wherever but Bill and I are going to Beirut."

Loretta gave him a hard look and then her eyes softened. "You'll have to go through Israel. It's the only way in with your weapons. Do me a favor. If you don't find what you're looking for go to Egypt."

Dell only nodded and then moved close to Loretta. "If I've done something wrong... well, I'm sorry."

"It's not you. It's me. I've never done that before... I mean I've never slept with someone I'm working with. Don't take it wrong. I enjoyed every second of it and under the right circumstances I want it again. I know your buttons and when I pushed yours I guess I pushed mine, too."

"I like the way you push."

Loretta asked, "You're not mad?"

"Hell, yes. I can't think of anything worse than a beautiful woman doing those things to me." Dell let a small smile out—for him it was a big smile—and she pressed against him.

"Thank you."

Chapter 8

Bill was so excited about leaving the U.S. for the first time. He stared at his newly issued Diplomatic Passport and smiled. "This is going to be great. I've never been anywhere and now I'm going to be talking like a native."

He had spent hours with his Arabic tapes and almost as much time at a nearby restaurant practicing. The owner had spoken to Dell and Dell made it clear that he was to overlook the mistakes Bill made and he asked if one of the owner's daughters could spend some time with Bill helping him. For all of Dell's depression and desire to die, he cared about Bill, although he would never admit it to anyone. Bill was a fast learner—who knew?

Bill was plain-spoken and had his own problems but he attached himself to Dell from the first day they were made partners. He had watched Dell's back and kept the brass off him when he was *doing his thing*. Dell even found humor in Bill, but again, he wouldn't admit it. For all Bill's faults, Dell had a boatload more. In truth, Bill was the reason Dell was still alive, but even in that Dell didn't hold it against him.

Bill said in Arabic, "Soon we will be in the land of our brothers and sisters. They shall witness the charm of the *White Snake*."

"I'd keep that name to yourself. We're not going to Hoboken."

"Well, I know that! Who would have thought I'd be going to the Middle East? Say Dell. Why are these flight attendants giving me the eye and not serving me liquor?"

They were on an EL AL flight to Tel Aviv and Bill was trying out his Arabic. It wasn't working.

Dell gave him a sour look and finally said, "Bill, hold off on the Arabic for a while. At least 'til we get to Lebanon."

"Okay, but how am I going to learn if I don't practice?" Dell just hunkered down in his seat and entered his own little world.

At Ben Gurion Airport, two uniformed policemen escorted Bill and Dell to an office on the second floor. One of the officers pointed to a desk where a pretty, young blonde woman sat waiting to check their passports and paperwork.

Bill walked up to the desk and said, "Salaam Alaaikum."

The woman sat back in the chair, looked at him and then Dell. Dell just shook his head.

"Do you have any idea where you are..." She looked at his passport, "Mr. Anders?"

Bill put on his brightest smile and said, "I'm in the Middle East on my way to Beirut. You are very pretty and I appreciate you not wearing that shawl thing. You're too pretty to cover your face."

She sat back again and stared at him for a moment, then looked down at her paperwork and slowly smiled. "Mr. Anders..."

"Please, call me Bill."

"All right, Bill. You are in the city of Tel Aviv in the country of Israel."

The few words that Dell had said to him during the flight finally sunk in and he turned the color of a ripe tomato. His mind started swimming and the young woman rushed around her desk and put her arms around him and helped him to take a seat. "Are you all right, Bill?"

"I... I... I am so sorry! I had no idea you would be a Jew! Is it okay to say that?"

Her laughter pealed through the hallways until she had to sit next to Bill. When she had calmed down a bit her sparkling dark eyes turned to Bill and she said, "Yes. That is okay to say, but I would leave the Arabic alone until you are in a place where it is spoken. My name is Sarah and you are a funny man. Could I show you around my country while your paperwork clears?"

Bill looked at Dell with hope in his eyes. Dell nodded. "I would enjoy that very much."

She returned to her desk, stamped all the necessary paperwork, inspected their passports and handed Bill a note with her name and phone number. She stood and said, "Mr. Sharpton, welcome to my country. These officers will escort you to your house. Everything is arranged for your departure in three days." She handed Dell his passport and turned to Bill. "Bill, here is your passport and I welcome you to my country. I hope to see a lot more of you, *White Snake*." She pronounced the Arabic nickname perfectly. Dell only shook his head again as they followed the men out. Bill couldn't wipe the smile off his face.

This was Dell's first trip to Israel and it surprised him at how friendly the people were. Young and old seemed to be enjoying life and wanting to share that joy with most anyone they met. It surprised him because all the time he had spent with Arab Muslims he had never heard one good thing about the Jews who had stolen their land.

At first, he tried to stay in the safe house and not venture out, but Sarah brought two friends with her and they insisted that Dell go with them to see the country. Bill said if Dell didn't go out he wouldn't either because he knew what Dell would be doing while cooped up in the house. Dell knew the danger they may be going into when they entered Lebanon, so he relented for Bill's sake.

The next morning Bill was not to be found in the house but finally showed up around ten in the morning. Sarah was with him and she assured Dell she considered Bill's safety her prime responsibility. She confided in Dell that Bill was the funniest, kindest man she had ever met. She also said she would guard him with her life.

"Listen, Sarah; whatever you do, please don't teach him any Hebrew. That could get him killed." Sarah laughed and said she understood. She left to check in with her office. Dell knew she was Massad, the Israeli spy service, but that was to be expected.

There wasn't a lot of preparation to do so Dell had agreed to go out with Bill and Sarah on a quick tour of Israel. Dell's youth had been spent with people who, if they didn't hate the Jews, thought of them as intruders. The Zionists were people who uprooted and displaced Muslims of the area.

What he found were people who loved their country and would die to defend it—much like the Arabs. They visited the Holy places of three religions and there was a special feeling of being close to God. Dell had given up hope of believing in anything except the black mist that he strived for, but even he felt the touch of a higher power in these sacred places.

Sarah was a beautiful woman with long blonde hair, a tall lean body and a personality that could draw the evil thoughts from anyone and dissipate them into the hot dry air. She seemed smitten by Bill's wide-eyed fascination and love for everything he saw.

Dell knew that Bill was intelligent in his own way but his upbringing had left a great hole in his knowledge of the world. He also had a yearning that was finally showing itself as he was exposed to life outside the States. Bill had only joined the Terrorism Task Force because Dell had, and he put his trust in Dell to teach him what he needed to know. Dell only strived to die without taking Bill and others with him.

Dell asked Bill, "Where did you go last night?"

"To Sarah's apartment."

"Where else?"

"We went to meet some of her friends for dinner but then we came back to her place. I had no idea Jews were so friendly. I think I like it here. I need to take a nap," he said with a sleepy grin. Dell guessed the *White Snake* didn't get much rest last night.

At the Lebanese border, Dell and Bill received their weapons and extra clips of ammunition. The soldier who walked with them to an enclosed van said, "Your passports are stamped as entering Lebanon three days ago and there are no Israeli stamps. You were never here. Sarah has asked that you explain this to Bill. She wants him to return safe and unharmed. Be very careful over there. It is a dangerous place, especially to people who are fond of Jews. The driver will take you to the outskirts of Beirut and a taxi will take you to the house your people have set up. Good luck." He turned and walked away.

Bill said, "I'm going to miss Israel. And Sarah. She might be the one. What's really going on, Dell? Why are we going to Beirut?"

They got in the van and as they rode Dell explained what he knew. He spent a long time talking about the hatred between the Jews and Arabs. Bill sat quietly thinking and finally asked, "Do you think we're going to die?"

"Not if I can help it. When we get back maybe you should start learning Hebrew. You did seem to hit it off well with Sarah."

"No way. I'm going to learn Jewish."

Dell settled back and he tried to enter the mist. It wouldn't come. Being in the desert and near the people he cared for made him content. He only dreamed instead of having nightmares. Then his dreams changed—he was back in the mist.

Bill shook him lightly. In Dell's dream he saw armed men hiding near a house with a blue door and a taxicab parked across the street. They were set up in ambush waiting for someone.

Dell opened his eyes to the smiling face of Bill. He looked out the front window and could see they were in the outskirts of a city with narrow, dry, dusty roads and people all about. The traffic was light and it was near sundown. He leaned forward and asked the driver where they were. He told Dell they were in Beirut and only a few blocks from the place he was to let them out.

They turned onto a wider street and the van began to slow. Dell could see a taxi parked across from a house with a blue door. He grabbed the shoulder of the driver and said, "Don't stop."

"But this is where I was told to drop you off."

Dell had his pistol out and pressed against the back of the man's neck as he repeated, "Don't stop." The van continued down the road at a slow pace. They came upon a large bazaar filled with people buying produce for the evening. "Stop here."

"But this is a dangerous section and many do not like Americans."

"How do you know we are Americans?"

"I was told."

"Stop the van!" The driver quickly pulled to the side of the road. "Get out, Bill." Dell stepped out of the van and said, "Drive away and forget about us. If I see you stop, I will blow your head off." The van pulled away and hurried out of sight.

Dell and Bill moved into the bazaar carrying small satchels with extra clothes. People eyed them suspiciously but Bill gave them an Arab greeting and a big smile. No one tried to stop them. As they walked Dell said, "We're doctors from Canada and we are going to work at one of the Palestinian refugee camps."

"What if they want me to operate on somebody?"

"Shut up, Bill, and follow my lead. And stop talking to everyone. It's not done here."

Dell purchased some fruit and a few sweets just to have something to keep Bill busy. They made their way through the bazaar and found a taxi on the other side. Dell had the taxi stop at a small shop a few blocks away and went in, leaving Bill in the car. He returned with two cell phones, chargers and a few other items. He told the driver to head down to the coast to a once thriving tourist area in Beirut. As they rode in the back of the car, he disassembled his special phone given to him by

Loretta and one at a time tossed the pieces out the window. He did the same to Bill's phone.

Bill leaned over and said, "I had Sarah's number in mine."

"We'll call her later and warn her to be careful. Someone knows we're here. They were waiting to kill us where we were to take the taxi." After the last piece was thrown from the window he told the driver to pull over at the Hilton.

He paid the taxi and watched it drive away. Bellhops were trying to secure their bags but Dell shooed them away. It was dark now and he led Bill across the busy street and hailed another taxi. He told the driver to drive towards the Bir Hassan district.

Little could be seen of the city at night. There was some obvious destruction but the old Beirut was coming back to life. Dell saw a large night bazaar and told the driver to stop. He paid and indicated for Bill to get out and carry both bags.

They entered the teeming market and were soon lost in the crowds. Dell found a clothing shop and made a quick trade of everything they had with them including the baggage. He even traded the clothes they were wearing for a few western style pants, shirts, underwear and shoes. The shop owner was pleased with the trade.

Dressed now in good but used clothing, they bought some fried fish and chicken at a tiny stand and twice Bill leaned in to say something but Dell shook his head. Bill had no idea what was going on but he never doubted Dell's ability to keep him alive.

They moved out of the crowd and secured another local taxi. They proceeded to the Raz Beirut district where the American University is located. Dell had the taxi stop near the university and they walked down a side street.

"What is going on?" asked Bill.

"I have a bad feeling. I think we're being tracked and that makes me nervous."

"Of course they're tracking us, but if you think it's bad then I'm with you." That was another thing Dell liked about Bill.

He rarely argued about Dell's feelings. It had saved his life before. They walked for forty minutes and Dell found a small hotel for westerners and locals.

The next morning Bill woke to find a small breakfast waiting and Dell sitting facing the window. Dell was *not-at-home*. Bill ate breakfast even though his stomach was protesting and then looked through the items they had purchased and slowly brought Dell out of the mist. When Dell looked him in the eye, Bill asked, "What is going on? What is it we're doing here?"

"We're going to find the street where I saw the men. I think the map might tell us where they plan to set off the bomb. We're also going to try and stay alive long enough to catch these people."

"Sounds like a plan! I'm ready to practice my Arabic."

"Whatever you do, don't speak Hebrew... Jewish. Maybe you shouldn't say anything."

"Dell, I came here to learn more Arabic. Not walk around like a dumb American."

"We came here to find terrorists, so whatever you do, don't act like an American."

"I'm just saying..." Bill let it drop.

They spent the day walking in the area of the American University and visited several internet shops. Beirut was coming back to the beautiful city it had been before the days of all the fighting between the Christians, Muslims, Palestinians, Israelis, Syrians, and anyone else who just wanted to blow stuff up. There was plenty of evidence of hard fought battles as many buildings were still in shambles, but the people seemed to be getting along—at least for now. Dell found a brochure with a picture of the street where he had seen the men and the map.

Bill was all smiles as usual. He was getting better at speaking Arabic and even the people who might have taken offense just naturally liked Bill and his friendliness. Several very pretty women—young and not so young—offered to show Bill around the city but Dell quickly put a stop to that. This was not a vacation. Dell also purchased more clothing for them.

They returned to their hotel room, checked out, and Dell found another hotel on the south side of the city. Bill had eaten something that didn't agree with him and it was making him a human gas factory. Somehow he thought it was cute. "Dell, pull my finger," Bill said with a grin.

Dell just muttered something about not being able to take him anywhere and Bill pulled his own finger and giggled.

Late in the afternoon they dressed in traditional Arab garb including a keffiyeh, head wrap. Dell had to warn Bill not to play with his clothing. Each secured their weapons for easy access but out of sight and then set off to look over the street Dell had found. His plan was to just have a look and then stake out the shop. The sun had darkened their faces but nothing could hide the color of Bill's blue eyes. Dell had told him if anyone should ask he was to say he was from Macedonia, where blue-eyed Muslims were common. It took ten minutes to explain where Macedonia was and that it was not important to speak the language. He told Bill to only speak Arabic and try very hard not to speak at all.

While they walked, Dell could hear Bill trying to quietly pronounce Macedonia in Arabic. Dell's dialect was so perfect that people only guessed he was from an affluent family because of his lighter skin. Bill's Arabic was improving rapidly but his accent was that of a foreigner.

They made one circuit down the street and Dell could see Bill sweating and wanting to talk to people. He took him to a small restaurant just down the street from the shop he had seen in his *vision*. As they enjoyed the strong coffee of the region, Dell slipped into his own little world.

There were five men and the woman he had seen before. One of the men, who was dressed in a tan dishdasha instead of the normal white, was placing a map into his briefcase while several others stood guard. Dell just caught sight of the city map but couldn't quite see the name. He could see that it was somewhere in the U.S. The men stood in deference to the woman— which was unusual—while she spoke to them heatedly.

Dell opened his eyes because Bill was shaking him. Bill said in Arabic, "This seems like a bad place to be sleeping."

Dell spoke quickly in Arabic, "It is time. Be ready and let your eyes see." Switching to English he whispered, "This is it. Follow me and be ready to shoot." He hurried from the restaurant and moved directly to the shop. Dell passed through the doorway with his weapon drawn but within the folds of his garment. The shop sold tobacco, hookahs and a myriad of other products.

Chapter 9

The shop owner caught sight of the pistols and spoke in a loud voice. "You have come to the wrong place! There is nothing for you here. Be gone." Dell never stopped as he moved to the curtained room in the back of the shop. Bill was close behind him.

At the sound of the shop owner's voice, the man in the tan dishdasha and another man ran through a doorway at the back of the shop that led to the alleyway. Two men drew weapons and faced the curtained door. The woman waited at the exit.

Dell never hesitated. He was firing his weapon as he entered the room. The two men went down and he stared at the woman still dressed in a Burka. Their eyes met for only a fraction of a moment and someone clubbed Dell from the side. Dell went down and the man raised the club to finish him, but Bill put a round through his head and he dropped like a stone. Bill checked the area and it was clear. Kneeling down to check Dell, he strained to pick Dell up and he let out a long, loud flatulent sound followed quickly by an odor that made Dell scramble to his feet. As the foul odor invaded the small room, they heard harsh voices from the shop. The owner said, "The infidels are there."

"Stay here and let no one enter," said another voice.

Dell grabbed Bill's arm and yanked him through the exit. The alleyway was clear and they ran west making several quick turns as they went. Dell could hear loud .voices that sounded like there were men all around them but he and Bill never stopped. Several times Bill's untimely flatulent attacks sounded off with loud reports. Del turned his head and said, "Why don't you just fire your pistol so they can find us?"

"I'm not..." Bill let another loud fart out as he finished. "It's not me. It's the food." Another burst came forth. "Sorry." Dell almost smiled at Bill's dilemma.

The shouts were getting closer. Dell tried several doors but they were bolted closed. He stopped twenty feet from a sharp turn in the alley and raised his pistol. There were the sounds of men rushing at them from both ends of the alleyway. He moved into a cramped passageway that led to another alley.

They were moving deeper into the labyrinth of the alleyways and buildings. The area looked like it had been close to the recent war, with rubble strewn about on the path. Dell stopped to catch his breath. The sound had faded but it was obvious people were still looking for them. From just ahead, around a corner they could now hear a large group moving their way.

A door opened just across from them and they both swung their weapons towards it. A small boy stuck his head out, looked both ways and then hurriedly motioned for them to follow.

Having no other option except to stand and fight, both men rushed into the opening with their weapons ready. The door slammed closed and they heard the bolt slide home. The darkness took their sight for a moment and a noise caused Bill to twist around, causing another loud fart to emanate from him.

A child's voice said, "Do you have money?"

Dell said, "Yes. If you help us." He looked around as his eyes adjusted to the dark. They were in a bombed-out room where only minor efforts had been made to repair.

"Follow me and no talking. And tell this one," pointing at Bill, "not to leave a stink trail. He could get us killed." The young boy laughed as he passed through a hole in the wall of the room. Dell and Bill could hear shouting just outside the doorway so they followed without questions.

Dell had not gotten a good look at the boy but as they passed through the light of the setting sun he saw a small boy dressed in rags but moving without effort. They traveled into several other buildings by way of holes torn in them by bomb or rocket blast. It was getting dark but the boy moved with surefooted efficiency and did not slow until he came to another doorway that appeared to lead out into the street.

He put up his hand and motioned for Dell and Bill to wait and rest. He slipped out and closed the door behind him. Bill whispered, "Do you trust this kid?"

"We don't have a lot of choices... just be ready to fight and whatever that was you ate... don't eat it again. It's starting to make me sick." Dell uncharacteristically chuckled.

"If..." purrrp, "I knew..." poot, poot... "what I ate..." puroopop, "I would stop." He started laughing softly, holding his hand over his mouth and couldn't stop. Each laugh brought more gas and awful smell. Dell tried to stifle a laugh but it escaped and he too had to cover his mouth.

The door swung open and both men turned their weapons on it as the young boy stepped inside. "Come. I will find a place for you to hide." He turned and hurried away. Dell and Bill were close behind him.

They crossed the street into more narrow alleyways and were soon completely lost. After almost an hour, the boy came to a halt and pulled them down so he could speak. "I will help you escape but you must promise to help me."

"What is it you want?"

"I will tell you later, but now you must promise."

"If we get away from here safely then I will do what I can for you," said Dell. The boy looked at him through the darkness and then turned to leave. Dell put his hand out to stop him and asked, "What is your name and why are you helping us?"

"My name is Sami Hasan Salim Salama. I told you why I help. I want a better life for my sister and me. I watched you a long time and I think you and your smelly friend are different. You are spies, yes?"

"No, Sami, we are not spies but it won't be good if we are caught here. I am Dell and my noisy friend is Bill. I won't lie to you. If I can help I will, but getting us out of here is our main priority. We are trying to save lives and we need the map one of those men had with him."

The sound of voices approaching from a nearby street prompted Sami to move out without another word. Only a jerk of his hand told them to hurry. They followed close behind in the dim light.

Sami took them right to the edge of the buildings. The light of numerous fires showed they were near a large encampment where many people lived. Sami moved along the walls of the damaged buildings until he came to a large opening that had been blown out by explosives. He motioned for them to enter a space where the smell of animals was pervasive. In the pitch black, Dell and Bill reached out as they followed Sami and felt what might be goats. What they stepped in was unpleasant but Sami moved with confidence.

At the back of the large room was a heaping pile of hay and bags of grain. There was a barrier to keep the animals from getting to the feed. Sami moved to the stacked hay. Reaching down he lifted a heavy wooden covering exposing a small hole in the floor. He said, "Go down and follow the tunnel a short way. It will lead to a cave. There is an oil lamp and candles and also water and a little food." He looked at Bill and smiled. "This will be a good place for your friend to stay. He will smell like the other animals and no one will suspect he is here." Bill smiled and ruffled Sami's hair, then he jumped down into the hole.

Dell looked at Sami and said, "I give you my trust and therefore my life. I will call you friend when this is over. Inshallah."

"Inshallah. If a girl comes, do not harm her. She is my sister, Fatima." And then Sami closed the opening and they

83

heard him moving hay over the cover. Bill led the way in total darkness and said, "I sure hope this kid knows what he is doing."

"Bill, I still have my gun and if you let one go in my face I'll be forced to shoot." Bill moved out quickly without a peep. They traveled only about ten feet and came to a larger opening. Bill felt around until he found a small bowl with stick matches and struck one. He saw a small oil lamp that looked a little like an elongated, small teapot and lit the wick. The feeble light it gave off showed them that the cave was a big room perhaps ten by ten. There were mats on the floor and bedding in the corner.

"It looks like the kid lives here."

"Maybe only when the shelling begins."

"Is there still a war going on?" Bill asked.

"There's always a war here. The Syrians, Israelis, Palestinians, Lebanese Christians and Muslims. Someone is always trying to kill someone else."

"How long are we going to be here?"

"Did I get here before you? I don't know but the kid is our only hope right now."

"Dell, you know we can't get this kid out of here. Hell, we don't even know how to get out. What are you going to do with him?"

"If he saves your life I'll do whatever I can. Maybe your pretty friend Sarah can help."

"I wouldn't mind seeing her again. I do seem to have a way with these women." Another loud, long fart escaped Bill and the flame from the small lamp brightened.

"Yeah, you're a real ladies man all right."

"Dell, I've got to go."

"Hold it in. We don't know how long we'll be here."

"That's not an option! I mean I really have to go."

Dell looked around and saw a bucket in the far corner and pointed at it. Bill had a strained look on his face as he moved to the bucket. He started to raise his dishdasha and stopped, looking at Dell. Bill pleaded, "Turn around. I can't do this with an audience." Dell turned and grimaced at the noise that came from the corner and the smell made him put his arm over his nose.

"Dell, how do I...? There's no paper."

With his arm still covering his mouth and nose Dell said, "Use the bucket of water beside you and stop talking about it. The smell is bad enough."

Dell heard the water splashing and Bill said, "Don't worry. You won't even notice it in a few minutes. By the way, this is disgusting. "

"Maybe if you lie down it might help your stomach."

"Right." Bill moved over to the sleeping mat and lay down. Dell sat with his back to the wall of the cave and watched the entrance. He couldn't allow himself the pleasure of his own little world.

Hours later Bill awoke and saw Dell filling the small lamp with oil. "How long have we been here?"

"Five hours."

"Has the kid come back?"

"No."

Bill sat up and wrinkled his nose. "Man, it stinks in here." Dell gave him a disgusted look. Bill said, "Lie down and sleep. I'll keep watch. Is there anything to eat?"

"You're not eating again 'til we get out of here." Dell switched spots with Bill and was soon asleep.

Bill looked at the low table and saw what looked like fruit and round balls of bread or pastries. He was so hungry he ate the entire plate of food.

Dell dreamed of his youth with the Bedouin. It was a hard life but it suited a young man like Dell. He had often gone back to the States with his parents but he missed the rugged beauty and the people of the hot sands.

Sometime later he woke to the sounds of a struggle and even before his eyes had cleared he had his pistol out and ready to fight. What he saw made him stop. Bill was lying on top of a young woman with his hands holding her arms spread away from her body and his mouth covered hers. Dell moved next to them and said, "You do seem to have a way with the women here."

Bill jerked his head up and Dell replaced Bill's mouth with his own hand to cover her mouth. "Help me out, buddy. She's trying to scream." She struggled under Bill trying to get free. There was fear in her big, dark eyes.

Dell turned her head so she could see him and said in Arabic, "Be still, pretty lady. We mean you no harm. Sami brought us to this place. We mean you no harm." Her struggling stopped as she saw the truth in Dell's eyes and she nodded. Dell slowly removed his hand and she remained quiet. Bill was lying on top of her and staring into her beautiful eyes. "Bill... Bill. Let her up. Bill!"

Bill stared at the girl underneath him. Her skin was dark and dirty. Her teeth were blackened and a few were misaligned and her breath stank. Her hair was filthy and ragged, but her eyes were... beautiful. He could feel her full breasts as she squirmed under him. Bill finally turned his head to look at Dell and said, "What?"

"Get off the girl."

Bill let out a long, strained tooting sound as gas escaped once more. "Oh. Sorry! I just didn't want you to scream."

"Tell her in Arabic."

"Forgive me, pretty lady. By the word of Allah I mean you no harm. Forgive me." He released her and sat back.

She jumped up and with blazing eyes said, "Forgive? You try to rape me and put your mouth on mine and you ask for forgiveness?"

Bill looked at Dell, not understanding, and Dell said, "He is new to this world and does not know your customs."

"Is it common where he comes from to attack a woman?"

"Only if we think we are in danger. He speaks the Holy language but not very well."

She took a step forward and slapped Bill hard across the face and then she looked into his eyes and gave him a tiny black-toothed smile. "Tell him to keep his hands to himself.

86

Why does he smile so?" She sniffed the air, wrinkled her nose and asked, "What is that smell? Did you bring a dead animal down here as well?"

"My friend ate something that disagreed with him." As if to confirm this, Bill let out another squeaking toot. His face turned red but he said nothing.

"Well, inform him not to eat more. He smells so that my animals won't come near the feed. They fear a wild animal is near."

"Only a *White Snake*."

"What...?"

"Never mind."

At hearing his nickname Bill gave a big smile to Fatima but then backed away and let another loud fart escape.

"What did she say?"

"She says you smell like a dead animal. And you must only speak Arabic." Bill turned red again and that brought a giggle from Fatima. He looked over at her and kissed his lips and touched his heart and then moved his hand towards her. Now her eyes widened and her color deepened. Dell let out a groan.

Dell said, "His name is Bill and he is just learning the ways of the sand. He is asking for forgiveness at the odor he is causing. Please do not take offense at his gesture. I will try to instruct him in proper manners."

"Are you a true believer?"

"I am a Christian but lived with the Bedouin in my youth."

"You are an infidel."

"In your thoughts, yes."

"Have you come to this place to kill Muslims?"

"I look for information about terrorists. In my eyes I have only respect for the Arabs."

"But you kill Muslims, yes?"

"I won't lie to you. I have killed terrorists who call themselves Muslims."

"Then you have come to the right place but you will need many more weapons. Have you killed the innocent?"

The question caught Dell off-guard and he slumped in reaction. Then he asked her, completely ignoring her question, "How do you know I have a weapon?"

"This one," pointing at Bill, "carries two and you do not look to be one who would run from danger."

He looked at Bill and then back at Fatima. "We do have pistols but Bill only has one."

"When he lay on me and held my hands I felt a pistol and another large weapon."

"He only has a small pistol."

"I know what I felt and he has two..." She stopped and suddenly his name *White Snake* came back to her. Her head whipped around to look at Bill and then her color deepened even more as she covered her face with her hands. She leaped to her feet and blurted out, "I must go!"

Both men jumped up and barred her way. "It is dangerous for us if you leave. Your brother Sami told us to stay here."

Her beautiful dark eyes looked at Dell in fright and she glanced over at Bill and again hid her face. Bill said, "We will not harm you. Please forgive the smell." Bill hadn't followed the conversation and thought she was offended by the odor.

"I will tell no one—but I must leave. I will take the bucket to empty... I will tell no one."

Dell nodded to Bill and they stepped out of her way. She grabbed the bucket and as she stooped down to leave Bill said, "Forgive me." She stopped and shyly looked at him and then she hurried out.

It was then that Bill noticed she had a pronounced limp and she seemed to have a deformity in her back. "Dell, she's not too pretty but those eyes are intense. Did you notice that limp and her back and those teeth? Why was she turning red like that?"

"Because you pretty much asked her to marry you."

"I did not! All I did was do that thing with my right hand you taught me to do. Was she angry?"

"Sit down." Bill took a seat. "Here's another lesson in Arabic customs. When you ask forgiveness or say hello to others you touch your heart and kiss your fingers. It is a sign of sincerity. Never kiss your hand and touch your heart unless it's to someone you love or have great respect for and never to an unmarried woman."

Bill thought about it and couldn't really see the difference but if Dell said it he knew it was true. "Okay, so what do I do when or if she comes back?"

"Stay away from her and only speak when she asks you something—which is likely to be never."

"But she's a woman and we have to be nice to her." The look Dell gave him made him groan. "Oh, all right. What are we doing here stuck in this cave? Don't you think we should be hightailing it out of here?"

"We can't leave until dark. I don't like this either but that map is important and I'd like to find out who that woman is. I've never heard of an Arab woman giving orders for this kind of attack." He looked around the small room and then said, "We don't have a choice that I can see. Just be ready to fight and run if necessary. Sami is our only hope of getting out of this with our skin."

They settled down and Bill took the first watch. "I hope she brings that bucket back."

A few hours later they heard a noise and positioned themselves. Sami called out that he was alone and he moved into the room. "What have you done? There are men looking for you everywhere." He sat a basket down and looked from one to the other. He wrinkled his nose and gave Bill a hard look.

Dell said, "No one knows we are here."

"Someone knows. There is a big reward offered for you two. I could be a rich man, but I have given my word and I will see my part through. I expect you to do your part as well."

"We'll do everything we can and I'll make sure you have money when we leave."

"Money will get me killed. My sister needs to get out of here."

"Why is it so important for your sister to leave?"

"You saw her." He pointed at Bill and gave him a hard look. "He has touched her and now she acts like a fool."

"She hides herself from those who might take her as a wife. Everyone thinks because she is deformed she would only be good as a slave. She is getting old and I must find a place for her so she can marry and use her intelligence. She is my only family and she is smart. I want her to have a chance at a good life, but now this... this one has tainted her."

"Me? I didn't do anything but make sure she wasn't armed. And I'm sorry about my stomach. I'm not used to eating some of this food. She looks young. She couldn't be that old."

"If my father were still alive he would kill you, but I understand about infidels. I put it on you to see her safe and get her out of this fighting." Sami motioned for them to sit and sat the basket between them. "Eat."

Dell reached for some rice and chicken and began to eat. Bill looked at the food. He was hungry but he remembered what happened the last time he ate. He looked at Dell, shrugged his shoulders and reached with his left hand for some of the food. Dell slapped his hand away and said, "Right hand! Always eat with your right hand."

"But I'm left-handed."

"Just do it."

Sami said, "I believe I have found the one you seek. He carries a case with him and shows it to no one. It is said that he has a treasure in it."

"Do you think he carries a map?"

"I don't know but he is being very careful with it—always has at least one bodyguard. Because I gather things for many sides in this conflict, I can move among them. They think me only a child trying to earn enough to eat." He puffed out his chest with pride and said, "I have twenty goats! That is more than most families have but I have to hide that from them or they would not trust me. My sister tends my goats. I will take you to this man after dark. Do you have a weapon that is not so loud?"

Dell said, "No. We didn't expect to be fighting our way out of here."

"That was foolish of you. Here you must always be prepared for the worst." He reached up and pulled two pieces of cord from around his neck. He withdrew two long, thin, curved-bladed knives still in their sheaths and handed one to each man. "You owe me for these."

After the meal Bill looked over at Dell and said, "Dell, it's happening again."

"What's happening?"

A long blast of gas escaped Bill and he said, "That." The smell was more powerful than before. Bill stood and walked around the small room hoping it would settle his stomach. He began to feel a bit better. With his back to the entrance he concentrated on his stomach when the scent of sandalwood touched his senses. He turned around and looked into the beautiful dark eyes of Fatima. It startled him so that he let out another great volume of fetid gas. The noise rose and fell in a low bass sound. His tomato face came back and he backed against the wall, not looking at her.

The giggles that came to him caused him to look up and see a blackened smile and those eyes that were bright with humor. She asked Sami in a different dialect, "Does he always make these noises and turn that color? He looks like a ripe pimento but he smells like a dead cat."

Dell said, "He does turn that color sometimes but he is having trouble adjusting to the food here." Fatima looked at him in shock as she realized that he spoke in the same dialect.

Fatima was now wearing a hijab, a scarf Arab women wear that covers their head but not their face unless they pull it across. She pulled the hijab to cover her face and approached Bill. She stood, waiting until he looked up at her. When their eyes met, Bill tightened his butt, but the gas escaped in what sounded like tiny blasts from a cornet. Fatima laughed and pulled her hijab tighter. Then she opened the sack she was holding and gave Bill a small pouch. He opened it and saw a white powder inside. Fatima spoke with her eyes downcast, "This will help with your... problem. Take it with water." She handed him a bottle of water.

Bill looked at Dell to be certain of what she had said and Dell said, "Take it." Bill ate the powder, drank the water and the relief was almost instant.

He looked at Fatima and said, "Thank you." He touched his heart and kissed his lips.

Fatima said, "You are learning. Perhaps I will work with you to improve your speech."

"Thank you."

Fatima turned to Dell, lowered her hijab and said, "We must get you out of here. The entire city will know of the reward for you both. You cannot stay. We are all in great danger if you do."

"There is something I must do before I leave."

"Is it worth dying for?"

"Yes."

Sami spoke up. "I will take this one to find what he needs. You will take the *orchestra* and go into the hills but..." He looked at Dell. "He must not violate my sister!"

Dell said, "I want Bill to go with me. It's not a good idea to separate. I will need someone to watch my back."

"That is why I go with you. I fear two men traveling tonight would draw too much attention and this one smiles too much. Fatima will see him to safety and we will join them when you have what you came for. It is the only way."

Dell spoke with Bill and made sure he understood what was happening.

Bill protested but Dell explained it was the only way to get out of the city.

Sami asked Dell for money to buy a few things they would need and he was soon off on his mission.

They would have to wait for three hours before leaving so Dell settled back to enter his favorite world. There was too much pain in this world that constantly reminded him of his brother and the war he had been in.

Dell's entire family was deeply religious. Even as his father placed him with the different tribes within the Arab world, he always spoke to Dell about their commitment to Christ. Dell, when he was ten years old, asked his father how he could be a Christian and do the things he did. His father would always say that he did those things for his country and that he would be forgiven at his judgment.

After his father's death, Dell attended Ohio State University majoring in Arabic and took a number of courses in religion including both Christian and Muslim faiths. He completed his degree in three years and then joined the U.S. Army as an enlisted man. He served in Iraq and Afghanistan as an Army sniper and LRRP, or Long Range Reconnaissance Patrol.

Dell left the Army after only a few years and returned to the desert to try and understand his role in the military. Dell spent a year in Sudan with his Bedouin family. He returned to the States and found his calling in the Arab Gang Unit of the New Jersey State Police. It became the Terrorism Task Force.

Dell felt the familiar tug and his dreams took on a lighter shade. Before he returned, he saw a small body lying in the dust of a filthy street and a dog trying to drag the body away. Dust was jumping all around the dog and the body.

"Dell. Dell... It's time to go. Com' on back."

Dell grabbed for his pistol but it wasn't there. His vision cleared and he looked into the eyes of Bill. "I wish you would stop taking my weapon."

"The day I'm ready to die I'll leave it where you can get it. Sami's back and he said it's time." Dell sat up and looked at the concern on the faces of Sami and Fatima. Bill said, "He is okay. This is... not unusual for him."

Fatima, with her hijab pulled over her mouth, said, "We must work on your language. Are you sure this *Desert Rider* will be ready for what he is to do?"

Bill said, "*White Snake* says it is so."

Sami's head snapped around when he heard Bill's nickname and then he pulled Fatima to the corner and spoke in a dialect that Bill did not understand. He was angry but Bill could see the humor in Fatima's eyes.

Dell was on his feet and said to Sami, "You can trust this one. I have spoken of the need to preserve this child's innocence."

Sami threw an old dirty robe at Bill and said, "Do not violate my sister!"

"I will protect her with my life."

This seemed to satisfy Sami. He said to Fatima, "If we are not at the meeting place by sundown tomorrow, then continue to the place that is known by no one and wait until we arrive." He turned to Dell and handed him a worn western style shirt and pants with a short jacket to conceal his weapon. "This will be better where we go. I will be your son, but you must follow my lead." He turned to Bill. "You will be Fatima's grandfather and chew this." He threw him a pouch. "It will taste bitter but it will fill your mouth so your speech will be difficult to understand. You must act a bit drugged but there is nothing in what I have given you to change your judgment. Making your animal noises will help if someone tries to question you." Sami turned to Fatima and said, "It is time. Fatima, take this one and go, but remember my words. I should not like to have to kill him."

Fatima kissed Sami on both cheeks and motioned for Bill to follow.

Dell told Bill to do whatever Fatima said. Bill followed Fatima out. Dell could hear the goats bleating as they were herded out into the night. They waited ten minutes and then Sami motioned for Dell to follow.

As soon as they entered the dusty street, Sami took Dell's hand and made a clicking noise. A small dog rushed out of the shadows and excitedly jumped at Sami. Sami knelt down and pulled Dell down as well. The dog looked suspiciously at Dell but Sami spoke to it and it was soon wagging its tail and nuzzling Dell. Sami said, "This is Haji. He will watch over us. If he pushes you, run to a place of concealment." Without another word Sami started off down the street.

They walked for twenty minutes and met only a few men out in the street. Several times Dell felt eyes watching them from the rooftops. They passed several coffee shops crowded with men talking loudly over the whining music coming from a radio or CD players. No one seemed to give them any notice, but at one point several armed men stepped out to block their way. There were no street lights so in the dim lighting Sami put his hand on Dell's forearm to caution him not to take action.

"Why do you come here?"

Dell answered, "My son and I go to see my sister, who is giving birth tonight."

"Where does she live?"

Dell looked at Sami and then at the three men. "I do not know the place. That is why my son goes with me. He lives here. I am from Golan."

Sami spoke to them telling them the name of the section where they were heading. It was a refugee camp not far away. The men turned and went back to where they guarded the byway. Haji barked excitedly and ran forward. Dell and Sami followed.

After several twists and turns, Sami pulled Dell into an abandoned building very close to another coffee shop. He said, "The man we are looking for comes to this shop very late but only stays for a short time before he goes to his home not far away. He will pass by here and I have seen him carrying a small business case. He always has at least one guard. Can you deal with two men without making a lot of noise?"

"Does he have the map?"

"That is what I have been told. You must silence both men or we will be dead quickly."

Dell pulled the long, curved blade. "I will do what I must."

As Dell looked out on the narrow street and listened to the high-pitched music coming from the shop, he thought back to the days he had spent with his adopted father, Tahnoon Al

Zayed. He had spent many months in the deserts of Egypt and Sudan learning from the Khawalid Bedouin. He would return to America from time to time but he would always come back to the desert. Dell came to love these people and the other Muslims he came in contact with. They were not the terrorists the western world considers most Muslims. They had a strict way of life and little that came to them from the modern world had any effect. As the years passed, the tribe moved across the Red Sea to Jordan and then to Syria and Israel. A great drought forced many of the people from Syria into the cities of Jordan and Israel, and Dell had lost contact with them for many years.

A soft growl from Haji brought him out of his daydream. His eyes searched the street and he saw four men walking towards them. Sami touched his arm, and just before he pulled Dell into the shadows of the room, Dell saw a glint of reflected light from a rooftop across and down from where they were. The men passed by and Dell moved to the opening again. He saw a rifle barrel trailing the men.

Sami said, "That is the man we seek. He has three bodyguards. We cannot overcome that many."

"How long do you think they will be in the shop?"

"Perhaps twenty minutes—no more."

"Is there another way out of this building?"

Sami said, "Of course, but it will take a little work to break through. Come, I will show you." He led them to the back of the building where Dell could see pinpricks of light in the wall's surface. "The wall is very weak here. We can break through if we must. But if we are caught in this next building we will be killed without a chance to explain."

"Why?"

"Look for yourself."

Dell put his eye to one of the small holes in the wall. The room was brightly lit and there were at least twenty young women laughing and talking gaily. They wore no coverings on their heads and Dell could see that most were very pretty. He looked questioningly at Sami.

"This is where maidens are brought to be selected as brides for the right price. This is the reason I must get Fatima away from this city. She hides her looks but it won't be long before she is brought to a place like this."

"Who would bring them here?"

"Families in need of money or if the girls are orphans they are taken from the streets."

"And they would do this to your sister?"

"Of course. It is the way here."

"Are they guarded?"

"There will be a few men outside but everyone knows the penalty for entering without invitation."

They moved back to the opening and Dell whispered, "When this starts you grab the case and wait for me by that wall." He nodded towards the back of the room.

"You will need help in this."

"You must do as I say, Sami. If I have to worry about you it will make it more dangerous. I don't want you involved with the killing. It is something I must do." Dell squeezed Sami's shoulder to let him know that he must trust what he said.

Sami puffed out his chest and said, "If you must worry about me then something is very wrong, but I will do all you ask."

Dell smiled.

Twenty minutes later Dell watched the man with the case emerge from the coffee shop with his three bodyguards. The man laughed and joked with his men as they started back down the street.

Dell was ready to attack, but just before the men reached the opening automatic weapon fire tore through the silence. It lasted only a few seconds and then in the deadly silence that followed someone from the roof top called out, "Get the package."

Two men ran out towards the dying men from a doorway up the street. Men burst out of the coffee shop but the gunman on the roof sent a burst of fire into the coffee shop above the heads of those who had come out to see.

As the men in the street scrambled to get back in the shop, Dell stepped out into the path of the two men racing to where the man and his bodyguards had fallen.

Dell never hesitated. He sliced through the throat of one man and continued his drive of the blade into the other man, taking him in the neck as well. He caught a movement to his side and saw Sami rush out. One of the wounded men reached out for him but Haji tore into his hand. Sami picked up the case. The man on the roof fired a long burst. Sami went down with dust jumping all around him. Dell reacted, pulled his pistol and fired six rounds at the shooter.

Sami was lying in the dusty street with Haji trying to pull him towards the building by the sleeve. Dell ran to Sami, grabbed his collar and dragged him through the doorway. Sami never let go of the case.

Dell's rage was turning on him for letting this kid get killed but then Sami rolled over and smiled up at Dell.

"Do not worry, Mr. Dell. It is an old trick to keep a gunman from shooting more."

"Are you hurt?"

"Just some cuts from the rock chips. I am well."

Dell did something he hadn't done in a very long time; he hugged the child to him and thanked God for his safety.

Shouts from the gunman could be heard and then the automatic weapon turned on the building that Dell and Sami were in. Bullets ripped through the sundried bricks and dust filled the air. Dell raced past Sami and lowered his shoulder into the wall sprinkled with tiny lights. The wall gave way so quickly that Dell stumbled through the screaming women and was at the entrance where two giant men stood in surprise. Dell hit them with his body but it was like hitting a solid wall that wouldn't give. Arms wrapped around him but then deeper throated screams than the women were making came from the two giants. Dell felt the pressure release and Sami was there pulling him past the two men who had fallen to the floor in agony.

Sami was putting his knife away as he led Dell up the street and then down an alleyway. They never stopped until Dell was nearly spent. Sami pulled him into another abandoned building and pushed him against the wall. "Rest for a moment. We are still not safe but I will take care of you."

Dell, huffing, rasped out, "Give me the case."

"Rest. You will have the case when you keep your word. I will not betray you." Sami moved to the entrance and looked out. Dell wanted to go after him but he had to rest before he dropped. He had trusted the boy this far and once again he had no real choice. He looked over at Haji sitting next to him. His canine lips were pulled back in an almost smile with his tongue hanging out as he too caught his breath. Dell reached over and rubbed Haji's head, smiling along with the dog.

Dell looked at the entrance and Sami was gone. He looked at Haji and saw no concern so he settled back to rest. He could hear gunfire in the distance.

Fifteen minutes later Sami returned and said, "There is a great battle and people are searching for us. Are you so important?"

"No one knows we're here and no, I'm not important."

"Perhaps you are not so important but many people know you are here. I heard men talking about two American spies that assassinated the leader of the local faction and stole diamonds worth millions. Now there are many people looking to collect the reward. Were the men who killed the leader working for you?"

"Didn't you hear the bullets flying all around us? That gunman was trying to kill us. No one should know Bill and I are here unless... unless the people I work for told them. We need to get out of here."

"Now you have involved me and my sister. I heard them call me by name. If you do not help us we are dead! Come. We must leave this place."

"How long before we meet Bill and Fatima?"

"I don't know. We cannot follow them. I will have to take you into the desert. I know people who may help us.

Fatima can take care of herself but if that... *White Snake*
touches her there will be trouble."

"Bill's a good man. He's just new to this world. I'm sure
he will respect your sister."

Chapter 10

The light chased the darkness from the east and the
goats needed to rest. Fatima and Bill's escape from the outskirts
of Beirut had nearly ended in disaster when she saw armed
soldiers approaching them out of the night. Fatima whispered
hurriedly to Bill not to speak.

Fatima had changed into a cloak that gave her a heavy
look and she walked behind Bill in the manner of a wife. Bill
instinctively stooped a bit and used his herding staff to support
his gait. He kept his head lowered.

The leader of the small group of armed men approached
and said, "Salaam Alaaikum."

"Alaaihum Salaam." Bill said in a hoarse whisper and
then he had a coughing fit.

"Why do you travel in the middle of the night?"

Bill turned to Fatima and gestured to her to speak. She
said, "We travel to our old village to seek medicine for my
husband. I think he has the spotted sickness." Bill again broke
into a fit of coughing.

The men stepped back and let them pass without
another word. One said, "Death walks this night. Let us hurry
from this place."

Bill later said, "You are very quick. Thank you, wife."

"Don't get any ideas... *White Snake*... Bill Anders. I must
think of another name for you. Either one you have now will

only bring suspicion. You may continue to call me wife but do not touch me. Do you understand?"

"I understand and will give you the respect you deserve for saving my life." They spoke no more until they arrived at the wadi Fatima had been aiming for.

Fatima moved out to lead the small herd into the rough country ahead. In the moonlight Bill could see her heavy limp and the bulge in the small of her back. She looked to be in pain as she walked in her shuffling gait. If it weren't for her dark, rough looking skin, her limp and those black teeth, she might have a chance at life in this crazy place. He felt sorry for her but each time he pictured her all he saw were those eyes. They seemed to look deep inside him when she spoke and they laughed even when she blushed. If he could find a woman with those eyes and a body to go with them, he would be happy. Too bad she limped and looked so bad. He would make an effort to be kind to her without being forward. He was a long way from understanding the ways of these people.

The Arabs he knew in New Jersey weren't anything like these desperate people. They knew how to appreciate a man like Bill. Well, they put up with him and got a big laugh from his nickname. He had been alone for a long time and had thought about trying to get to know one of the Arab women back in the States, but they had that... commitment-now attitude. Couldn't he maybe test drive a few before he committed? He thought about Sarah. Now, the Jews seemed to have the right idea. She was pretty and right away let him know she wasn't looking for a husband—just some fun.

Fatima on the other hand—he really liked that name— liked to laugh at his predicaments but at the same time didn't want to get too close. Of course, he couldn't blame her. He needed to find out what that was he ate and what it was that she gave him to fix it. He could really have a lot of fun with the other *Staties* on the force back in Jersey. If Fatima looked better and didn't limp, he could see her being fun to be around. He guessed that was too much to ask for, especially the black teeth.

Bill asked, "How long do you think we will have to wait here?"

"We will stay here until the sun rises tomorrow. If my brother does not come by then, we will move again."

The next morning Fatima woke Bill and said, "I have decided to call you Hakim. It means wise in my language, but I'm not sure if it will fit. Remember that name and answer to no other. I must take the animals to forage and gather more food for us to eat. You remain here, and if anyone comes, cough as you did before. No one will come near you for fear of your disease. You must drink water during the day. If you do not, the heat will kill you as surely as a bullet."

Bill slept for a few hours but the heat of the sun woke him with a great thirst. He drank from the water skin but it had a bitter taste and he only took a few swallows. As he looked around, the sun stabbed at the ground and he had to shade his eyes. The pack donkey that accompanied them had moved to an outcropping of rock and stood three-legged in the small bit of shade.

Bill raised the robe over his head but it only intensified the heat. He got up and squeezed into the shade beside the donkey. The animal gave him a forlorn look but did not move. The temperature dropped dramatically in the shade. It was almost tolerable. The donkey stank but Bill could see the waves of heat rising all around outside the small shade so he stayed beside the animal, preferring the smell to the heat. He was thirsty and several times he thought about drinking, but the bitter taste he remembered kept him from the water skins.

He had to move several times during the day to stay within the shade. At one point he sat below the donkey, which provided the only shade, but the animal seemed not to notice. Bill's thoughts ran away from him and he soon just endured the heat. He felt light-headed but even that went away as the day progressed towards evening.

He woke to a cool cloth wiping his face and chest. It was like a refreshing rain in the desert heat. His eyelids were stuck together and he couldn't open them. He tried to raise his hand to his face but Fatima said, "Be still, Hakim. I will make it better." Bill tried to speak but his tongue would not respond. "I am so sorry, Hakim. I should not have been away so long. There were men watching me and I had to move far from here."

Bill felt the cloth wash against his eyelids and then a thin trickle of bitter water ran into his mouth. He tried to turn his head away but Fatima held it firm. "You must drink. I warned you that you must drink. You will die quickly in the desert if you do not." Bill drank the bitter liquid and slowly it began to revive him.

Finding his voice he whispered, "Why does it taste so bad?"

"It has a little salt and quinine. It is the drink of the desert. I had forgotten you know nothing." She gave him more water and he didn't stop drinking until she took it away. He slept.

Opening his eyes, Bill could see it was sunset. He looked up at the brilliant sky and watched fiery orange battle with the soft blue and the darkness that crept in from the east. He looked around and saw Fatima working over an open fire preparing a meal. If he didn't hurt so much, he would have enjoyed the scene. Fatima looked back at him and smiled. Bill thought that even with her black teeth there was something about her he liked. He had never had anyone care for him like that and she seemed to be truly worried about him. Too bad she wasn't pretty. Laying back to enjoy the coolness of the evening Bill was soon asleep.

He woke and looked up into the dark pools of Fatima's eyes. When his eyes opened, she hid her smile with her hijab. His head lay in her lap and she offered him more water. Then she spooned a liquid broth into his mouth and he hungrily took it in. "You will be better tomorrow. I will teach you the ways of the desert and help you with your speech."

"Where are Dell and Sami?"

"I do not know. Even here there are rumors of a great battle near the place we lived. I think it has to do with *Desert Rider*. How is it he comes to have that name?"

"He doesn't tell anyone much of his past. But when he was young he lived here and learned from the... I can't remember what they are called but they traveled in the desert and lived in tents."

"Bedouin?"

"That sounds like what he called them."

"And now you kill Muslims for your country?"

"We try to protect our own people from all terrorists, including some Muslims. Dell doesn't say much but he's always made it clear that we are not fighting Muslims. He calls the ones we fight... I forget but he says they are not of the true faith."

"And how do you feel about the true faith?"

"I have met many Muslims in America and most of the people I meet are good. I have learned to respect them and they even give me a little of that respect. Dell taught me that. Meeting you and Sami has only given me more respect for your people."

"All Muslims are not the same and we must use great care if we disagree with the fanatics. America should stay out of our lives and not try to change the way we live."

"You—I mean the fanatics, brought this fight to us and we try to protect our people. I do not know all the history of what causes these terrorists to do what they do, but I am trying to learn."

"Perhaps there is truth in some of what you say, Hakim. I will help you understand."

"What does Hakim mean?"

"It means wise. I think I have picked a good name for you."

"Don't you like my nickname?"

Bill's head bounced off the hard sand as Fatima stood and walked back to the small fire. As she threw sand to douse the fire she said, "It is time for you to sleep. Tonight I will keep watch. It gets cold at night so try to stay warm. We will leave early if Sami does not arrive."

Bill shivered in the crisp, cold night air, but at one point he felt a warmth flow through him and his sleep became undisturbed. He woke while it was still dark and found that Fatima had curled up next to him. He looked up at the night sky that was filled with more stars than he had ever seen. He put his arm around Fatima and pulled her closer. Her warmth was like a contentment that washed over him. As he returned to sleep, he thought it was too bad she wasn't pretty, but he could get used to her warmth.

Waking again, he saw the sun rising in the east. Fatima was tending a small fire. She was humming a soft tune and he smiled. Bill rose to his feet and couldn't believe the pain in his body. He groaned and Fatima looked at him, drew her hijab across her face and said, "It will get easier but you must drink water all through the day. If you do as I tell you, you will learn the way of the desert."

"I am yours to command." The sparkle in her eyes told him he had said the right thing.

As they started the herd of animals off, Fatima said, "Our next meeting place is several days away but I will go slow for you and we will speak as we walk." She had wrapped Bill's head in a traditional head wrap and insisted he wear the robe. She told him it would protect him from the sun.

The heat softened his pain and he began to look around at the unfamiliar land. It was harsh and bleak and he wondered how the goats and donkey could find enough to eat in a place that had nothing but sand and rocks.

They camped in another wadi and Bill insisted he would help keep watch over the flock. During the night, Fatima woke to loud noises made by Bill's stomach. She went to him with more medicine and water to drink. Her smiles and his embarrassment were hidden by the night.

As they travelled, they would walk behind the small herd, and Fatima spoke of the beauty of the desert and richness of life found there. From time to time she would stop and point out the striation of color in the ridge lines and give Bill some of the history of the land. They topped a hill and saw deer and wild goats on a far ridge and in the distance he could see the green of trees and vegetation making a line through the rocky hills. Fatima explained that the green was the Litani River and they would be near it in a day or two.

For two days they walked the rolling dry hills of central Lebanon as they made their way south toward Israel and Jordan. Bill listened and learned as his eyes opened to the beauty that Fatima spoke of. He practiced his Arabic which often brought a laugh from her. He even tried a few jokes, but they didn't go over very well. She would sometimes look at him like she was trying to judge him or make a decision about him, but she would only look with her face covered. It suited her to show only her eyes and there were times Bill forgot about her limp and deformed back. If he only thought about her eyes he could hear the goodness in her.

They entered valleys of greenery that the goats and donkey found to their liking. The animals rested often in the shade of the hills and Fatima stopped at each small spring to replenish the water skins and made sure that Bill drank large quantities of water after she added salt and a small quantity of quinine.

Several times they saw small villages and Fatima would leave Bill with the flock and go in to buy meager supplies. With what little they had she made good meals of rice, meat and dried vegetables.

They had traveled until the afternoon and were preparing to stop in the shade of a deep cut. Fatima walked to a rise to view the surrounding area when she saw armed men approaching in a military vehicle several miles away. The men might pass without seeing them but she would take no chances.

She told Bill to chew some of the root Sami had given him to blacken his teeth. Knowing she must hide Bill until the men passed, she told him about the approaching soldiers. Fatima led Bill to a very small cave under a massive boulder and pushed him inside and then jammed dried brush into the entrance.

Throwing on her robe, she moved the flock farther away down the wash. Her limp became more pronounced. She heard the vehicle approaching so she gathered her flock and set up a quick camp.

The men rushed in to confront her but only found an old woman alone with her goats. "What are you doing here all alone?"

"Who else will tend my flock and find food for them? Will you?"

"Who is helping you?"

"My nephew. He has gone ahead to find water."

"We saw no one."

Fatima, with a cackling laugh said, "You drive around with a great dust cloud following you and think a person of the desert cannot avoid you. He will be here before nightfall if you wish to wait."

"We are looking for two foreigners from the west. Have you seen anyone in your travels?"

"I see many foreigners while tending my flock. All come from the cursed land of Syria or Saud. What western infidel could survive here?"

"Be careful of what you say about the men of Syria. We are here to protect you from the Zionist dogs who want to take this worthless country."

She again cackled and said, "An old woman has no fear of the ones who would come and spoil this land. We will be here long after your bones are bleached dry by the desert sun. I have seen no one in four days. Now leave me in peace and go about looking for Zionists and westerners." She turned her back on them, spit a black stream of liquid into the sand and began tending the small fire she had started.

They left but Fatima knew they would watch for a while. She did not want to leave Bill in the cave because of the heat and his not knowing what was happening, but she had no choice. As the afternoon progressed, she heard the far-off sound of a motor. She quickly climbed out of the valley, as agile as a monkey, and watched the soldiers meet up with two other vehicles and then drive away towards the west.

She hurried to the cave and dug the brush away. When she cleared the area she saw two black scorpions race out of the opening and hide in the rocks. She reached in and pulled Bill out. He groaned but could offer no help. Fatima cried out, "Have you been stung?"

"I... I don't know. I... think so. It hurts but I knew I couldn't cry out. It would have put you in danger."

Fatima knew the bite of a black scorpion was not as deadly as the white ones but the pain would make anyone, man or woman, cry out in agony. Pulling Bill into the sunlight, she yanked up his robe exposing his body. His entire back was red and swollen and she quickly found where he had been stung four times.

In her pack she had a pouch of tobacco which she quickly chewed. The taste made her ill but Fatima refused to spit it out. The tobacco mixed with the black gum she chewed and made a paste that she applied to the stings. This would draw out the poison but he would be very sick or he might even die. He must have been bitten soon after entering the cave. She bound the paste with strips of cloth and helped him onto the back of the donkey. Fatima tied Bill's legs and arms to the beast and started off to find water.

Bill would moan from time to time but made no loud noises. Fatima knew how much effort it took to hold that kind of pain in. He was protecting her. It was nightfall before she found a secluded area she knew would have a small spring. There were pines and grass covering the floor of the small arena and the depression would help hide the fire. Fatima needed to prepare an ointment made of goat fat, herbs and an antibiotic. Bill needed to eat and remain warm to survive the night.

While the medicine boiled down to a paste she prepared a soft bed of pine boughs against a large rock that retained the heat of the day. She laid out a blanket and moved Bill onto the bedding. He was shivering and unable to contain the moans of pain.

She had to remove his clothing to check for more stings and she wrapped her hijab across her face to hide her embarrassment, but she did what must be done. He was under her protection and she must do whatever she had to—it was the way of the desert.

This white westerner made her laugh on the inside. He was sincere but ignorant to the ways of her people. What would it be like to live in his world? Fatima could speak English but hid it from everyone except Sami. She read everything she could about America and it was her dream to go there with Sami to live a safe life. Maybe these two men were the key to making that happen. Bill was her responsibility and she would do what she must to protect him. Perhaps she might even tell him the truth.

After applying the medicinal paste, she covered him with his robe and a blanket and then brought meat and soup for him to eat. She helped him sit with the heated rock against his back and spoon-fed him. She tore off the pieces of goat meat and chewed them until they were soft and fed them to him. He was delirious and mumbled about her beautiful eyes and willowy body in English. It embarrassed her to think that someone—even a foreigner—thought of her in that way.

Spending her adult life hiding so many things from others had become natural. What would this one do if he knew the truth? Fatima had spent all her young life hiding any beauty she might have to discourage the men who were constantly looking for girls to sell as wives to the older men. Disguising her beauty for so long, now she too was convinced that she was ugly and unwanted.

She shooed Bill's mumbling and moans and soothed him by stroking his hair and neck. It seemed to work and as she laid him down he briefly opened his eyes and smiled. His smile warmed her.

By the time she had cleaned the camp and prepared for the night watch she could hear Bill's teeth chattering from the cool night air. Touching him she found his body on fire. Fatima went to the spring and washed her body for prayer and asked to be blessed in what she must do to help this man.

Removing her clothing and adding them to the blankets, she moved in next to him and pressed her body to his to aid his warmth. Bill's contentment was immediate and he was soon in a deep sleep. She thought her skin must be glowing red but he felt good. Is this what it is like to be with a man? Snuggling in beside Bill, Fatima felt his arms come around her in comfort and heat. She too fell into a deep, peaceful sleep.

During the night Bill awoke and for a moment tried to remember where he was. The stabbing pain in his back reminded him of being in the small cave, but in his arms was an incredible heat. He moved his hand along the smooth perfect skin of a woman. In the twinkling of the starlight he looked down into the face of a beautiful woman. In his confusion he thought he must be dreaming. Or perhaps Fatima had found another woman to lie with him. This was no child he held in his arms. He felt the womanly breasts pressed to his chest and felt the muscled lines of her body. Arab women hid so much beneath their robes. She snuggled closer to him and he drifted off to sleep again.

At some point during the night, Bill's bowels loosened and he woke to the terrible smell but then he felt hands touching him. They were moving him and cleaning his mess. Bill couldn't remember anyone ever caring for him in that manner, not even his mother. The person removed the soiled blanket and replaced it with another and then gently rolled him back to a comfortable position. Drifting back to sleep he asked, "Who would do this for me?"

Chapter 11

Sami, Dell and Haji moved steadily north skirting the city at night and hiding in abandoned buildings during the day. Sami would go out and secure food and gather information. He returned in late afternoon of the second day after their escape. "The battle to the south is slowing but people are still looking for us. They know what you look like and I think it is more than a map they wish to get back from you. You must tell me the truth about why you are here."

Dell told Sami all that he felt he could divulge without endangering his mission. He finally said, "Give me the case and let's see what is in it. Maybe it will tell us what is so important that there would be a battle over getting it back."

Sami left but returned quickly with the case in hand.

Before he could say anything Dell said, "I will never forget my promise to help you and Fatima. You have already saved my life and even though that is not what I seek I will make sure you are protected." Sami handed the case to Dell without a word.

It took Dell ten minutes to jimmy the case open. There was no map inside but the case held several leather-bound notebooks, a stack of American greenbacks and a small pouch filled with diamonds.

Sami said, "No wonder they want the case back. There is enough money to make any man rich."

Dell ignored the money and looked over the notebooks. Most of it was in code but one of the books contained the code-breaker. He ran through it quickly and sat back in wonder. He said, "This looks like a list of several cells of terrorists and their locations and how to make contact. It may even contain the instructions to activate them. I must get this back to my people."

"You will use this to kill Muslims?"

Dell sat down and told Sami about his youth and the love he had for his adopted people and respect he had for Arabs. He finished by telling him of the danger these fanatics were causing to the Muslims around the world. "They are bringing hatred to the Muslims in the west. Many of my people do not understand the difference between the fanatics and most Muslims. There will come a time when these terrorists do something to enrage Americans so much that their hate will reach out and we will become the thing we fight so hard to stop. I don't want to see that happen. That is why I fight against these people I do not consider Muslims. I have lived with the Khawalid and met many people of the desert that I love and don't want to see the world punish them for the actions of a few who are misguided by hate."

Sami stood and said, "I will return. We need supplies and I need some time to think." He turned and left. Haji stayed by Dell's side.

Sami returned at sunset with a rucksack of supplies. "We must travel east into Syria and then make our way down towards Golan. Fatima will not stay long where she waits but will go on to the next place and then back to our home. Are you truly adopted by the Khawalid? Who is the man who adopted you?"

"I have told you the truth, Sami. My tribe lived in Sudan and Egypt but I have heard they have moved to Jordan in recent times. My father's name is Tahnoon Al Zayed but I don't know if he still lives. He was an old man in my youth."

This satisfied Sami and he motioned for them to move out. Haji leaped out of the building and led the way east. Around midnight they broke out into the desert and did not stop until near daybreak.

As the sun started its journey, Dell stood on a rise to view the hills of the rocky desert opening up before him. He breathed deep of the coming heat and tears came to his eyes as the brilliance of the day blasted the night to the far west. The big azure sky took over before he turned back to help Sami set up a day camp.

Sami had watched him the entire time and witnessed the same thing he felt touch Dell's heart. He was a true *Desert Rider*. His word was the same as his life—unbreakable.

That first day as they slept and kept watch from the shade of a hill, Dell was alive as he had not been in many years. The heat of the desert soaked into him, softening the brittle fabric of his soul, and his beliefs began to return, but his conviction to see this journey through remained constant. When he tried to enter his black mist, it would not come. Dell looked at Sami. He found him watching and smiling. Sami was looking inside of Dell and he didn't shy away.

"We will have to travel a long distance to find my sister and your friend. She knows this land better than me but I have doubts about your friend. Do you think he would take advantage of being alone with Fatima?"

"Bill would not do anything unwanted. He is a good man."

"But when he finds that she is twenty-two and not a child can he be trusted?"

This caused Dell to pause in his thoughts. Bill was in search of love—something more than a quick encounter—but the desert does strange things to a man. He hoped Bill would not fall victim to its heat and beauty. "I would trust him more than any other man with your sister. Perhaps he will not see through her disguise. You have done well to keep her secret hidden from others."

"I saw that she likes him. I have come to trust you, but if he spoils her... then I make no promises to his safety."

At daybreak Bill opened his fevered eyes and his entire body ached. Even turning his head was an ordeal, but he wanted to find Fatima. Fighting the pain, he looked to the east and saw the tiny form of a girl stooping by a spring. She was wrapped in a gauzy cloth that turned translucent in the rising sun. She was washing her incredibly long dark hair. The scent of jasmine carried on the breeze to where he lay. Rinsing away the soap, she dipped her hair into the pool and moved so the light of the sun blinded Bill for a moment. Then she stood blocking its rays once more and Bill saw all of her small figure. She could be no more than five-two with a willowy body that made her seem taller. Her body was that of a complete woman. This pixie looked like an angel come down from heaven to enjoy the new day—perfect in every way. He wondered where Fatima had gotten to. Bill's eyes closed and drifted away again. The woman's body raced through his dreams.

Fatima raised her head to see him sleeping.

Fatima had pressed herself to a man—to aid and care for him—but now she felt something more. She had cleaned him and touched... Had she sinned or was this the one man she was meant for? How could she know such things? She had spent her life duping all others into thinking she was an ugly child. Now she wanted this one to know the truth but it could not be. He was an infidel—a westerner—and he would soon leave this land and turn away from her. She couldn't let him trick... No, the truth was she couldn't trick him because he would be gone from her world all too soon. She would keep her disguise and not let him know the truth.

Fatima sat for a long time musing about what would become of her and letting the sun dry her body. Finally, she rose and dressed, securing the hard leather pad around the small of her back, tucking her hair under so it appeared much shorter, rubbing sand and dirt into her hairline and finally chewing the paste to blacken her teeth. She prepared a morning meal of soupy gruel and goat meat.

The heat had come to the desert and she erected a sunscreen from the night blankets to protect Bill. Then she knelt down and gently woke him. "Hakim, you must eat." Bill opened his eyes and for a moment she could see the look of a man as he looks at a woman. He smiled and winced as he tried to move. The look left him and a friendly smile returned to his face. "How do you feel, Hakim?"

"I feel like I have been run over by a truck. What happened?"

"You were stung by..." she thought of the English word. "By *scorpions*. You made no sound when the soldiers came. You were very brave."

Being in the cave and the stabbing pain in his back returned to him. Remembering harsh voices, he knew Fatima would be in danger if he made a sound. "I didn't want the men to harm you. You have saved my life."

"Very brave." She helped him to sit up and lean against the heated rock. Once again, she fed him by hand and she was forced to hide her face with her hijab.

He looked around and asked, "Where is the woman who was here?"

"What woman do you speak of?"

"The beautiful one that was bathing at the spring."

"There is no one here except me and your eyes tell you I am not beautiful. Enough talk. You must rest." She pulled the hijab tighter across her face. Bill smiled at her and closed his eyes.

There was enough forage for the animals so they remained where they were through the day. Fatima was in constant motion caring for the animals and Bill. She would bring in small rocks heated by the sun and place them on Bill's back over the wounds left by the scorpions. By the evening he was up and moving around. She insisted he bathe but left for the surrounding hills before he started.

After sundown they ate and Fatima continued her lessons long into the night. She was a confident woman but often hid her embarrassments in the folds of her scarf. She prepared the bed for Bill and quickly moved into the shadows to keep watch.

Looking around, Bill hoped the woman he had seen would join him. He left the corner of the blanket pulled back in invitation for Fatima if she became cold in the night. He woke once and found her snuggled in next to him. He enclosed her in his arms and drifted back to sleep with a smile.

Over the next several days they slowly made their way deeper into the hilly desert. Fatima would occasionally climb a steep hill with impressive agility and speed to survey the surrounding area. Most of her time was spent teaching Bill how to watch over the herd of goats and refining his Arabic.

In the desert, with nothing but its beauty to pull Bill's attention away, his skill with Arabic improved as his strength returned. He also began to see past Fatima's physical problems to the beauty within her. Her humor was slowly coming to him as his command of Arabic grew. She was full of life but seemed determined to hide it from him. His admiration grew but he forced himself to keep his distance, not wanting to force his attentions on her. Her limp and other problems became less noticeable, but she remained hidden in her robe and hijab. The closer he came to knowing her the more the beauty of the desert lands came to him. He was getting a taste of what Dell's life might have been like in his youth.

Sami and Dell crouched in a gulley alongside a roadbed as two four-door pickup trucks passed slowly by. After they had passed Sami said, "Those were freedom fighters of Hamas. The reward must be great for them to come so close to the Syrian soldiers."

"I thought Syria was helping Hamas against Israel."

"It changes from day to day, but Syria only helps Syria and they want the Zionists gone so they can control the lands all the way to Egypt. They put up with the Palestinians only as long as they do as they are told. When the Zionists fall there will be another war, but the Palestinians will not fare well in that fight."

"How far is it to where we will meet Fatima and Bill?"

"We must cross this land to Golan. If they are not there, then we will go into Jordan to our people."

"You are not Palestinian?"

"No." Sami would say no more on the subject. They settled back to watch and wait for nightfall.

"*Desert Rider*. What is it you seek? I can see you are pleased to be here in this land but your mission is to kill Arabs."

"My mission is to stop something that I believe will bring a terrible war to the people of this land. I respect the Arab people and understand the life they wish to maintain. Few from my country know anything about the Arabs except to think they all wish to kill us and destroy our way of life. Most have no idea that most of the Arab people want many of the things the west has to offer, but they cannot express what they think for fear of the fanatics punishing them. It will take many brave people in these lands to step forward to stop the destruction. I fight and, yes, I kill those who would bring death and fear to the people of my land. I wish there was another way but until we are helped in this fight the Arab people are in danger too. If the west is baited into unleashing its power, then there will be blood and death here that will never be forgotten.

"For now all I want is to get back to the States and stop the people who would terrorize us. It is important."

Sami said, "I can see how the desert affects you. It is difficult for me to understand how someone from the west can care about this land and its people and still kill those who live here. Perhaps I will have to think more on this.

"I worry about my sister and this man you call friend. He doesn't seem very bright and he smells like something dead. Are you sure he won't harm Fatima?"

"Bill has never left my side when there was danger and he is the only person I trust. He will not harm Fatima and will watch over her. He doesn't know much about the Arab people but I would put my life in his hands. He will learn and maybe Fatima will learn about the west through him. He is the closest thing I have to a brother. He is open and doesn't hide his feelings. Some people think he is not smart but it's not true."

After two more days of travel Fatima led the herd to another quiet place with a small spring and grazing in the area. Scouting the location before entering, it looked as if no one had been there in a while so she led Bill and the herd into a secluded spot and made camp. Once again, the heat had taken its toll on Bill and he had lagged behind for most of the way.

117

Fatima wondered what this strange, noisy man thought of her. Although he was polite, he seemed at a loss for what to do most of the time. He had much to learn but he listened intently to what she taught him. As a result, his Arabic vocabulary was increasing, but more importantly, she could see his eyes starting to take in the true beauty of the dry land. Still, he didn't realize the danger he was in. If he were found here in the tribal lands, she would have to fight to protect him.

His friend, *Desert Rider*, had made promises to Sami but she didn't believe he would fulfill them. They would leave at the first opportunity and Sami and she would be in danger once again—perhaps more than ever before. They had left their tribe because Sami feared Fatima would become just another ill-treated concubine or unloved wife to one of the men there with whom they had no true connection. He wanted a more promising future for her and for himself. His crazy dreams of going to America were just that, but even though she was the older of the two, she still took great pride in the fact that her younger brother did all he could to protect her and her honor. This was not the normal way of the desert. Sami found her books to learn English and some of the ways of the west: all for Sami's dreams. She did not believe they would ever get away from this life and she had thought of offering herself to a man so that she could protect Sami. He was all she had in this world.

Now these men had come to fill his mind with hope and she knew they would betray them in the end. But she had given her word to protect this... smelly man. He was funny in his own way and she was enjoying teaching him her language and about desert life. She even thought about letting him know some of her secrets, but he was a stranger, and she had no way of knowing what he might do if he knew more of her true self. The more she learned of Bill, the more she saw into his heart, but who was she to think a westerner infidel—no matter how interesting—would give a care for her or Sami? She would not go anywhere without her brother. Fatima had taken a pledge to protect Sami with her life.

Perhaps when they saw these two safely away she would offer herself to one of her tribe. She had no desire to become one of many wives but it would bring Sami back into the tribe and he could become a man of substance. He was the smartest person she had ever met and she knew he could hold his own in the tribe or anywhere he went. What if it were true... that these men could take them away from the wars and fighting and hard, harsh life of the desert? Would it be worth the risk?

Fatima looked over at Bill, Hakim, and discovered that his fever had returned. She drew fresh water from the spring and took it to him. As she reached him he toppled to the side. She hurriedly opened his robe to examine his back and saw the red lines of poison that coursed across his skin. This sometimes happened when the scorpion's bite left too much venom or infection set in. He was deathly pale and his breathing had become very shallow. Placing her ear to his chest she could barely hear his heartbeat. She chastised herself for not paying more attention. He needed medicine she didn't have. Bill would die without it.

Fatima quickly erected a tent from the ground cloth packed on her donkey and then made a fire to brew a medicinal drink and a broth to give him fluids and nourishment. Thoughts of lying with him again to keep him warm made her pull the hijab tighter to hide the heat of her face. She fought the thoughts that she enjoyed being close to him with her body pressed against him. He was not for her and she would be a fool to think otherwise. But he was interesting and she wanted him to live.

She washed his body and left water on him to be cooled by the heated breeze. Next she filled the water flasks and placed them within his reach, along with dried meat to eat if he should wake. Gathering all the blankets, she covered Bill to keep him warm. After all was done she said a prayer and asked Allah to watch over this infidel and let him live. She swore an oath to look after him if he would be allowed to live and promised to teach him the ways of her world.

Fatima, finally prepared, hobbled the donkey, gave Bill one last drink, washed his body one more time and then set out across the desert at a fast walk. It might take as long as two days to return with medicine and other supplies that would be needed.

During her absence Bill's fevered dreams were a mixture of phantoms, ghouls, unbelievable beasts and occasionally a beautiful tiny woman would come and lie with him to ease his pain. At one point he heard voices and spoke out in Arabic for water. All he received was laughter and warnings he would soon be dead.

Bill survived in darkness and watched the wraiths coming closer and closer with empty grins of anticipation. These wraiths seemed disappointed that it was Bill and not the other one who tormented them.

Death appeared and moved closer to him and then suddenly the tiny sprite was there to threaten death and curse it to stop and be gone. The beautiful lissome creature faced death, screamed out her challenge and drove death from Bill. Her angelic face looked at him with tears streaming down her face as she knelt and touched him. He knew her but couldn't remember. He tried to call death back to ease his pain but she turned his face and kissed him. The pain eased and coolness touched his body. All he could see were those dark pools looking at him and then he slept.

Fatima had traveled all through the night and the next day to reach the distant town where she found an apothecary. The desert people had been taught since childhood what herbs and medicines were needed to treat the ailments of the desert. Using the last of her coins, she had to beg a meal from an old lady of the village. She didn't stop to rest but turned back to the dry lands after filling her water skin.

By the time she returned, she was stumbling and at the end of her endurance. Taking only quick notice that her goats were gone along with the donkey, Fatima ran to Bill. Throwing the covers from him she could see death was almost upon him. She quickly brewed the medicine that might bring him back.

Fatima sang softly to him as she worked and then washed him down to take the fever away, hardly noticing his naked body and the places she touched. After feeding him the medicine and a broth of dried goat meat, chills had returned to his body. As the sun receded and the heat began to leave the desert, she stripped to nothing and lay down pressing her body to his. She fell asleep as his arms wrapped around her.

In her dreams he touched her in places no man had ever been, and it gave her comfort. Wrapping herself around him, she pressed all of her to him. It was good and her dreams were at peace.

She woke a few times during the night to his murmurs. He spoke in English about black teeth and a twisted body and how he wished it was made whole for him to enjoy. She silently cried that he thought her ugly and wanted someone of beauty to lie with him. He was not for her. But then he would quiet and come to her again and hold her tight and even kiss her forehead. She knew in his delirium he would not remember the hurt he spoke, but she also knew it was his truth and it tore at her heart. She would not allow him into her world. He was an infidel and could never... love an ugly girl like her.

Later he spoke in Arabic of men who had tormented him and stole Fatima's animals. He spoke her name and it touched her deeply, but weariness was still upon her and she slept without dreaming.

Chapter 12

As the heat of the day rushed back, she woke to loud voices and threats. She jumped up quickly, reached for her knife and saw Sami and Dell struggling. Sami held a long knife and was trying to get to her. She looked down and saw Bill's nude form lying beside her still asleep.

Sami roared out, "Cover yourself! Are you a whore of the streets? I will kill you both!"

Fatima looked down and at last noticed she too was nude. She jumped at the widened eyes of Dell and the hateful looks of Sami. She quickly wrapped herself in a blanket, grabbed her clothes, and before she ran she covered the nude form of Bill. She bolted around a boulder to dress and cover herself properly.

Sami screamed, "I will kill this... this *White Snake*! He has violated my sister and turned her into a whore. This infidel will die—I swear it!" He struggled to bring his blade to bear on Bill and Dell finally had to hit him and knock him unconscious. Dell took a rope and bound Sami's hands behind him and pulled him into the shade.

Fatima heard the struggle and after dressing, blackening her teeth and placing the pad at the small of her back, she rushed out to see what had happened. Her mind was still muddled from fatigue but she saw Sami bound and Dell standing over him with a blade.

She drew her own blade and ran at Dell screaming, "Do not touch him! We have promised to protect you and this is how you repay our kindness? Get away or you will die!" She rushed at Dell and he easily disarmed her and pushed her to the ground beside Sami.

"I mean you or your brother no harm. I am trying to protect my friend and you. What is wrong with him?"

"We have done nothing wrong!"

"What is wrong with him? Why does he look so ill?"

"He was bitten by two scorpions and I could not remove all the poison from him. He was dying and I went to a village to get medicine. He would have died without it." Her face flamed and she pulled her hijab to cover her entire face. "He has not seen me and has done nothing improper. He was sick with fever and I used my body to keep him warm... That is all... I swear it!"

She looked down at Sami, whose consciousness had returned, and saw his eyes burning into her. "I swear it, brother! I pledged to protect him and that is all I have done. I swear it on my life. He knows nothing of this. Hakim was unconscious and knew not what I did. I was only protecting him, Sami." She scrambled closer to Sami and bowed to the ground with her forehead at his feet.

Sami looked at Fatima for a long moment and then looked at Dell and said, "You will release me now. I must think on this but I will not kill him or this... woman. You have my pledge."

Dell said in an ancient dialect, "The desert brings strange truths to a man and Allah shall show it as true. Secrets live in the dry places and it is there they will stay." He switched to the normal dialect and continued. "I know this man and his word is that of steel. I have seen the actions of your sister and sees she speaks the truth. I tell you the truth." He untied Sami and stepped back.

Sami leaped to his feet and Dell offered him his blade back. Sami grabbed the blade and put it in its sheath. He looked at Dell, then Bill, who was still sleeping, and finally at Fatima. His eyes softened for an instant and he said, "See to this man you so boldly protect." And then he walked away into the desert.

"Fatima, he will be all right. He knows the truth. Please, continue to help Bill."

"I call him Hakim."

"Please help Hakim."

Fatima stood and went to build a fire to prepare more medicine.

Dell asked, "Why do you hide yourself so? You are a beautiful woman."

She spun on Dell and with great authority in her voice said, "You will not speak of this again. You will give me your word that what you have seen will not reach Hakim." Her voice softened. "I ask this of you, *Desert Rider*."

"I give you my word. Will he live?"

"Hakim will live."

"What happened to your animals?"

"They were stolen while I was away seeking out medicine."

"Who took them?"

Sami stepped from behind a boulder and said, "Bedouin have taken them. The signs are clear." Fatima spun at Sami's voice and she ran to him and again dropped to his feet. "Rise, Fatima. Your word is enough for me. I can see this... Hakim had no part in this and you only did what you must to save him."

She looked up at him with tears flowing down her cheeks. For Sami to speak her name meant he had truly forgiven her.

It was almost amusing to Dell as he watched this boy take on the posture of a grown man and for a young woman to prostrate herself to a child, but he kept his humor hidden. The desert called to him through these young people and his heart softened watching them. All the time he had traveled with Sami he had tried to retreat to his black mist but it would not come. He was slowly beginning to live again.

Fatima turned back to Hakim and attended him with easy touches as she spooned more medicine to his lips. Dell could see Bill relax at her touch and this made him smile a smile that could not be hidden. He looked over at Sami and saw his hard stare. Dell said, "It is good to see the word of the desert people has not diminished. I would proudly call you brother if you would allow."

Sami's eyes softened but he turned away and gave a soft whistle. Haji ran in from the shade of a boulder and leaped into Sami's arms, squirming in delight. He then jumped down and ran to Fatima, forcing her to laugh and hold his wiggling body for a moment. Next Haji ran to Dell begging to be lifted. Dell picked him up and hugged Haji.

Sami walked to Dell and said, "Haji leaves me no choice but to accept your offer of brotherhood. It shall be so." With his right hand he kissed his lips and touched his heart and then offered his hand. Dell repeated his gesture, took Sami's hand and then pulled him into an embrace.

Dell said, "When Hakim is able, we will retrieve your herd, brother."

"Why would we do this thing, brother?"

"A man must never let thieves take his wealth. He must walk proud for others to see."

"You are a true desert rider. Yes, we will get my herd back and then I can sell them so Fatima will have money when she goes to this new land of yours."

Late in the night Bill stirred and sat up. He could see other forms sleeping nearby. He called out in a raspy voice, "Water. I need water." Fatima was there before he finished speaking. She offered him a flask of cool water and he drank deeply. "Thank you, Fatima." The way he spoke her name gave her a thrill but she remained quiet. "I dreamed there was a woman lying with me. She saved my life. Was it you, Fatima?"

"There was no one with you. You have been very ill and I have given you medicine. You will live."

"But the woman? She was so real."

"There was no one with you. I rolled a blanket and pressed it to you. Fevers cause strange dreams in some. Now lie down and rest. In the morning you will be better." He didn't argue. She helped him lie back and Bill was asleep before his head touched the ground.

The light of day woke Bill and he looked around to see Fatima limping to the small fire preparing a meal. His dream of a woman with such a fine body lying by his side stayed with him but as he looked at the girl with the limp and bent back he knew it could have only been a dream. He wondered what it would be like to be with someone like her and knew he could never get past her infirmities. He did enjoy talking to her and if he didn't think about those black teeth, he really enjoyed her company. She seemed such an intelligent person. Maybe when she was older she would find someone who could overlook her infirmities. He hoped so.

Bill turned his head as Sami entered the camp. He smiled at Sami but a glare of momentary hate was all that was returned.

Bill asked, "Where is Dell?"

Sami pointed to the other figure sleeping on the ground. "He is resting. How do you feel?"

"I am weak but alive. What happened to me?"

"Ask your protector." Sami walked away without another word. Haji ran over to Bill, wagged his tail and ran after Sami. Sami gave the dog a hard look but said nothing.

Fatima, with her hijab pulled across her face covering all but her eyes, came to Bill with a broth and a few pieces of meat. She kneeled down to offer him the meal but would not look at him directly.

"Are you my protector?"

"Who would say such a thing?"

"Your brother."

Bill could see her face darken as she looked up into his eyes. Her eyes trapped him for a moment but then they looked away. "It is true. I have pledged to protect you since you were with me when you were bitten. I will remove this pledge if you prefer."

Smiling at her he said, "No. I've never had anyone be my protector. I am honored that it is you. If you will allow, I will be yours as well."

"It is not necessary. You have no need for an ugly, deformed... It is not necessary. Here is your food. You must eat to regain your strength."

She started to rise but Bill reached out and touched her sleeve. She looked at him and he said, "Why do you say that? I will be your protector. And do not speak of yourself in that manner again. No one would say such a thing to you."

"You have said those words. You must ask my brother if that is what you wish, but I need no protector. I can take care of myself." She rose and his hand slipped away as she walked back to tend the fire.

I said those words? No. I would never say that... even if it is true. He watched her limp back to the fire. *I am a complete ass. I must find a way to apologize to her.*

After Bill had eaten and rested he woke and saw Sami sitting in the shade talking to Dell. He called out to Dell and they both came to where he was lying under the shade of the tent.

"I want to ask something of you, Sami. I'm not sure of the proper way to say this." He looked at Dell but he offered no help. "I want to be Fatima's protector. I was told I must ask your permission."

Sami stared hard at Bill and finally said, "Have you violated my sister?"

"No! I give you my word. She is not my... No. I would never do that. You both saved my life and I ask this without conditions."

"Your Arabic is improving. You still talk as a child but I can see someone," he looked over at Fatima, "has been helping you. You may think of me only as a boy, but I have lived as a man for many years. Fatima is my only family and I will not allow her to be hurt. Are your words true?"

Dell broke in and said, "Bill. Maybe you should think about this. Do you have any idea what you are asking?"

Bill spoke in English. "Well, I might not know all there is to know but I do want to help her and Sami. I think it is something I must do."

"As her protector you would have to be willing to lay down your life for her and fight anyone that might try to harm her. You will have to help her in any way she requires. Only Fatima or Sami can remove this obligation you ask. It's no small thing to these people."

"I would be dead and my bones drying out in this desert if it weren't for her. Dell, I want to help her."

"Protecting her would not mean you could... She's not a child."

"Dell, you've seen her. She's not... pretty and that's not what I want."

"She's not...?" Dell had seen her in her true form but he remembered that Bill hadn't seen her except the way she hid herself. "All I can say is this is no small matter." He saw the confused look on Sami's face and said in Arabic, "I believe him, brother."

Sami turned to Bill and said, "Hakim. Is this true? What you ask."

"I give my pledge that it is true. I will try hard not to speak as a child and I will look to you and Fatima for guidance. I will protect Fatima with my life."

Sami looked at Fatima and saw the sadness in her eyes. He knew she understood the English that had been spoken. "Do you believe this man?"

Fatima nodded and replied, "Your ugly sister believes him. I will say when this is over. When he finds a woman that pleases him I will release him."

Sami turned to Bill and studied his face. The sudden thought of his nickname caused anger to darken his complexion. "You shall be her protector but if you violate her or hurt her you will answer to me. From this day on I will only call you Hakim... Hakim the Protector. I never want to hear you speak the nickname you are called. It is done!"

Bill looked at Dell and saw a real smile on his face. He hadn't seen Dell smile in a long time and wondered what he had gotten himself into. He held out his hand and Sami took it. Sami said, "Now get dressed. You are Fatima's protector and no more!"

They rested through the heat of the day. Bill and Dell spoke about their need to hurry back to the States. Dell showed Bill the ledger, money and diamonds that he had taken from the man in Beirut.

As the sun set, Sami announced that it was time to go after those that had stolen from him.

Dell said, "We must hurry. Bill and I have important business to take care of. Do you have any idea where they might have gone?"

"There are only a few places these men could be with my herd. They had their own herd as well and must follow the water and feed. They think Hakim is dead so I do not think they will travel fast. It should take no more than a night and a day to find them, if Hakim can keep up. The two *protectors* will stay together if he lags." He looked at Bill and then Dell. "Are you prepared to fight?" Both men nodded.

They started in the cool of the evening. Dell, Sami and Fatima carried the burden of their gear on their backs. Bill carried nothing but he soon began to lag. Fatima stayed by his side but wouldn't allow him to help her carry anything.

They stopped only twice in the night but as the sun rose they made a quick camp and Fatima prepared a meal while Bill slept. After a short rest they started off again. Fatima made Bill wear a hooded cloak to protect him from the heat and the sun. Again he lagged behind.

As the day was dying, Bill and Fatima finally caught up to the others. Sami and Dell were atop a dune surveying a peaceful camp with a large herd of goats and a few donkeys. One of the donkeys brayed and Sami swore, "That stupid donkey has caught our scent! I shall roast him when this is over."

Bill refused to be left behind but he agreed to go into the camp with Fatima as a ruse to distract the men.

He shuffled into the camp with Fatima walking behind him after Sami and Dell had made their way down near the camp and were in position. Bill entered the firelight and called out weakly. "I come in peace."

The men stood with knives drawn. "Who are you that you would enter a man's camp at night without announcing himself?"

"I am ill and my voice would not carry. You have found my animals. I must thank you for watching over them."

"Tell the woman to step out where we can see her!" Fatima limped forward and pulled back her head cover. One of the men laughed and said, "Old man, is that the best you could do?" The heat of anger flared within Bill but he said nothing.

The one who appeared to be the leader spoke. "We have only our animals. We were of fortune to find several goats in the desert near death. In my kindness, I decided to add them to my herd in hopes they would survive. We have nothing of yours."

"I see a fine herd and recognize my animals. And as you can see, they recognize me." A number of goats had come in to stand close to Fatima. The donkey butted his head against Bill and brayed.

"You do have a way with the donkey," another man said with a laugh, "and the goats have picked one of their own." This brought a laugh from all three men standing ready to fight.

The leader said, "Enough. Be gone or there will be trouble and you don't look fit enough. And your accent is not of this land. Where do you come from?"

Fatima spoke. "He comes from the land west of Egypt and these animals are his!"

"Shut your mouth, ugly child!"

The men advanced on Bill and Fatima and Bill pulled his pistol from under his cloak. They stopped and the leader smiled as he saw the pistol waver and shake. "That is a fine weapon you have. I shall take it, after you are dead."

They came in a rush and Bill fired wildly and missed but then Dell and Sami were on the men. Dell didn't want to kill so he used the butt of his knife and hands. Haji sprang in to harry the leg of one man. Two of the men turned to meet them and the other rushed at Bill and Fatima with a wild cry. Before he reached them, the donkey jumped forward and butted the man in the gut. He went down but recovered immediately. As he started to stand, the donkey whirled and with its hind legs kicked out and caught the man in the head. He dropped like a poled ox.

Dell had clubbed his man and the other was lying on the ground screaming from a knife wound to his leg that Sami had inflicted. It was over quickly. Fatima took all the weapons and Sami searched their clothing and found several more nasty looking knives. Fatima attended to their wounds after Dell tied their hands behind them. Bill sat in the sand, spent. The donkey came over and nuzzled him.

Sami said with a laugh, "I withdraw my words about roasting this beast. He has done well and given over his loyalty to Hakim. He is yours."

Bill said in English, "Thanks. That's just what I needed: a donkey." Fatima laughed and translated to Sami and he too laughed again. She realized what she had done and looked at Bill to see if he had noticed. He was rubbing the donkey's head, nearly asleep as he sat. She was relieved until she looked at Dell and saw him giving her a hard stare. She turned from his look and attended to Bill. Dell said nothing.

A rush of hoofs brought them all, except Bill, to their feet. Men wrapped in desert garb drove their horses into the camp and surrounded the small group.

The men were armed with long, wicked looking blades and one man held a rifle pointed at them. They pressed in close using their horses to hold the captives. Their faces were covered but their eyes left no doubt as to these men's deadly intent.

One man spoke. "What is this? Thieves stealing more of my herd?"

Dell lowered his pistol, motioned for Sami and Fatima to lower their blades and said, "We steal nothing. We come to get back that which was taken from us."

At the sound of Dell's voice the man turned to study him. There was a familiar ring to his voice but it had been many years since he had last heard it. He motioned for his riders to back away a few paces. He laughed and said, "An old man, young boy, a foreigner and an ugly girl child make a strange band. Who claims these animals are his?"

Dell said, "They belong to my brother and not all are his. We've come to collect that which belongs to my brother."

Dell looked at Sami and could see he knew he should not speak. He looked to be a child and these men would not believe the animals were his.

At hearing yet another man calling Fatima ugly, Bill rose up and pointed his pistol at the man who had spoken. He said, "Take care of what you say about this woman! I am her protector and your insults will not go unpunished." Fatima tried to go to Bill to quiet him but one of the men pressed a sword to her chest as another used the flat of his blade to slap the pistol from Bill's hand.

The leader spoke. "What a man of men is this old one! He speaks the true language but with a muddled tongue."

131

Fatima said, "He is ill and only means to protect me."

"But he speaks much like a child. I do not believe he is Arab." He motioned to one of his men, who jumped from his horse and stripped off Bill's outer coverings. He did it with such force that Bill collapsed to the ground.

Fatima again tried to go to him and yelled, "Leave him! He is ill and I will kill you if you harm him!"

The men laughed but when the leader saw Bill's blue eyes he became intense. "What is your name old man, and where do you come from?" Bill gave no answer. "You look to be an infidel from the west. You travel our lands claiming you are the protector of this... child. I think she is your slave, but the why of it gives me pause. Are you a spy from the Zionists? What is your name?"

Bill had gotten back to his feet and looked steadily at the man. "My name is Hakim and I am new to this land but this girl is no slave. It is as I say."

The leader turned back to Dell. The deadly look coming from Dell gave him a moment's pause. "Keep your eyes on this one. I think he too is more than he seems." He raised his rifle to strike Dell but Haji attacked his horse causing the animal to jump to the side and rear up, nearly unseating its rider. Sami gave a sharp command and Haji ran to him and sat at his feet.

The man got control of the horse and looked around at his riders to see if there was any humor in their eyes. He shouted, "Drop your weapons and control that dog or I will kill it!"

Dell dropped his pistol and several knives. Fatima and Sami threw their weapons in the sand as the man dismounted. The man looked at Dell and said, "Speak again, stranger."

Dell used the dialect of the Khawalid Bedouin. "What is it a man with no manners would have me say?" The riders growled and moved in towards Dell.

The leader held up his hand. "What is your name?"

"I have many but I am known as *Desert Rider* to my people." Another surge of anger came from the men.

"How is it you know the language of the Khawalid and speak it so well?"

"Would you expect anything less of a man of the Khawalid?"

"Remove your head wrap so I can look upon this man who claims to be my kin."

As Dell did as he asked the leader removed his head wrap as well. They stood and looked at each other for a long moment. Then one of the riders said, "I know this man. He is..." The leader raised his hand to silence the rider.

The leader asked, "Do you recognize me?"

Dell had been studying him and finally he spoke. "You are Mohammad Al Zayed, my brother." They rushed at one another and embraced as most of the others looked on in surprise.

Mohammad turned to his riders and spoke, "It is true! My brother has returned to the desert. Be at peace. We must celebrate!" He turned to Fatima and made a slight bow and then turned to Bill and bowed a bit lower. "Forgive our words about your charge. Be at peace. I invite you to my house as a guest."

Even Bill knew that to be a protected guest guaranteed their safety. He stood and Fatima rushed to him to help support him. "Hakim has taken the poison of two scorpions and is still weak from the ordeal."

One of the riders laughed and said, "Is that the reason he has taken such..." He never finished as Mohammad leaped and pulled him from his horse and hit him in the face three times. No words were said but the man recovered quickly, turned to Fatima and Bill and touched his heart and kissed his lips asking for forgiveness. Bill touched his heart and swept his hand away in acceptance. Then it was as if it never happened.

Mohammad saw that Bill was still suffering from the effects of the scorpion bites and the heat so he called to one of the men and told him to prepare medicine. He turned to Dell and said, "We have medicine that will take this poison from

133

Hakim but he will suffer for several hours before it takes effect. One of my men will attend him until he is recovered."

Fatima broke in and said in a strong voice, "Hakim is under my protection. I will attend him." And then she turned to Sami and lowered her head. "If you will allow it, brother."

"Attend to him." Sami turned to Mohammad and said, "Forgive me, Mohammad Al Zayed. If I speak out of turn it is only because this woman has made a pledge that I feel she must honor."

"She is your sister to command. Nothing will be said otherwise."

Bill was given the broth and almost immediately he fell into a deep sleep. Fatima made a place for him close to the fire. The men built another fire for the preparation of the meal.

Mohammad sent one of his men off and then the celebration began. They butchered two goats as the rider returned with pack animals and extra horses. Normally if a woman was present she would prepare the meal but the riders would have none of that. They paid homage to Fatima for their harsh and unkind words. She attended their prisoners—caring for their wounds and seeing that they were fed. Then she remained close to Bill, attending to him. A number of times she was forced to push Bill's donkey away. He tried to move in next to Bill and was stepping in the fire. Fatima finally took the donkey off and hobbled him after giving him some grain found in the loot of the robbers.

Dell brought Sami in and announced that he had taken Sami as his brother and that the animals were his. Sami told Mohammad that the goats were his but he had given the donkey to Hakim. There was laughter all around.

Mohammad said, "You are wise for your age. If my brother says you are his brother, then you too are my brother. Welcome to the Khawalid, Sami Al Zayed."

Dell and Mohammad talked long into the night and from time to time their laughter woke the others briefly. There were also moments of great sadness as Dell learned of the family he had lost. His adopted father, mother and many of his uncles were gone; either from old age or accidents.

At one point during the night Bill cried out as chills took him. He also soiled himself but remained in a deep sleep. Fatima woke Sami and told him of her concerns about Hakim. She asked what he would have her do.

Sami said, "He is yours. Attend him. He is not to know." Fatima kissed her younger brother and moved to Bill. She cleaned him as she had before, changed his bedding and kneeled in prayer next to him. She stood and looked around at the sleeping men and then at Mohammad and Dell. They were waiting to see what she would do. Fatima pulled her hijab across her face and slipped under the covers to lend her heat to Bill.

Mohammad said, "That is a strange sight. Does this ugly child care so much for Hakim?"

Dell smiled, not revealing his secret about Fatima, and said, "It is indeed strange, but she has pledged herself to protect Hakim. He is a good man—much like a brother to me."

"Do you trust him to be alone with this woman? This might bring trouble if others know."

"I trust him with my life and have done so for many years. He does not know all he should but he will not bring shame to your house. I give my word."

"That is enough. I will counsel my men and nothing will be said to draw her anger. It's too bad she is so... unpleasing to look at. She would make someone a good wife." Dell only smiled and nodded.

Fatima was at the fire preparing breakfast before first light. Bill was sleeping peacefully as the others came awake. Some of the men whispered to one another but Mohammad spoke quietly to them and nothing more was said.

Near evening Bill was up and, although a bit weak, he felt like his old self. The men packed and started off back to their home. Fatima walked with one of the men herding the goats. Sami rode proudly with the others. He was not treated as a small boy of only twelve years but as a man.

135

When they arrived at the compound word spread that *Desert Rider* had returned home. Bill was taken in by the children and received many interested stares from the women. His red hair and blue eyes were a source of fascination. Fatima stayed away but watched him to see if his needs were met.

Dell was able to charge his phone and call in to set up an extraction. Loretta was not available, but William took care of the details, including picking up Sami and Fatima. He told Dell that the terrorists had gone to ground for the moment and the threat level had been reduced. Arrangements were made to meet in Haifa.

Bill put in a call to Sarah about crossing the border and transportation to Haifa. She sounded excited to hear from him.

Dell had to take photos of Sami and Fatima and transmit them for paperwork. He was told that it would take three or four days to have everything ready.

The Khawalid took in Hakim, and he seemed to have teachers everywhere he went. He also learned to ride a camel, which he took to quite naturally. The children gave him little peace but he enjoyed the attention. He would look around for Fatima but she was always busy with the women.

The Bedouin no longer moved about the desert in a nomadic lifestyle. Wars, governments and drought had made that all but impossible. Many Bedouin had settled in towns and villages in Syria, Jordan and Israel, and a few like the Khawalid bought land and took up farming and raising livestock.

Bill watched Dell having long discussions with Sami and Fatima but he was not invited to join them.

Fatima found Bill sitting alone at sunset and went to check on his needs. "Hakim, you look happy. Does this place please you?"

"It does, but I miss the openness of the desert. Even in my illness you helped me see the beauty of the land. I want to thank you for that."

"I am glad you found some beauty there." She did not look at Bill.

"I also found kindness I have never received before and friendship and... warmth that I never knew I needed. Thank you, Fatima."

Fatima pulled her hijab across her face but said nothing for a long time. She spoke in a soft, uncertain voice. "Would you have me release you from your vow of protection? I am with people who will care for Sami and me."

"What about going with us to the States? I thought that was what you wanted."

"That is Sami's dream. What place would someone who looks like me have in your world? Perhaps I will stay here." Fatima turned her head to hide the glistening of her eyes but Bill felt her tears.

"You would do well there. I could help you with education and adjusting and maybe even take you to a dentist. And how could you leave your brother? You know he will go."

Without looking at Bill she asked, "Hakim. Why would you do these things for such an ugly girl as me?"

"I have asked you not to say that. You have taught me that beauty is much more than physical appearance. You have your own beauty in your caring and dedication to your brother... and to me. I owe you much for saving my life. I am glad I have met you and we will be good friends in the States. You will need a guide and what better guide than a friend who speaks perfect Arabic and English." Fatima laughed and shyly looked over at Bill. Those eyes trapped him as they sparkled in humor. "You see, Fatima. Who would make you smile in the U.S.? And perhaps you will meet someone who would appreciate someone as..."

"Ugly as I am?"

"As kind, funny and brave as you."

"Perhaps. Would that please you, Hakim?"

"We've known each other for a short time but I care about you." Fatima squirmed and moved away slightly. "I care about you as a friend and if you found someone who could appreciate you for your qualities... then I think it would make me happy." The thought of Fatima laughing and playing with another man gripped him in anger for an instant but he didn't know why. She could be a good friend but she just wasn't the type of woman he was looking for. If only she... was pretty and not a child.

Fatima had turned to watch Bill as he spoke and saw the different emotions pass across his face. She wondered if he might ever want her. Perhaps if she told him the truth; but Dell had warned against that until they were in the U.S. Perhaps then.

The next day Bill asked Mohammad and Sami if he could take Fatima on a ride around the Khawalid's land to see the farming and ranching. Mohammad agreed but told Bill they would need a chaperone. Five children, three girls and two boys, along with five riders and a pack animal set off at dawn with Fatima and Bill.

Bill was disappointed that they weren't getting to spend time alone as friends, but he was soon caught up in the spirit of all the people going on the outing. It was an adventure to the children and they made sure Fatima was laughing at their antics and skill on horseback. She truly looked happy. She laughed and looked at Bill and he saw beauty in her but it passed almost as quickly as it came.

Dell spent long hours enjoying his adopted family and joining in the work it took to run a farm. The black mist never visited him. He sat with Mohammad one evening speaking about Dell's work. Mohammad said, "I see you follow your American father in many ways. Why do you hunt Muslims?"

"I hunt those who would hurt my country and the people of the west. I do not consider them Muslims. Do you?"

"They are Muslims, but what they do is wrong and should be stopped. We Arabs are always fighting and many have found a way to turn their hate on the west. It is hard to forget the past."

"My brother, I believe that this hate and the attacks will bring a final anger to America and other western nations and they will turn on the Arab world. The destruction that will follow will not be isolated to the evil ones. I don't want to see that happen. I tell you the truth. I believe these terrorists will bring your world and mine to death's door and there may be no return. I try to stop this the only way I know how.

"These few days here with my family have brought me joy I have not felt in many, many years. I would like to return one day and live my life here."

"*Desert Rider*, you will be most welcome! It will be a time of great celebration. Be at peace and do what you must to protect both of your peoples."

"Mohammad, have you heard of a woman leading jihadists?"

"You ask things that will help you kill?"

"I don't know. Possibly. I have seen this woman twice and she gives orders to men whom I believe are terrorists."

"Are you sure it is a woman? There are men who use many disguises."

"This was a woman. Even covered as she was it left no doubt."

"Then this would be a most unusual thing for an Arab man to take orders from a woman. It could happen, I suppose, if the need is there, but I have never heard of such a thing. I will ask some others."

"You have my phone number. Call me any time and not just for this. I have missed you and my family."

"I will tell you what I hear. I tell you the truth, *Desert Rider*. You must return to the desert to prolong your life. You must!"

Chapter 13

Dell, Bill, Sami and Fatima sat in the food court of Canyon Haifa, the largest shopping mall in Israel. They had spent the morning buying luggage, clothes and everything needed to prepare Fatima and Sami for a new life in America. Fatima's eyes were as big as saucers as she looked around with her new hijab pulled across her face.

Sami talked animatedly with Dell about how he could set up a small stand and sell almost anything there.

Sami and Fatima were both timid and afraid at first to be in Israel, but saw quickly that no one looked at them with hate or distrust. It was so different from where they lived in Beirut. They even saw donkey carts and goats being herded at the outskirts of the city.

Bill felt a pang of regret at having to leave *his* donkey behind. He never got around to naming it.

Fatima saw his concern and said, "Don't worry, Hakim. The donkey will be well cared for." She laughed. "I have never seen a donkey so upset as when you left. I thought he might break down the gate as we drove away."

Bill left to do some shopping and Fatima turned to Dell. "How will this work? What will Hakim think of me when he knows the truth?"

Dell smiled. He found himself smiling more and more these days. "Bill is in for a big surprise but he will be all right, except maybe for the part about you speaking English."

Sami looked at Dell and asked, "How do you know this?"

Dell spoke in English and said, "I'm not as dumb as I look." Sami gave him a confused look and through her laughter Fatima translated.

"No, my brother. You are not dumb. I will stay close to my sister to make sure Hakim does not try to violate her."

"Sami, you must learn to trust people, especially Bill. He is a good man."

"Oh, I trust Hakim, but even a man such as he can be tempted by the beauty of a woman." He turned to Fatima and said, "I think you should wait for a while before you reveal your secret."

"I will do as you say, brother, but how will that be possible? My disguise will be found out at the airport, will it not, *Desert Rider*?"

Bill returned and handed small gift bags to Sami and to Fatima. "This is something you will need in America."

They each pulled out a beautiful expensive watch, one masculine and functional and the other a beautiful piece of feminine jewelry. Sami smiled broadly in delight and hugged Bill, but Fatima hung her head in embarrassment. "This is too much for me. Hakim, you should not give such a gift to a woman."

"I give these gifts to my friends. Now at least show me a smile so I know you like it." She turned her face to Bill and beamed. Her hijab slipped to expose her blackened teeth but Bill didn't seem to notice. "Now that's more like it," he said in English.

A tall, slender man wearing a cowboy hat sat down with them and said, "Howdy, partners. You look a mite lost. Maybe I could help you find your way home."

Bill looked closely at the man in the Stetson hat and said, "William! You never cease to amaze me. What are you doing here?"

"Well, little buddy. I'm your ride home. Are these the two young'ins that won a free trip to America?"

Sami and Fatima looked at Dell in confusion. Dell said, "These are the young man and woman who saved our lives. William, meet Sami Al Zayed and his sister, Fatima."

"Al Zayed? Isn't that the name of... never mind." He turned to Sami and Fatima and in perfect Arabic said, "May Allah bless you each day for watching over my friends. I hope the one with flaming hair did not embarrass you."

Bill answered in Arabic, "You who would kiss men should take care of your words."

William's surprised face made them all laugh and then he sat back and joined them.

"You've come far, *grasshopper,*" remarked William.

Fatima pulled her hijab from her face and William gave her a double-take. He asked, "What did you say your name was?"

"I am Fatima."

William looked at Dell and started to speak but the look Dell gave him told him to put off any questions until later. William looked again at Fatima and wondered where the beautiful woman in the photographs had gone. He decided to wait to ask more.

He then said, "You will have to travel separately to the States. Dell, you and Bill will travel by private jet so we can debrief you. Orders from headquarters. Sami and Fatima will travel commercial out of Ben Gurion, but they will have an escort all the way. There will be people to meet them when they arrive and they will be protected."

Dell said, "I have my own people meeting the flight. I don't want your group getting anywhere near them. They have done their duty and know nothing about our agenda."

Bill said, "Shouldn't we be traveling together?"

William said, "Not going to happen, Bill. Don't worry. Two of our best agents will see them all the way to Newark. They'll be safe."

"I'll hold you to that, William."

They walked out to the entrance of the mall and saw four white Suburbans waiting for them. Dell said, "Why don't you put a big lighted sign on them that says U.S. Embassy?"

"Believe me. It's the safest, fastest way to travel around here."

Dell turned to Sami and Fatima and said, "We will be together soon. When you arrive in America there will be friends of mine to meet you and take you to my home. We will be there very soon. I give you my word." Sami rushed to Dell and hugged him. It was the first child-like expression Dell had seen Sami make. It touched his heart. Fatima offered her hand but Dell pulled her to him and hugged her. Sami ran to Bill and hugged him too. Fatima touched her heart and kissed her lips and Bill silently returned the salutation.

Before Dell entered the small jet he took William aside and said, "Fatima is in disguise. She has lived like that for years trying to protect herself. Bill knows nothing about how she really looks and I want it kept that way until the time is right. Understand?"

"Whatever you say. I've informed my men to take them to a place where she can change. After your men take over, it will be up to her to change back. If she is stopped there might be questions, but I think we can deal with that. Why is she hiding from Bill?"

"It was important not to confuse Bill while we were here, but I think there is more to it. I only found out when I saw... I saw her without the disguise."

They boarded the private jet and William gathered all the information he needed on the flight home. He told them that the cell they had been watching was quiet and there were no signs of an imminent attack.

Dell asked, "Where is Loretta?"

"That's a good question. She's been on assignment since you left. I've spoken to her on the phone twice but she doesn't say much. Why do you ask?"

"Just wondering."

Chapter 14

Loretta sat strapped to a hard wooden chair. She was nude and had a dark bag over her head. She could feel the effects of the drug that had been administered starting to wear off. Her thoughts were muddled.

As her awareness came back to her, she heard people moving around and the sound of weapons being checked.

Then she heard a sound that froze her heart. "Please don't hurt my sister! We didn't do anything wrong."

It was the voice of her son, Sam. She struggled and tried to cry out but the gag in her mouth was tight. She continued to struggle until someone slapped her hard across her face.

The bag was removed and the bright lights dazed her for a moment.

"Mommy! Oh, Mommy, make them stop! They're hurting us!"

Loretta looked across the room and saw her children tied to chairs. Sam had blood trickling from his nose. Kiri was crying and her face was bruised.

Loretta struggled and cursed through her gag. An Arab woman stepped in front of her and slapped her again. Then she removed the gag.

"I will kill you if you hurt my children!"

A man stepped up to the children and brought a cane down across their legs. They screamed in pain.

The woman said, "Continue with your threats and your children will enjoy more pain."

"What do you want? Please don't hurt my children!"

"My name is Aisha and I am the head of the warriors you've been looking for." She saw surprise on Loretta's face. "Oh, yes. I know all about you and your Seer from New Jersey. I know many secrets." Aisha turned to look at the children and then back to Loretta. "You will do as I tell you or your little Sam and Kiri will suffer much more."

"I will do nothing to..." Loretta froze as Aisha raised her hand and the man raised the cane again.

"Wait! Please don't hurt my children! They have done nothing to you."

"I care little for the children of infidels. Their lives are worthless to me. I use them to get what I need. You will do everything I tell you and perhaps they will live. Disobey and they will suffer greatly!"

"What do you want?" Loretta said in defeat.

Chapter 15

When Bill and Dell arrived at a small airport outside Washington, D.C., they were taken to NSA headquarters for additional debriefing. Dell asked again about Loretta but no answers were given. He made a call to Herman Lum, one of the men from the New Jersey Task Force, to check on Sami and Fatima.

They had been whisked through the airport and were now at Dell's apartment. A policeman had shown them around and was now stationed outside in a squad car. Dell called his apartment but no one answered the phone. He called the officer and asked him to go to the apartment to check on them. He would call back in five minutes.

Dell called back and the officer answered and told him everything was fine.

The officer said, "The kids didn't want to answer the phone."

Dell spoke to Sami and then Fatima. Fatima said, "*Desert Rider*, you have a beautiful home."

Dell smiled as he thought about the crummy apartment he lived in. To Sami and Fatima it must seem like a palace.

"I want you and Sami to think of it as your home for now. Get some sleep or watch TV and I'll be there in a few hours. And Fatima, you should start to call me by my name. It's Dell. Also, speak English."

"Very well. My English is not so good. Mr. Dell, I am afraid what will happen when Hakim finds out the truth. I think he will hate me for deceiving him."

"Let's worry about that later. For now, get some rest and we'll think of what to do when I get there. And Fatima, I'm sure that Bill will not hate you."

"Yessa, Mr. Dell." Fatima was accomplished with English but she hadn't had an opportunity to speak it. Dell liked her accent very much.

He found Bill sleeping in a chair in the hallway. "Com'on, Bill. Let's get out of here. There's a car waiting to take us home."

"I need to go check on Fatima... and Sami."

"They are at my place and one of the guys is watching over them. You go home and get some sleep. Oh, and start speaking English again. The Commissioner has already called and we're supposed to meet him in the morning at his office."

Bill looked at the NSA people bustling past the doorway. "What about all these people?"

"We're going back to work and not saying anything about where we've been."

"I bet the Captain will be glad to see us."

"Yeah. I bet."

Chapter 16

Dell needed rest but Sami and Fatima were wide-eyed when he got to his apartment. He took them on a quick tour of the area and stopped at one of the local shops to eat. It was hard to keep his eyes off Fatima. She was five feet one inch tall, with long, silky black hair and an uncertain but sparkling smile that made her all the more beautiful. Her teeth were small and gleaming white. He commented on how pretty she looked and she instinctively reached for her hijab that wasn't there. Dell had told her it might be best if she didn't wear it, but after seeing all the eyes drawn to her, he thought maybe it would be a good idea after all.

Fatima asked, "Mr. Dell, why is everyone looking at me? I feel very... uncomfortable without my hijab."

"Fatima, you are a beautiful woman and perhaps, until you grow accustomed to life here... perhaps a hijab might be a good idea. You must be careful. In some ways the States are a bit like Lebanon. There are people who would try to take advantage of you and Sami. We will sit down and talk about what you and Sami will do and I will find an Arab lady who could guide you. We'll see."

"I have lived my life in a dangerous place, especially for women. I know how to protect myself and Sami. I have fear that Sami will be the one who needs guidance. But Mr. Dell, what will Hakim think of me?"

"Does it really matter so much what Bill thinks?"

Fatima blushed and once again reached for the missing hijab. She looked up into Dell's eyes with those large, dark pools that sparkled in the light of the shop. "I do not know how to answer that. He... he thinks me ugly and deformed, and in his illness he spoke of these things. I fear the truth might disappoint him. Telling untruths has been a way of life for me since our parents were killed. I am most afraid that I may not be able to change. I... care for Hakim... but I would never make myself a burden for him and..." Tears began to run down her cheeks but she held Dell's gaze. "Oh, Mr. Dell, I have deceived him. How could he ever trust or care for someone such as me?"

Dell wanted to hold her and give her comfort but he didn't want to embarrass her any further. He handed her a napkin and patted her hand. He tried to think how Bill would react, and as he looked at her he knew that her beauty—both inner and outer—would overcome any shock or dismay Bill might initially experience. Dell wanted Bill to find happiness. He couldn't imagine a better source than in the truly beautiful heart of this desert jewel.

Living as a recluse had suited Dell, but now with two young people in his apartment he could feel the need to return to the world; yet at the same time he didn't want that at all.

"Bill takes his duty to you very seriously and I do believe that no matter what his first reaction may be that duty will come through. Is there more to your feelings than simply disappointing or hurting him?"

"I don't know... Oh! That is not true, Mr. Dell. I don't want to be his duty and I do have... feelings. He is like no man I've ever met. Perhaps all Americans are like him but I do not believe that. Sometimes when I..." She thought back to the times she had lain with him in his illness and warmth spread through her and her embarrassment increased. "When I aided him in his illness there were times he looked at me as more than an ugly child. I have had dreams of there being more but I fear I have gone too far in my deceit... too far." She broke down and Sami put his arms around her. She threw her arms around Sami and cried in loud sobs. People were starting to look but when they saw Dell's eyes they turned away.

"It will be all right, Fatima," said Dell. "I know enough about Bill to know that these things will work out and I also know that he cares more for you than simply as a protector."

"Do you really think so?" she asked, hopefully.

"Yes, I do. I think it might be best to give him some time before everything comes out. I will find a way to give you and Sami time to adjust to your new life, but remember this: I will also be here for you, and as my brother and sister, I will protect you."

When they returned to the apartment, he gave them each a cell phone with both his and Bill's numbers programmed in the contacts.

The next morning Dell went to Bill's place and had to bang on the door until he finally heard a muffled voice. A groggy, bleary-eyed Bill opened the door and said, "What time is it? All of my clocks have different times on them."

"It's 0900, buddy. We've got to get a move on. The Commish is expecting us at ten."

"Let me take a quick shower. I went straight to bed and I guess I haven't moved since."

On the ride to see the Commissioner Bill asked, "How is Fatima... and Sami?"

"They're fine. I took them out to eat last night and brought them breakfast."

"I've got to get over there and see her... them."

"Give them a little time to adjust. You know that they're going to be on their own soon."

"I'm still Fatima's protector and... I don't know. It doesn't seem right not having her close by."

"You're going to have to expect a lot of changes in them now that they don't have so much to worry about. I'll take care of getting them set up. Sami needs to go to school..."

"I'm going to get Fatima in English classes right away. She needs all the help she can get so she won't be... looked at so much. You know. I've gotten used to her and she is sort of cute in her own way." Dell smiled again but said nothing.

They walked into the front office of the Commissioner and Gina gave them a bright smile but then put her finger to her lips. Loud voices were coming from the Commissioner's office.

Captain Teasdale was shouting, "I put in a request for two more men to replace those two losers and you turned me down!"

"Teasdale, you need to watch that tone of voice with me!"

"You want to fire me? Go ahead! I can't run this task force without men. I'm going too..."

"Settle down, Phil. No one wants you to quit. I need you. I've told you before it's out of my hands. The Feds are calling the shots with Dell and Bill." Captain Teasdale opened his mouth but Commissioner O'Hara stopped him by saying, "I don't like it any more than you do, but that's how it is. I'll loan you a couple of men if that's what you need, but Dell Sharpton and Bill Anders stay on the team."

Dell watched as Bill walked into the office just as Teasdale yelled, "Well, where the hell are they?"

Bill leaned over to Teasdale's good ear and yelled, "We're right here, Captain."

Teasdale hit the ground and reached for his piece, but stopped as he looked up at Bill.

"Good to see you, Captain. Here. Let me help you up." Captain Teasdale leaped to his feet, grabbed his heart, and Bill had to reach out to steady him. "You okay, Captain? You look a little pale, and man! Look at that ear!" Captain Teasdale had had half his ear shot off by a suspect on an operation with Dell and Bill. Dell had saved his life.

"You son of a... Don't ever sneak... Where the hell have you been and where's that maniac partner of yours?" Bill was looking behind the captain and Teasdale spun around so quickly that his knee hit the desk with a resounding bang. Dell had just walked into the office. He came up behind Captain Teasdale and asked in a calm voice, "Are you all right, Captain?"

Teasdale spun back around, banging his knee again and nearly fell over in pain. Bill and Dell helped him to take a seat. Captain Teasdale didn't say a word. He just grimaced and held his knee.

The Commissioner asked, "Where have you two been? Look at those tans. You look like you've been on vacation in Florida."

Bill said, "We do look pretty good, don't we?"

"Shut up, Anders. Answer me, Dell."

"Pat, you know I can't answer that. You've got the number to call. I'll tell you this. We haven't been on vacation."

"I hate the Feds. I hate all this secret *spook* crap. Just tell me if you're doing any good."

Bill piped up, "You'd have been proud of us, Pat."

"You call me Pat one more time, Anders, and you'll be sifting through garbage when you're not up to your ass in Feds! I let Dell get away with that because we go all the way back to Hoboken. Me and you don't cross the street. You got that?"

"Sure, Commish. I was just trying to help."

"Dell, what the hell is wrong with him? I think you're a bad influence."

"I probably am, Pat, but I couldn't do it without him."

Captain Teasdale stood up and said, "Do you see what I have to put up with, Commissioner? Now he's got Anders acting like a fool."

"We'll talk in a minute, Phil." He turned his attention back on Dell and Bill. "You two report back to work. Try to let me know the next time you do that disappearing act, will ya?"

As Dell closed the door the shouting match erupted again inside the office. Bill asked, "Wonder what blew up the captain's skirt?"

Dell looked at Bill and said, "What is with you? I'm the pain in the ass. You're supposed to calm the captain down."

"I don't know. I feel... different. I think I'll swing by your place to check on Fatima and Sami."

"You do that. I'll meet you back at the office in forty-five minutes."

Bill had a bright smile on his face as he rushed away. Dell made a quick call to Sami and told him to take Fatima out for at least two hours because Bill was on his way over.

Dell was feeling the compression of his job starting up again. He hadn't *spaced out* for over a week—ever since he entered the desert. Even now that he was back he was only feeling minor tendrils of depression. Having Fatima and Sami around kept it at bay. Dell had always shied away from outside contact. His life as a recluse by night and a cop by day suited him.

Bill walked gloomily into the office of the Terrorist Task Force and a loud roar rose up from the other officers. Many came over to pat him on the back and ask questions. Bill finally made his way over to his desk that sat opposite of Dell's. Dell was looking at him with a smile on his face.

"What? Man, this is a crazy place. I come in here and it's like homecoming weekend and then I sit down to see a smiling Dell. I hope the world don't blow up before I find out what's behind that smile." He leaned in towards Dell and said in a low voice, "Fatima wasn't there... or Sami either. I called her cell number and she said she was with Sami taking a bus ride around the city."

"How did you get her cell phone number?"

"You know I've got a key to your place. I have to use it every time I pick you up. Well, I saw two new phone boxes and figured you got them phones—and by the way, that's really nice of you. So I..."

"Bill, take it easy. They are safe and I'm getting things set up for school for them both. I'm also arranging for an English tutor for Sami."

"What about Fatima?"

"Yes, her too."

"Well, count me in, buddy. I'm not going to let you pay for all this on your own."

"Okay. I'll make you a deal. When I need help, I'll let you know. I've got money put away and, well, I like Sami and Fatima."

"No way are you keeping me out of this!"

Dell said, "Can we talk about this later? I've got everything covered for the moment."

"Okay," Bill said. He thought about all that had happened and finally said, "What's the matter with me, Dell? I feel... I don't know. I miss having Fatima around."

"Do you think you might be in love with her?"

"Dell! She's still a kid. And I don't think she's my type."

"What is your type?"

"Well, someone who's not young enough to be my daughter and those black teeth... No. Forget about the teeth. I could... I like her smile. I was happy out in the desert, even after getting bit by those scorpions. I had some dreams that she was..."

"Sharpton, Anders! Get in my office, pronto!"

Dell asked, "I wonder what the captain wants?"

"You just let me handle him."

As they walked towards the office Dell looked over at Bill and wondered what had gotten into him. They walked in the office. Bill slammed the door shut and took a seat. Dell stood and waited for the explosion.

Captain Teasdale opened his mouth to scream at them but the look on Bill's face kept the words from getting out.

Bill said, "Close your mouth, Captain. You could injure your jaw holding your mouth like that. What's up?"

"What's up? What's up! What is going on here?" He looked from Dell to Bill, from Bill to Dell and finally took his seat, waving Dell to do the same. "Dell, what is going on? Where have you two been?"

Bill answered for Dell. "I think the Commissioner has already explained the part about where we've been and as for..."

Dell held up his hand and Bill stopped talking. "Captain, we've been on assignment and that's all we can say right now. We've been through some hairy stuff and I think Bill is a little keyed up so give us a break. We're back and you just tell us what you need us to do. Hopefully we're back for a while and we're all yours. By the way, how's the ear?"

"What the hell is going on?" Captain Teasdale had leaped to his feet and felt like he was in the twilight zone. Sharpton had never tried to explain anything to him and

Anders had never raised his voice. "Did the Feds give you two a shot or something?"

Bill said, "Dell. See if you can figure out what he wants. I need a drink." He got up, left the office and kept going right out of the squad room.

"What can we do for you, Captain?"

"What is wrong with Anders?"

"He's had a pretty enlightening experience. Don't worry about him. He'll be fine. What can we do for you?"

Captain Teasdale sat back down. His head was spinning. "I need you to go over to 51st Street and check on a robbery at one of the *raghead's* shops. It's called..."

"Captain. You're going to have to find a new word for Arab-Americans. I don't like that word and I can promise you if you use it in front of Bill... well, just don't do it."

"What the hell is going on? I'm so confused. Okay... There was a robbery at the Al Salam Bazaar and it doesn't play out as an ordinary holdup. I've got Clay and Broadman on it but they can't speak the lingo. They're not getting anywhere. You and Bill get over there and check it out."

Dell stood up and said, "Right away, Captain." And then he went looking for Bill.

Captain Teasdale watched him walk away and wondered what was happening to his world. He thought, *The Feds must have done something to them.* He rubbed his half-ear and closed his eyes.

Dell found Bill in a nearby bar and got him into the car. Bill said, "How's the captain?"

"He's a bit confused—but that's nothing unusual."

"I didn't mean to jump down his throat, but man, I've got too much on my plate."

Their route took them right by Dell's apartment and Bill was looking at the people passing by on the sidewalk.

"Hey, that was Sami and some pretty girl! Where's Fatima?"

Dell had seen Sami and Fatima walking on the sidewalk near his apartment. After Bill asked about her, he knew there was going to be trouble if she didn't tell him the truth soon. Bill had his cell phone out and Dell said, "Don't worry. She's okay. Listen, we'll swing by after we check out this robbery. No need to bother them now."

"Well... Okay."

Dell said, "There's some things you need to know about Fatima and Sami. They had a hard life and had to keep secrets to protect each other. Fatima, in particular, had to do difficult things to protect herself..."

"What are you saying? I know how hard it must have been to live over there all alone, but things will be different here. Those two kids deserve a chance at a good life. What kind of secrets?"

"We'll talk about it later." Dell didn't want to spoil the surprise but he did hope Bill would understand.

At Al Salam Bazaar, Dell told Bill to walk around but not let anyone know he could speak Arabic. His reputation was spreading in the community.

Bill was greeted by a number of men and women and they all praised him as the great *White Snake*. He was enjoying his interaction with the people and without revealing himself he asked about the robbery. Several people pulled him to the side and whispered information to him. A couple of young women shyly approached him to offer a tidbit but also to offer more. Bill blushed at a few suggestions and his blush brought friendly laughter.

Bill went to Dell, who wasn't getting anywhere with the shop owners, and pulled him aside. "I've got the 4-1-1 on the perps."

"You've got the what on the who?"

"Com'on, Dell. You know what I'm talking about."

"Yeah, I do but I've never heard you talk like that before. Okay. What've you got?"

Bill told him it was a local gang trying to break into the protection racket and had the names of the boys involved in the robbery. Dell asked, "How did you get all of this?"

"Hey, they don't call me the *White Snake* for nothing. I even had a couple offers that, well, I couldn't believe."

"What kind of offers?"

"You see that pretty, cubby woman over there?" He nodded towards a pretty young woman and she looked directly at Bill, smiling. "Well, she wants to..." He leaned over and whispered to Dell what she had offered to let Bill do to her.

"Get outta here!"

"I swear! Scout's honor."

"You need to get rid of that nickname."

"Don't I know it. What if Fatima or Sami hear that name again? The last time Sami heard it he wanted to slit my throat, but I think it's too late. Everyone here knows me by that name and you wouldn't believe what some of them were saying. They trust me and say I need a good Arab wife to tame the snake," said Bill with a beaming smile.

They caught up with Broadman and Clay and gave them the information on the robbery and the names of the suspects. The officers were duly impressed and happy to switch from scratching around for leads to chasing them down.

Chapter 17

As they walked out of the bazaar, a jet-black Suburban pulled up to the curb and the back door opened up. Dell looked in and saw Loretta on the phone waving them in.

As soon as the door was closed the Suburban pulled away and sped down the street. It turned right towards the interstate. Loretta hung up the phone and practically leaped into Dell's lap, kissing him hard on the lips. Then she pulled Bill over and kissed him as well. "We heard you two were dead, but I knew you'd be harder to kill than having a few refugees taking shots at you. I'm happy to see you." She took her seat again and gave them a critical look. "Looks like you've been busy. The notebooks you retrieved will put an end to several cells operating around the world if we can get to them in time."

"What about the money and diamonds?" asked Dell.

"What money and diamonds?" she said with a smile. "How do you think I keep up appearances? And fund many of my... little known operations. Speaking of which, take this as a reward for your work and loyalty." She handed them each a beautiful inlayed hardwood box. Bill opened his and found a new titanium cell phone, a small stack of bills, a black carbon treated CZ-85, 40 caliber pistol and a small velvet bag with five diamonds that looked to be over three carats each. Dell had the same in his.

"What's all this for?" asked Dell.

"What my team secures in the way of cash and goods I keep. How do you think all my operations are funded? There are probably only two people in Washington that know about us and they're the types that don't kiss and tell. I believe if my men get a little reward from time to time it will keep them honest and on the right side."

"Bill and I don't need any of this. Do we, Bill?" He looked at Bill and saw the disappointment on his face. He was holding the CZ in one hand and caressing it with the other.

"I guess not."

Loretta said, "This isn't an option, Dell. It's approved procedure."

Dell said, "We're not taking any of this stuff. That's not an option."

"The cell phones are Government Issue and you will take them. I figured Bill may need a reserve if all that I hear comes true."

Bill asked, "What are you taking about?"

"Rumor has it you might need a *bride-price* before much longer. I know all about the two you brought back with you. Quite a prize."

Bill and Dell turned on her but Dell put his hand on Bill as he spoke, "They have nothing to do with any of this. They're just two kids who helped us out—saved our lives—and they don't know anything about anything that we're working on. So keep your hands and people off them."

"Easy, Dell. I know all of this. No one from our group will go after them. As a matter of fact, I had most of their records pulled and classified so it looks like they've been here for a couple of years. From what I hear, Bill here is a lucky man."

"I'm lucky to be alive, if that's what you mean."

"I was talking about that pretty little..." She stopped when she saw the look on Dell's face. "You mean he doesn't know?"

"Know what? What's going on? Dell, what's she talking about?"

"We'll talk later, okay? It's not important and Loretta's got a big mouth."

Loretta said, "So you keep the cell phones and no reward? You know there are no hidden tricks. But have it your way. That information you brought back will save the United States millions in damages."

Dell settled back and looked around. "Where are we going?"

"We've got to talk about the case you're working on. The cell has gone to ground and we think the threat might have been a hoax, but then we have to make sure. Besides, I think a little alone time might be just the thing for you."

Bill asked, "What about me?"

"Oh, don't worry. William has a whole list of things he wants to go over with you."

"Oh, swell."

Loretta's laughter resounded inside the Suburban.

When they arrived at Loretta's *house* Dell made a phone call—with his old phone—to Sami and explained that he and Bill would be gone for a while.

Sami excitedly told Dell some of the things they had been doing. He said that the young man that was watching them was very nice and showing them around. Fatima even liked him. Sami told Dell not to worry. He said, "America is not so dangerous if you have lived in Beirut." Sami even spoke a few sentences in English that he had learned from Fatima and TV. Dell was smiling again when he hung up.

He came out of the elevator with the smile still on his face. Loretta looked from one man to the other. Bill said, "Get used to it. He's been smiling more lately than I... Heck, I didn't even know he knew how to smile."

"I would think you would be the one smiling."

"What's that supposed to mean? I'm getting tired of being the butt of a joke that I don't know about."

From behind them a familiar voice said, "My word, old chaps. If it isn't *White Snake* and *Desert Rider*! How fortuitous I am to be in your presence."

Bill said, "Bite me, William."

"Oh, please, Bill. Come. Let's have a cuppa tea and talk. I'm sure Loretta has... um, bigger plans for Dell."

Loretta leaped into Dell's arms and kissed him hard. "I've really missed you."

Dell said, "Where have you been? No one seems to know."

"That's the way I like it. I've been following up on the cell we are chasing and looking into the list you brought back with you. Do you have any idea how valuable that information is? We'll be able to follow or take out a number of big players."

"I really didn't get a chance to look at the list," Dell said. He had actually made a copy that no one knew about. He had the feeling that it might come in handy. CYA was something he didn't normally do but the deeper he got into this *spook* stuff the more he felt he needed to.

"What's wrong with Bill? He has changed and that girl is beautiful."

"I wish I knew what is going on with him. He reminds me of me and that's not good. I'll have to keep a close watch on him. The woman is beautiful but Bill has never seen her without her disguise. She had a hard time living in Beirut and had to hide her looks. I think Bill has fallen for her but I don't know what will happen when he finds out the truth."

"Speaking of changing. I've never seen you so caring. I like it. Bill will flip for that woman when he gets a look at the real her."

"I don't know. He's been burnt before and the truth means a lot to him. She's just what he needs but it will be a struggle for him when he finds out. Enough chit-chat. What do you want us to do?"

"One of the cells on the list operates out in Iowa, of all places, and that may be the perfect place to hide whatever it is they are up to. I want you, Bill and William to go out there and see what you can find. But first, darling, I want to take your temperature. I've missed you more than I thought I would."

Loretta and Dell came out to the conference room and found Bill and William laughing.

"You two look like long-lost friends. What's going on?" Loretta asked.

William, now with an American accent, said, "I think Bill is seeing the real me, finally. We're going to do just fine when the time comes."

Bill said, "I guess I can work with him. He did help us out in Israel."

"Well, that's just wonderful. When you put your life on the line you need that trust in your partner," said Loretta.

"Dell and I are partners," Bill quickly corrected, and added, "Hey, Dell, did you ask her about the woman you saw?"

Loretta turned to Dell and asked, "What woman?"

"She was with the men I saw when I went after the map. I don't think it was anything."

"But you said it looked like she was in charge," Bill said.

"The more I think about it... I just think she happened to be at the wrong place at the wrong time. I've all but forgotten about her." Dell moved over to the sideboard and poured a big glass of Jameson.

Loretta watched him the entire way but said nothing. Then she said, "I'm going to need you two to go to Iowa."

Bill said, "I thought the only thing dangerous in Iowa is corn."

"One of the cells from your report is now operating there. If you think about it, it's the perfect place for terrorists to hide and plan. Who's going to look for them there?"

Bill was going to ask about Sami and Fatima being left all alone but he saw the look Dell passed him so he asked instead, "How long are we going to be there? I mean, are we going to take them out or just watch them?"

"For now you'll watch them, but if my information is correct, they are planning an attack that could come at any time. It might take a week or longer to find out what they're up to. If it has anything to do with the big bomb, you'll have more people and agencies rushing in. I want you to find out what you can before this gets spoiled again."

Dell asked, "When do we leave?"

"In a day or two. William will be joining you. He can fit in almost anywhere."

William put on a Midwestern farmer's accent and said, "I'm gonna teach you a few tricks, Bill. Before this is over, I'll have you running a combine and chewing tobacco."

On the ride back Dell said, "You've got a big mouth."

"Me? What did I say?"

"No more info to Loretta unless you check with me... Got it?"

"Sure, Dell. I thought we were all on the same team."

Bill remained quiet for an hour and then he blurted out, "I'm worried about Fatima and Sami."

"They can take care of themselves."

"Yeah. In Beirut maybe, but the States is something completely different for them, and someone needs to stay close to Fatima. I don't want anybody hurting her, you know, somebody saying the wrong things."

"I'm dealing with everything they need to get started in a new life."

"Why you? Why not me? And I haven't seen them since we got back."

Dell asked, "Can you pay for all the things they need: school for Sami, college for Fatima, clothes, tutors, computers?"

"I'm divorced. You know I don't have that kind of money, but I'll do my part. Heck, I'll take out a loan."

Dell said, "There's no need for that. I'm loaded and I haven't had any reason to spend my money in a long time."

Bill gave him a hard look and then looked at the floorboard. "I know."

Dell in a most un-Dell-like manner put his hand on Bill's shoulder and said, "We're in this together, buddy. I know I haven't been the best partner and I don't know how long this good mood will last so let me take care of the finances. I need your help on this and Sami and Fatima will need your help in settling down. Just don't worry about the money."

"You sure have changed. I think the desert air did you some good."

"It did. I think it did you some good, too."

"Dell, I can't remember the last time I had so much... fun isn't the right word. Contentment is better. Being out there—and in a weird way even being bitten by those scorpions—it all just felt right. Fatima... I've never had anyone take such good care of me. There's a lot more to her than she lets on. I never thought I could look at someone with her problems and really feel something. I know she's too young for me to think like that, but I think I want to take care of her. Does that make any sense to you?"

Dell thought about what Bill said and he wanted to tell him the truth. He could see that it needed to come out soon or Bill would be deeply wounded by the deception. It was time to bring Fatima out in the open and let Bill see the real her.

"Bill, there's a lot you don't know about Fatima. For one, she's twenty-two years old. She's not a child. She has spent her whole life protecting herself and Sami, and she had to change the way people thought of her to do that. I hope you will understand why she has done some of the things she's done. I know that she is worried about what you will think of her."

"Oh, I know all of that but... Did you say she was twenty-two?"

"She is. And you don't know everything."

"Twenty-two? She's so tiny and... All the rest doesn't matter to me. I know she had to protect herself but she would never deceive me now that we've been through so much."

"Just remember, when it all comes out she is still the same woman you knew in the desert and try to understand."

"No worries, mate. William taught me that," Bill said with a laugh. "Drop me off at my place. I want to get cleaned up before I see her and Sami. I'll meet you at your place in a couple of hours."

Fatima stood in front of Dell with tears of fear. He was sitting on the couch and had watched her pace the floor. Dell still had trouble looking at her without admiring her form. He knew it would come as a shock to Bill—he hoped it would be a good shock. Now she stood in front of him with tears and trembling lips.

"Mr. Dell. I have such a difficult fear about what Hakim will say." She switched to Arabic and blurted, "He will find me as a deceiver and will curse me for my lies. I miss the warmth of the sand and his... *Desert Rider*, what will I do?"

"You must be truthful with him and explain why you did what you have done. Have you fallen in love with him?"

Now the tears weren't tiny jewels that accented her face. They flowed down her cheeks and darkened her blouse. She tried to look at Dell but she couldn't hold his gaze. She knew the answer to his question and had known it since she was alone with Bill in the desert. His nickname had made her think he was a womanizer but now that she was here in New Jersey she heard the truth from many Arabs she had met. He was funny and tried so hard to learn their language. They told her of his mistakes and of his kind heart. He was so brave to fight for the community and he enjoyed the teasing. Always respectful of the women and he never intentionally did anything to cause problems. His nickname was something not of his making, but it came from the men who knew him. Bill was respected.

She knew in her heart that her dreams of a life with him were about to be shattered because of her deception. Why hadn't she told him the truth as soon as she knew what a good man he truly was?

Fatima wanted to run but her obligations and love for Sami wouldn't let her. She now looked to Dell for answers that she knew he couldn't give. He had become the brother he had proclaimed and she loved him for that. Dell was a good man and she must follow his advice, but a feeling of foreboding lay heavily on her. Fatima didn't want to lose this chance with Bill.

She said, "Yessa, Mr. Dell."

Dell smiled as he watched her fighting her dilemma. He was just as uncertain about Bill's reaction as Fatima. In the past Dell knew Bill would accept her reasoning for keeping things from him, but a new side of his friend had emerged from the desert. Bill reminded Dell of himself, which made him more nervous than he wanted to admit. Still Dell would do whatever it took to help Bill and Fatima through this. Fatima deserved a good and happy life. Having thoughts of Sami and Fatima as his brother and sister made him smile. It even came to his mind that they were more like the children he never had. If Bill screwed this up, Dell swore that he would kick his ass until he accepted the truth and admitted his love for Fatima.

Sami put his arms around Fatima and kissed her cheek. "I know not all that you have said but I see the truth of your words on your face. I remove my threat from Hakim. This will be a hard test for you both but I believe there is love between you and it shall be enough." Fatima wrapped her arms around Sami and sobbed. Sami said, "This is no way for a woman to present herself to a suitor. Go clean yourself, sister, and remember your brothers love you." Her sobs turned to bawling, but after a moment they blossomed into laughter.

"Thank you both. I am such a very lucky sister!" She ran to her room.

Chapter 18

Dell heard his apartment door open and a streak of white raced into the room. Haji leaped into Sami's arms and Sami laughed with joy as he tried to contain the lightning bolt of energy. Haji couldn't be contained. He leaped to Dell and his happiness came out in a growling whine as he wiggled in Dell's arms. He jumped to the floor, spun around three times and raced away following the scent of Fatima. They heard Fatima exclaim, "Haji! Is it truly you?"

Bill walked in smiling like his old self. Dell asked, "Where did you pick Haji up?"

"He was delivered to headquarters. I got a call while I was at my place. I'll say this for the Feds; they can make things move fast when they want to."

"Any problems?"

"Well, Wilson let him out of the carrier to play with him and the first thing Haji did was bite Captain Teasdale. By the time I got there he was sitting in the captain's lap. I've never seen Teasdale laugh so much. He showed me the bite marks and laughed about it. We need Haji around to keep the peace."

Fatima hadn't heard Bill come in and she ran into the living room carrying Haji. "Oh, Mr. Dell! Thank you for bringing Haji to us! I hope Hakim will be as..." Her eyes met Bill's and she stopped. Fear gripped her as she stood frozen.

Bill looked from the beautiful woman to Dell and asked, "Who is this?"

Dell said, "Maybe she should answer for herself."

Fatima could only stare at Bill. The tears returned in full force. Bill saw her crying and said, "Hello, ma'am. I hope I didn't startle you. I don't think we've met. My name is Bill."

Fatima lowered her gaze and in a whisper said, "I am Fatima."

"Wow. Really? Then there are two Fatimas." He looked at Dell and said, "Where is my Fatima? I haven't seen her since we've been back. Is she okay?"

"It is I. I am your Fatima," she explained, softly searching his eyes.

Bill looked at her for a long moment and the truth of it began to dawn on him. He wavered and Dell jumped up to help him sit down. Bill looked up at Dell and asked, "What is going on?"

"Bill, I didn't want anyone to be in danger over in Lebanon so I told Fatima to keep her disguise. Don't take it out on her."

"Take what out?" He looked at Fatima and asked, "Is it really you?"

As tears continued to flow from her dark eyes she said, "It is I, Hakim. I am sorry I kept this secret from you. I truly am. Will you forgive me?" Fatima touched her heart and kissed her fingers and then she looked at the floor.

"You're speaking English! And you... you're beautiful! What about the limp?"

"My legs are fine."

Haji jumped down and leaped into Bill's lap but he didn't seem to notice.

Dell said, "There's a lot you don't know but trust me; I thought it was for the best."

"Trust you? So what about Sami? Is he full of lies too?"

Bill's mind flashed through his life at all the times he had been deceived by people he cared about. Dell had never done that and now the woman that he thought he knew—and loved—had played him like a fool. That thought of love raced through his mind but it was the deceit that burnt through. And then another thought came to him. "You speak English?"

"Yessa, Hakim. But not very well. I will need help to speak better."

Bill's blue eyes blazed as he stood and said in perfect Arabic, "You drive a knife into my chest and then ask for my help?" He looked at Dell and said, "I take away all that has been said. I am no longer her protector. Perhaps this traitor will look after another... traitor. I wash my hands." He slapped and slid his palms apart and stormed out.

No one said a word for a long time. Only the sound of Fatima crying broke the silence. Even Haji was subdued. Dell finally said, "It will be all right. He just needs time..."

Fatima said, "Hakim has released me. I have been such a fool." She turned and ran to her room.

Bill raced through the streets but when he almost hit a pedestrian he pulled to the curb. His mind was a maelstrom of pain and questions. All the people who had meant anything to him throughout his life had lied or cheated or just plain deceived him. He had thought Fatima was different. Bill knew they were back there laughing at his stupidity. Having a good ole laugh on his account. He couldn't take it—not from her. Depression swept through his mind like a dark cloud. It took him down to the depths of despair and it suited him. Dell? The one person who had never deceived him. Even he knew the truth and held it from Bill. A mist enveloped him.

A few hours later Bill felt something tugging at him.

"Hey, buddy! You can't park here. What is wrong with you? Step out of the car and keep your hands where I can see them." Bill looked up into the barrel of a gun and then at the policeman holding it. "I said get out of the car now."

Bill said, "I'm on the job."

"Out! We'll see about that when you're standing in front of me. Come out easy."

Bill stepped out of the car. Showing his fore and index fingers of his right hand he reached slowly into his inside coat pocket and pulled out his shield and ID.

The officer checked Bill's wallet and then holstered his weapon. "Sorry, Detective Anders. You looked like you were in outer space. I hope I didn't mess up here."

"No, Officer...?"

"Felton."

"Officer Felton. I just had a lot on my mind and needed a place to think."

"No problem, Detective. This is a no-parking zone but that's no big deal. Stay as long as you like." The officer returned to walking his beat.

It was early morning and Bill got back in his car and drove away. He saw Jimmy's Bar and pulled into the alley. Jimmy, the owner, was locking the back door and at the sound of approaching footsteps turned and saw Bill. "He's not here."

"Who's not here, Jimmy?"

"Your partner. In fact, I haven't seen him in a couple of weeks. Is he okay?"

"Yeah, just peachy. I need a drink, so open up."

"I've been up all night. Had a big fight last night and I just got the place cleaned up."

"Sad story. Now open up."

Jimmy didn't want a beef with the *Staties* and he liked Bill so he unlocked the door and let him in. Bill reached over the counter and pulled down a bottle of Morriston Gold Scotch and grabbed a glass. He filled and emptied the glass twice and then looked at Jimmy. "When will you be back?"

"I got to open up at three."

"Lock me in and go home. I'll be here when you get back. Don't worry. I'll cover the tab."

"You got it, Bill. Just try not to break anything."

Fatima had cried all night and there was nothing Dell, Sami or Haji could do to help. She finally passed out at five in the morning, exhausted. Dell woke around noon and found Sami sleeping bedside him on the couch.

Sami woke when Dell stirred. "What shall we do, brother?"

"I don't know. Bill just needs some time to sort things out. I know he cares for Fatima and, well, he'll come around."

"What did you say? I have no English."

Dell explained and then changed the subject by talking about school and tutors for Sami and Fatima. He told Sami that he would have to go away in a day or two and wasn't sure when he would return. He also told him that he had made arrangements with one of the community leaders to provide trustworthy instructors for them both.

Sami smiled and said, "I will learn this new language quickly. Is school so important?"

"In this country it is very important. I have confidence in you to become an important man and to protect Fatima while we're away."

"You have no need to worry. I may be new to this place but I know how to protect my family."

Dell made out a list of people and numbers Sami could call if they needed anything while he was away. Sami pulled out his new cell phone and began to enter the names and numbers into it.

Dell thought about Sami and his eagerness to start making money and have all the electronic toys and *bling* he saw around him now.

Deciding he must help Sami understand, Dell had his first heart-to-heart talk with anyone. He explained to Sami what he, Dell, thought was really important to be successful and happy in the States, none of which involved *bling*. He had to laugh at the irony of delivering such a speech because until only a few days ago he hadn't been happy for many years. It had suddenly dawned on him that he was happy. Dell hugged Sami and laughed. Sami returned his hug and said, "You truly are my brother. Yes, what you say is true. I am happy now. Come, brother, tell me what I should do and it will be done. But I do like some of the... how do you say... *Bling*."

Dell talked about enrolling Sami in school right away because that was one of the keys to success. Learning English was a top priority. Dell asked Sami if he could do all this and not get frustrated. Sami said, "Because you say it, I know this is important. I will do as you ask but how will I survive? I must work to help you provide for Fatima."

"I will take care of providing for you and Fatima. Always remember that you are my brother and it is not only my honor but my duty. This is your home now and soon you will be able to stand on your own." He held up his hand when Sami started to protest. "I've lived like a man in a cave for a long time. But in that cave I saved my money and made investment trades and now I have enough money to do whatever I want. I want to see to your future and to Fatima's. I also want something else. I want Bill to have a chance at happiness and I think his happiness lies with Fatima."

"He shall not... I am sorry, Dell. I see what kind of man Hakim is and he is someone I dreamed might find Fatima, but her bride-price is high!" He looked at Dell and they both broke down laughing.

Dell took a shower and got ready to report in. The phone rang and Jimmy from the bar called to let him know about Bill. Dell told him he would meet him at the bar at three.

The phone rang again and Dell answered to the shouts of Captain Teasdale. "Do you know what time it is, Sharpton? Now that the Commissioner is backing you two, you think you can just do whatever you want. Well, let's get one thing straight..."

"Sorry, Captain. We've had a little trouble..."

"That dog is okay, isn't he?" replied the captain, suddenly concerned.

"Haji is just fine. I'm sorry about him biting you."

"Oh, that. He was just getting to know me. Say, when you come in how 'bout bringing Haji with you. And bring Anders too. Did you just say you're sorry? I never thought I would hear those words from you."

"I'll be there in about an hour, but it might be a few days before I can bring the dog."

"He's not hurt or anything, is he?"

"No, he's fine. He just needs a little time to adjust."

"Get here when you can."

Dell's cell rang again and Loretta said, "It's time to go. I'm sending a car for you and Bill."

"Tell them to meet us at Jimmy's Bar on..."

"I know where it is. It will be there in an hour."

Dell pulled in behind Bill's car and saw Jimmy walking up the alley. Dell joined him as he unlocked the door. "Wait here a minute, Jimmy. It might be better if I went in alone."

The barkeep opened the door and motioned for Dell to enter.

Inside the bar Dell saw Bill lying face down on the floor with a stream of drool making a trail across the floor. He delicately removed Bill's pistol and put it on the bar. Then he shook Bill hard and said, "Rise and shine, buddy. Time to go to work."

Bill reached for his weapon and when he couldn't find it he rolled over and tried to focus on Dell.

"Fuck you! And don't call me buddy, you backstabber!" He sat up and grabbed his head. "What happened?"

Dell looked at the bar and saw an empty bottle of Morriston Gold Scotch Whiskey and another that was half empty. "Looks like you had a fight with Scotch and the Scots won. Come on, Bill, we've got a plane to catch."

"Kiss my ass, *Desert Rider*."

"Have it your way, but you're going with me to watch the corn grow."

"Hang on." Bill looked around and then ran for the bathroom. He came out ten minutes later looking like death warmed over. "I need a drink." Dell poured him a stiff one and Bill downed it in one gulp. He pursed his lips and then made a beeline for the bathroom again.

Bill returned to the room just as William walked in the back door with Jimmy following. He looked at Bill and then said to Dell, "What have you done to him?"

"Me? I didn't do anything."

William looked at Bill and said, "It's that girl. Isn't it? I knew that was a bad idea. When did you find out?"

"Last night," Bill looked at Dell and slurred, "So he knew about her too? Was it on the damn news or something? Bill, the idiot, screwed again. Film at Eleven."

Dell said, "I'm sorry, Bill. It's my fault. We need to talk about this."

171

"About what? I don't want to hear another word about... her. Not one word! Get me the fuck out of here."

William smiled and said, "Your chariot awaits. I'll make arrangements to move your vehicles."

Chapter 19

Bill slept the entire flight and when they got to the old farmhouse that was set up for them he found a bed and crashed again. William looked over at Dell and raised an eyebrow.

Dell said, "He'll be all right."

William said, "That was a nasty bit of work you pulled on him. I don't want to see him go out and get himself killed because of a woman. I like him."

"He'll come around and I'll keep a close eye on him. He just needs some time."

"Time to see who else is putting it to him?"

"Shut up, William."

Bill woke with an aching head and heart. He didn't give Fatima a chance to explain. He missed her but she had lied to him. She looked so beautiful even with all the tears—why would she even think about him?

Bill twisted the sheets and tried to go back to sleep, hoping the next time he woke his hangover would be gone. He closed his eyes and there she was. Fatima's face cycled between beautiful and the way she was before. He missed her black teeth. He knew he had said all the wrong things and he had lost his chance with her. Did he really want her or the girl he knew in the desert? It didn't matter now. In a few months, with her looks, she would forget all about ole Hakim. It was for the best. With his track record with women it wouldn't have lasted long anyway. He tossed and turned his way into a fitful sleep. He loved her.

Fatima lay in her bed and couldn't stop the tears. She had lost him. Bill was the only man she had ever met who had looked at her like she mattered. He was an infidel... No! That had nothing to do with Hakim. She thought she would have to give up that name and call him by his American name. This was her fault. She had grown comfortable in her disguise. She walked around unnoticed. But here in this place called New Jersey people stared at her like she was a freak or something. Why are they all so rude to stare at her? Dell said it was because she was beautiful, but she didn't believe that. She had seen many women walking around and they were so tall and beautiful. She would never be like that and now what was the point?

Love had come to her and what had she done? Deceived the one she loved. She knew that these feelings would never leave her. How would she be able to face Bill again? The look and the words he spoke made it clear that he was finished with her—even before she could explain. Why had he not given her a chance to explain herself? Her anger grew and her tears dried for a moment. She did not need this white man. She had her brother... brothers.

Now the pain returned as she thought of the goodness in Dell and how she had just thought with hate about white men. But she loved that funny man who introduced himself while smelling like something dead. She chuckled, but just as quickly the pain returned and that brought her tears back. She loved him—her Hakim. How could she go through life without him? Would she ever find a way and forget the happiness that might have been hers to hold?

Bill woke as the first light of a new day crept through the window. He looked around, not sure where he was. Memories flooded him but he pushed them away. There was a job to do and all that had happened was over—over and forgotten.

Bill pushed the thoughts of the past few days into the recesses of his mind. He was a cop and when on the job these things had no place. He'd use his training to do what he was paid to do. Walking through the old farmhouse he found the kitchen.

Dell looked up as Bill entered the room. "How you doing, Bill?"

"Looks like I'm going to live. Got any aspirin?"

William grabbed an extra mug and poured Bill a cup of fresh coffee. "Check the cabinet to your left. The one on top."

"Thanks. How long have we been here?"

Dell said, "About sixteen hours. We're waiting for a contact to show up. Bill, listen…"

"Save it. I was out of line with you and I've put it away. I just want to do my job and watch your back. Can we forget about the other stuff?"

"Sure we can, buddy. I deserved everything you said."

"No, you didn't. You were doing your job. No hard feelings?"

"None."

"Now that you two sweethearts are back on the same side I see our contact coming."

Jamaal Harris was a large black man who walked with the ease of a fighter. He entered the house without knocking and proceeded to the kitchen where he greeted Dell, Bill and William in a loud Arabic voice. "I smell infidels! You who would steal the land of the Arabs and try to keep us from showing this country the one true religion are but fools in the eyes of Allah." He switched to English and continued. "Hey, good buddies. How the hell are you?" He pointed at Bill and said, "You need to get that one some clothes that fit in around here. He sticks out like a turd in a punch bowl. William, I haven't seen you in a coon's age."

Bill moved before anyone could react. He had his pistol out and pointing at Jamaal's head as he said in Arabic, "Those with mouths as large as the desert who come into our house uninvited do not always leave."

"Hey now! It was only a test. I always throw out a little Arabic to see who gets mad. And to see who understands. William. Tell my friend here that I'm one of the good guys."

Dell said, "Take it easy, Bill. He's legit. I saw his folder on the ride out here. Put the gun away."

Bill holstered his weapon and said, "I guess I didn't pass the test."

Jamaal laughed and said, "It's a lesson learned. Don't forget it or it might get you killed one day. Say, that's some good Arabic you speak. Where did you pick that up?"

"I don't know what you're talking about."

Jamaal roared out in laughter. "He catches on quick! I like him."

Bill walked back to the table, opened a bottle of aspirin and said, "He's too damn loud."

William said, "Okay, Jamaal. Tell us what we're looking at." William poured a large mug of coffee and put it on the table with cream and sugar nearby.

Jamaal took a seat, fixed his coffee and took a sip. He smiled and nodded to William.

Bill asked, "By the way, where are we?"

Jamaal said, "Well, ole buddy. We're fifteen miles outside Eddyville, Iowa, only about a mile from the famous Des Moines River and right smack dab in the middle of corn country."

"Great."

"These guys are good. How did you ever find terrorists in Iowa?"

William said, "We know as much as you do, Jamaal."

"I wish I had a dollar for every time I heard that. I've been out to their place but as we all know, if you ain't connected you don't get too far with these guys. I helped them learn some of the lingo of a corn farmer but as smart as they seem to be, they just can't get the dialect. I have seen their stash of explosives and it could blow a big hole in Iowa—not that many people would notice. They're five miles from the nearest house—kind of like here. Nothing—and I do mean nothing—around them except corn and the river.

"They are bored out of their minds so one day a week they go to Eddyville just to see the sights and have a meal at the diner on Front Street. Talk about excitement."

Dell asked, "Do you have any idea what their plans are?"

"Not much. I don't think anything will happen for a couple of weeks. I'm serious. If they set all the stuff off, it's going to make a dent in something big. I get the feeling they are waiting on instructions."

William asked, "Do they have internet?"

"A big satellite rig but everything I've seen is encrypted. I know they get messages every few days. We're getting all the traffic into the house but it's either porn or encrypted."

Bill asked, "Did you just say we're going to be here a couple of weeks?"

William answered, "However long it takes unless they shut down and try to hide the material."

Jamaal said, "What's the matter, Bill? You got a lady back home that's going to miss you or start looking around?" Bill gave him a hard look, then got up and went outside. "Man, he's got it bad. Is he going to be okay for this mission?"

Dell said, "Don't worry about Bill. He'll be ready when the time comes. So what do we do until they decide to move?"

They talked for several hours, finally deciding that Jamaal would take William to the house to look around and plant some listening devices. Dell said he would go along too. He walked out in the backyard and saw Bill sitting in a chair up against a massive corn field. He stopped before he got to him. Dell recognized that look and he didn't like it. "Bill... Bill. Come on back." He shook him and stood behind him in case he went for his pistol.

Bill said, "Have you ever seen so much corn? What the hell do they do with all of it? I mean, who eats that much corn?"

"From what I've read, most of it goes into making ethanol for gasoline. Some of it goes to feeding cattle and almost nothing goes to the store. That's why corn is so expensive."

"Seems like a big waste to me."

"A lot of people feel that way. Are you okay?"

"Dell, I'm on the job. I'm okay. I don't want to talk about it."

"You're going to have to talk about it. And I think the sooner the better."

"What do you need me to do—concerning this job?"

"William, Jamaal and I are going to make a patrol out to the cell's house and plant some bugs. I need you to go into town to the diner on Front Street and keep an eye on these guys. This is the day they go to town to eat. Give me a call if they leave early. Jamaal says there are five of them. Just observe and let me know when they leave. Can you do that?"

"If you don't trust me, send me home!"

"Bill, this isn't about trust. You've saved my life too many times. The truth is I care about you and I kept things from you and it hurts me to think that you were hurt by it. Fatima is a good woman and she cares about you too. And I think... I know you care about her. Let it go, Bill, and try to be happy."

"Happy? You mean like you? I don't want to talk about it. And if you're going to keep on about this then I'll have to ask for a transfer. I don't want to do that. I got screwed over and I'm finished with it so let it go. I'll change and head to town."

"Whatever you say."

River's Edge Diner was crowded with only two booths left empty. Bill took one and sat facing the back wall. He ordered a hamburger, fries and a bowl of chili. Just as his order came, he watched in the mirrored back wall as five men came through the door and claimed the booth behind him.

The waitress approached and asked, "I guess you boys want the usual?"

"Yes. Hamburger. Fried potatoes and chocolate milk."

"You guys should try something else. We have a special on barbecued ribs. They're really tasty."

"No! I mean no, thank you. We like the hamburgers very much."

"Okey-dokey. Just trying to help."

One of the men whispered in Arabic. "We should kill that cow for offering us pork!"

Another man gave him a look that made him slide to the corner of the booth. The man leaned back towards Bill and said in a soft voice, "Infidels are pigs. Wouldn't you agree, white monkey?" Bill didn't flinch or respond. He kept eating his burger. The man touched Bill's shoulder and spoke in English. "Excuse me, sir. I haven't seen you in here before. How do you do?"

Bill looked around and smiled. "Oh, sorry. Are you talking to me?"

"I was just saying that I haven't seen you around here."

"Sorry 'bout that. My mind's on my ex and how much money she got outta me. Yeah, I've been here most of my life. I just don't get into town on Wednesday much. Usually too busy working on my equipment. Can't afford new stuff since my ex took me to the cleaners." He could see total confusion on the man's face. "You boys ain't from around here, are you?"

"We've been here for a while but, like you, we do not get into town very often." He switched to Arabic and said, "You are a pig."

"I'm sorry. What was that you just said? It sounded like one of those foreign things. Are you all from Europe?"

"Forgive me. We are from Italy. You don't speak Italian?"

"Heck, I have enough trouble with American, although my daddy was in Italy back during the war. He liked it real well—except for the shooting part. Well, got to go. You fellows ever get out to Briar, stop in and see me. It's about twenty miles north of here. My name is Tom." He held his hand out and shook hands with each man. Bill got a box to take the rest of his meal with him and then waved to the men on his way out.

The one who had done the talking turned to the others and asked, "Do you know what he was talking about?" They all shook their heads.

Bill sat in an old pick-up a block away finishing his meal and keeping watch until the five men drove out of town. He called Dell, who reported he and the others had finished their task and were on their way back to the farmhouse.

Chapter 20

Fatima walked home looking at the sidewalk. She wondered if it would be better to go back to the Bedouin and start her life over. She didn't know if she would ever fit in here in the States, but for Sami's sake she would try. All the newness of New Jersey had little effect on her. She did enjoy being in a place where war and death weren't always near. It was a relief to walk the streets without worrying about someone abducting her to be sold as a concubine or a wife. Most of her thoughts were on Hakim and the life she had lost with him,

Dell had given them credit cards to buy food, clothing and anything they needed for school and settling in. She felt uncomfortable using it but Dell had insisted that he would be angry if they didn't use them to take care of their needs.

An Arab lady named Sari had come to help them get started in their new life. She had grown up in New Jersey and understood some of the problems they would be facing. The first thing she did was to take Sami and Fatima on a shopping spree to buy clothes that wouldn't make them stand out. Sami was thrilled with everything but Fatima found no joy until Sari took her to Georgian Court College in Lakewood and enrolled her in English and American history courses. Sari was very careful to explain the bus schedule to Fatima and even accompanied her for several days until she felt confident enough to go it alone.

The clothes Sari had picked out caused Fatima much concern. They were modern, tight-fitting skirts, blouses and dresses which drew too many looks from young men who watched her pass by. Fatima returned them to the shop where she had purchased them and exchanged them for baggy, looser

179

fitting clothes. She also wore her hijab almost every time she left the apartment. She couldn't understand all the stares.

As the days passed, she put the thoughts of Bill into the recesses of her mind—or she tried. He hated her for what she had done. She turned some of her feelings to anger but she knew who was at fault.

Sami found that he loved school and his English improved rapidly. Fatima helped him often but TV and study aided him the most. He tried to comfort Fatima through her heartache but this new world captured most of his attention. He knew what a prize his credit card was and guarded it well. He would not disgrace his brother, Dell, by losing it to thieves or over using it himself. It was hard to believe the outrageous prices of things. He could never afford clothes or anything without Dell's help. He shopped in the bazaars and was soon known for his skills at getting the best price. One shop owner, who had been particularly impressed with Sami's bartering ability, gave him an after school job selling items in one of the shops.

He worried for Fatima but she did seem to be adapting. He would find a way to make things right with Hakim. Sami knew in his heart that Bill was the man for Fatima. Sami would change the way Bill thought.

Sami even found work for Fatima in one of the women's shops. They often walked together to and from their work. One day Sari took them to the *city*. New York City was a place of wonder for them both. How could so many people live together without great conflicts erupting? In Brooklyn it was like going home, but without people trying to kill you. It seemed that every kind of people lived in New York City in peace. He watched the news and saw reports of some of the crime and laughed at the frightened people. They knew nothing of hardship and death. Sami loved New York.

He went to Fatima's room and found her crying late one night. He sat down beside her, put his arms around her and said, "Sister. Why do you cry so?"

"I am lonely."

"How can you be lonely in a place where there is so much?"

"Oh, Sami! I am so glad you are with me. I'm afraid of this place."

"You need a man to make you feel safe."

"I want no one... except you, brother."

"You want Hakim. He is a fool."

"No! It is I who betrayed him. He has forgotten about me and it is for the best."

"You are wrong, Fatima. He has forgotten nothing. He needs you. This I know. You will go to him when he returns and bow to him and ask him to forgive... although you have nothing to be forgiven for... But that is the way of a man. I command this of you."

"I will not!"

"So? You have taken the ways of the west and will not do as your brother tells you?"

"Please, Sami. I love you and honor you for all you have done to protect me, but this is not something I can do. Hakim hates me. Can you blame him?"

"He is a fool but his eyes will open to the truth. Do not give up your love."

"I will love him forever but I will not cause him more pain. Forgive me, brother, but this is something I... must not do. For Hakim. I will not bring him pain."

"I will speak to my brother of this. This is a new land and I must learn what is proper. Quiet now, my beautiful sister. Sleep, and may Allah bless you in your dreams. You are loved." Fatima fell into Sami's arms and cried but after a while she grew quiet and finally slept.

Chapter 21

Fatima's dreams were vivid. She walked far behind Hakim as he crossed a sea of tall grass. The grass was planted in rows and as he walked he would look behind and Fatima could see his tears but then he looked directly at her, shook his head and turned away. She could see his feet dragging in the dirt and he gave no care to where he was going. She saw a man step onto the trail between the tall grasses and lift a pistol to fire at Hakim. She screamed his name in warning but he did not hear. Fire leaped from the pistol...

Fatima woke screaming Hakim's name. Sami ran into her room with a large blade in his hand. When he saw it was only a bad dream, he went to comfort Fatima. She crushed him in her embrace and cried out, "Hakim is in trouble!"

"How do you know this?"

"I saw it!"

"But it was only a dream."

"No. We must warn Mr. Dell and Hakim. Please help them, Sami."

Even Haji was bouncing off Sami's leg barking excitedly. He took a bite of Sami's pajamas and shook his head trying to pull Sami from the bed.

"How can we warn them, Fatima? We don't know where they are."

"We must go to the place they work and tell their captain!"

"Very well. Get dressed. We will take Haji as well. Dell told me his captain likes Haji. It may help him listen."

Captain Teasdale stormed into the squad room yelling in a sleep-filled voice. "Do you people know what time it is? This better be important!"

Herman Lum, the night sergeant, pointed at his office and said, "Those kids came in and demanded to see you,

182

Captain. They won't talk to me except to say one of our men is in danger."

"Which one?"

"They wouldn't say. All they said was is it was important to talk to you."

"Who are these kids?"

"Well, only one is a kid. The other is... well, you'll see."

A streak of white and brown flew out of Captain Teasdale's office and nipped at his leg. Teasdale screamed, reached for his weapon and fell back into a chair. He held one hand over his heart as the other was searching for a target. He looked down at the dog, now calmly sitting and looking up at him. "Haji! What are you doing here, boy? You took a year off my life. Between Sharpton, Anders and you, I might die next week. What's the matter, boy?" Haji turned and ran to Teasdale's office. "If those idiots are playing a joke on me I'll have someone's..." He had just stepped into his office and looked into the frightened, beautiful eyes of Fatima. Captain Teasdale stopped dead in his tracks. She was maybe the prettiest girl he had ever seen and she was crying. "Now, now, Miss. No need to cry. What can I do for you?"

Sami came out of his seat behind Captain Teasdale and said, "You have to help Hakim..." Teasdale jumped and spun in surprise and anger until he saw the young boy standing beside him. Who the hell were these rag... kids? And then he remembered Sharpton telling him about the two kids that were living with him. *That damn Sharpton's been giving them pointers on how to scare the crap out of me! Where is that guy anyway?*

Teasdale limped to his desk and sat down. Haji was in his lap licking his face before he got all the way into his seat. "Haji, it's good to see you too, boy." He turned to the two young people and for a second was lost again in Fatima's eyes. "Now. What's this all about and who is Hakim?"

Fatima spoke in her sweet accented voice. "We must warn Hakim... I mean Bill Anders that he is in danger. You must warn him, pleasaa, Captaina."

"I have no idea where they are. Those two come and go without telling me shi... anything. So Bill Anders has a nickname. I thought the... Arabs called him *White Snake* or something. Now it's Hakim. That's a good..." He saw Fatima turning a bright blush color and heat come to Sami's eyes.

"Yesaa, he is called that by some but we call him... This is not important. He is in danger." The tears returned to her eyes. "Captaina, you must help us warn him. Pleasaa!" Haji barked loudly and then whined looking directly at Teasdale.

"Is Haji your dog?"

"Yesaa."

"Then you are the two kids Sharpton is watching over?"

"Yesaa."

"How do you know Anders is in trouble?"

"I saw it in a dream." She went on to explain in detail her dream and at the end she said, "A man was pointing a gun at him and then he fired."

"A dream?" *Oh, crap. She's been hanging around that damn Sharpton too long! But he has saved my life twice because of those stupid dreams.* Teasdale wanted to tell them to get out of his office but the fright in both their eyes told him this might be real. And Haji was agitated and he really liked that dog.

Fatima threw herself at his feet begging for his help.

Teasdale grabbed the phone and yelled as he helped Fatima to stand. "Get me the Commissioner...! Yes, I know what time it is.... One more word out of you and I'm gonna..." He looked over at Sami and Fatima and finished, "Just wake him up and get him on the phone!"

After twenty minutes of yelling back and forth over the phone and finally Teasdale admitting that Dell had a gift of knowing what was coming and that he believed the young girl had it too, he hung up. He looked at Fatima and said, "We're going to try to get in touch with them. No one knows where they are, but the Commissioner has a few ideas. Now, you two go back home and I will call as soon as I know something. Say, you wouldn't mind bringing Haji back once in a while, would you?"

Sami said in Arabic, "You have shown that you trust us. We are in your debt and it will be an honor to return and see the man who has helped us." Fatima translated and Captain Teasdale escorted them into the squad room.

"Wilson. Get a car and take these fine young people home. And Wilson, don't get any ideas. This pretty woman and Sami are friends of mine."

"You got it, Captain."

Chapter 22

William, Dell and Bill were suiting up. They had watched and listened to the cell for eight days and now they knew the bad guys were moving the explosives to a target but they didn't know where. Three men from the ATF had joined them and it was decided to go in before they drove away with the bombs. Jamaal would stay in the background, not wanting to blow his cover.

This wasn't the cell that the NSA was looking for. There was no radioactive material and no hint that they knew anything about a dirty bomb. William made the call to go in and not to bring Loretta into the loop. She might try to stop them because their only objective was to find the terrorists and the dirty bomb. He refused to let the ATF take the lead. They would strike in broad daylight because the area around the house was planted in tall corn. There would be good cover until they were within twenty yards of the house.

Bill would go in on foot to the right side of the house. Dell and the ATF team would race in with the pickup and they would be loaded for bear. William would also go in on foot to the left side of the house. He would give the Go signal.

At ten in the morning Bill started his move through the tall stalks of corn. He heard the pickup pull away, checked his

M-4 rifle and pistol as he slowly made his way to the house over a mile away. He used his small handheld GPS to guide him. No one would approach closer than one hundred yards until Dell sent out the signal that his team was in position and then William and Bill would move up to the edge of the corn.

Bill didn't sleep much the night before. It wasn't the operation that bothered him. It was lingering thoughts of Fatima. He shook his head trying to get her out of his mind. Bill imagined her back in Jersey having the time of her life. Anyone that pretty and that free would surely be having a great time, especially after everything she had been through. That's what bothered him the most. She had lived her entire life avoiding danger and doing whatever she must to survive, including deceiving him and he actually understood the reasons why. Still she had withheld the truth from him and that ate away at his gut. Why couldn't she have told him the truth when she lay with him in the desert, offering her own warmth, trying to save his life? Why should she? That was the right question and until that moment he wouldn't allow his mind to answer. Why should she? She didn't know him but still she had protected him with her life and reputation and saved his life. Why would she do that? And she was so beautiful... Bill shook his head to clear his thoughts. He had to be on his toes or someone could be killed. This was no time to let some deceitful woman get inside his head.

Bill felt the tendrils of depression start to surround him, but he tripped on a clod of dirt and went down, breaking the cycle that was coming too often these last few days. He stopped and listened. He felt something was wrong but... it must have been in his head.

Tarzic heard the noise off to his left and knew what it was. He had stumbled around in this cursed corn for days. Now it was paying off. Someone was approaching the house.

He had taken it upon himself to stay out in the corn at least three hours every day to learn how to move in it. He hated corn. He refused to eat it after his first try. It tasted like... like animal food. It was the perfect food for these infidels.

They were all animals and needed to be taken from this earth. Unlike some of his brethren he wanted them all dead. There was no hope in converting these westerners to the true faith. All they wanted was money, power and toys. If they came to his land they would die within a week. Their women were coarse and showed their sex openly. Each time he was forced to go to the village he became sick from looking at the fat cows and the pigs of men in the town. And they laughed all the time like they were insane.

He silently prayed and smiled. Soon he would be in paradise reaping his reward for the gift of his life. He would gladly strap on a vest and walk into the diner and kill the pigs. He prayed that the day would be soon. He wanted to look at their faces as he called out for blessings. The others could do as they wished but he would not leave this spoiled earth untouched. He would not!

Tarzic felt the sound before he heard it. Then he saw him; a single man with a military weapon. He lifted his pistol but the man looked back. Were there others? Tarzic lowered his weapon. He would follow and see what this fool was planning. The man was not a soldier. He moved like an old man in the city. Tarzic smiled. He moved out parallel to his target. He could kill him at any time but if there were others he would increase his glory by killing more infidels.

Jerry, one of the ATF agents, pulled the pickup into position three hundred yards from the house. He let the engine idle—ready for instant action. Dell settled back and looked at the electronic tracker. William was one hundred and fifty yards from his position but Bill was still three hundred yards out. Dell was impressed with this array of electronic equipment.

Dell called on the mist but it would no longer come. He was beginning to enjoy life without it but in his own way he did miss it. Sami and Fatima had changed his life. No. The desert had changed his life and it now called him home. He daydreamed of being with the Bedouin and of riding through the desert on a hunt.

A buzz brought him out of his daydream. It was his cell. He had never forgotten to turn it off before. He angrily pulled it from his pocket to turn it off but something made him open the message page to see who had sent him a text. It was Loretta. She was probably upset that he hadn't reported in. His thumb moved to power the cell phone down but then he pushed the read selector. The message was short. _Bill is in danger. Fatima._

"Jerry! Take me back to Bill's drop off point, now!" Jerry gunned the engine and made a quick U-turn. One minute later Dell lifted his silenced M-4 and said, "Get back in position and when you get the Go signal from William, don't wait for me. I'll be there."

"Roger."

Dell slipped into the corn and raced between the rows frequently checking the GPS to guide him to Bill.

Tarzic thought he heard something coming from a different direction and stopped to listen and get a fix on it. He swiveled his head but the wind had picked up and all he heard was the rustling of the corn stalks. He turned back to his target and moved in closer.

Dell slowed only a little but watched where he put his feet. He was definitely not a country boy and running through a crop of corn was as foreign as dancing the Samba to him. He was getting closer but the track of Bill showed he needed to move to the east. He broke through two rows of corn, aware that he was making too much noise, but he hoped the wind would mask it.

Tarzic stopped again. This time he was sure he heard something coming from behind him. It was time to kill this one and go after the other fool stumbling about. He had moved to within thirty yards of the infidel. The man had stopped and was looking down at something he held in his hand.

Tarzic stepped out for a clear shot, lowered to one knee, raised his pistol using both hands and took careful aim. He took up the slack on the trigger holding his aim steady and then...

Dell was huffing as he hurried down the row of corn. He saw the man step out about one hundred yards ahead. Dell dropped to a kneeling position and as he raised the rifle his thumb flicked the selector to three-round burst. He took a quick breath and slowly let it out. The target moved in the sights and he saw him raise his arms. He let the crosshairs move to the upper torso and squeezed the trigger. A short nearly silent burst thumped against his shoulder and he saw the target drop, but not before he heard the soft report of a pistol. He also saw Bill sag to the ground. Dell was up and running, switching to full automatic. Blood was soaking into the fertile ground and he saw three holes in the back of the man. One high in the shoulder. He was dead. Dell raced to where Bill lay on the ground. He could see blood seeping from his left shoulder.

"Bill... Bill, are you okay?"

"They got me, Dell."

Dell carefully examined Bill and could see where a round had pierced the shoulder flap on his Kevlar vest. He moved the flap and could see an in and out wound through the flesh of Bill's upper shoulder. It was bleeding steadily. Dell also noticed it wasn't a large round from a pistol that had wounded him. "Bill, you're..."

"Dell... Dell. I'm not feeling too good." Bill turned to look up at Dell and saw the concern in his eyes. He thought, *It must be bad for Dell to look like this.* "Dell. Promise me one thing."

"Bill. You're going to..."

"Dell. Listen to me. I want you to promise that you will look after Fatima. I've treated her badly and I wanted to make it up to her... but now..."

"Bill. You're going to..."

"Listen to me! You have to promise me. I'm in love with her... even if she is beautiful. I can't hold that against her and if I hadn't taken a bullet I would have wanted to..."

William sent out a two beep urgent Go signal. Which meant something was going down and they had to move right now.

Dell had been supporting Bill, but now he dropped him to the ground and said, "Got to go!" He jumped to his feet and ran towards the house while replacing the magazine in his rifle with a full one.

Bill lay on the ground for a few seconds and felt the pain to his shoulder. *Dell left me to die alone. How could he do something like that?* He pulled the vest back and saw it was only a flesh wound. He moved his left arm and there was pain but nothing he couldn't take. And then he heard loud reports of a heavy automatic weapon and spurts of silenced weapons. He jumped to his feet, retrieved his rifle and sprinted towards the house.

As Bill rushed out of the field he saw a man with an automatic weapon jumping out of the window on the west side of the house. He saw Dell around the corner heading for the east side. The man would be coming up behind Dell. Bill brought the M-4 up and squeezed the trigger. He let his aim pass through where the man was moving. He had time to notice the line of bullet holes he was making in the house as he tracked the man. The man was raising his weapon as the line crossed him and he took two rounds in the body. He dropped to the ground but was still moving. Bill touched the release and slapped a fresh magazine in all in one motion, released the bolt and depressed the trigger again, holding his aim on the man. His body jumped as each round hit him.

Dell had swung around and saw Bill. He smiled, gave him the thumbs-up and continued around the house. By the time Bill reached the house the heavy weapon fire was silent and he heard the ATF men calling, "Clear."

Bill slumped to the ground and Dell rushed to him. He led Bill to the porch and William came out of the house and saw the blood streaming down Bill's arm. "Bill! What have they done to you?"

Dell said, "It's a through and through in his upper arm."

William turned and called Jerry to get the kit.

As they finished patching Bill up William said, "That looks like a small caliber rifle wound." Dell gave him a hard look. Bill was resting with his eyes closed so William said, "You two need to get out of here before the locals show up. We don't need your names on any of the reports. I'll get Jerry to take you back to the house and then you head for the airport. I'll have a plane waiting."

Chapter 23

As the plane landed at a small airport near Newark, Bill said, "You saved my life... again."

"You saved my ass back there, too. And about that wound..."

"Oh, I'm okay. I guess it was shock that made me act like a girly-man."

"You did fine. Do you remember what you said to me about Fatima?"

"No. What?"

"You told me you loved her and that you..."

"I never said that! Why would a woman like her want anything to do with me? Besides, she... Well, she didn't do anything wrong, I guess, but I acted like a fool. She won't want to have anything to do with me. She's going to have a good life here thanks to you. If I said anything, just drop it."

"Bill, you've got it all wrong. Fatima is crazy about..."

"Enough of that crap! I want her to have a good life and find a good man. I'm going to stay away from her and... I hate seeing her cry. It's all my fault. Promise me you'll help her and let her live her own life. She's smart and... pretty and she sure doesn't need a dope like me. She'll find someone in no time. That's what she needs."

Billy gingerly moved his shoulder and felt the pain from his wound and then a thought occurred to him. "Hey, I guess I'll be off for a couple of days. Maybe I'll take Sami to the mountains and do a little fishing. He needs to get out of the city and see some beautiful country. Yeah, that's what I'll do. Look,

Dell. Do me a favor and don't tell Fatima I got shot. I still don't understand how that pistol round went through my vest. It must have had a defect."

"Bill, about that shot. I'm the one that..."

"You saved my life! That's all I need to know. Now promise me you won't say anything."

"I don't make promises but I'll keep my mouth shut."

The car pulled up at Loretta's house and Bill said, "We're going to be in here for hours. She'll be tearing us a new one for going off the reservation."

"I'll handle this." Dell told the driver to take Bill home. The driver started to protest but Dell shut him up with a look.

"Do me a favor and look in on Sami for me. I'll be here for a while. That kid needs some guidance and I'm not the role-model type."

"I'll take care of it but I hope Fatima's not there."

"Bill, you've got it all wrong. Fatima really..." Bill shut the door and the driver pulled away.

Loretta was waiting on Dell as he stepped out of the elevator. She didn't look happy.

Dell said, "Before you say anything, I made the call to go in. Those terrorists had enough explosives to level a city block and they were ready to use it."

Loretta said, "You should have let William make that call... but I have to agree with you. We'll talk more about this later. Let's have a drink and you can tell me all about it."

Bill went to his apartment, took a shower and redressed his wound. It hurt like hell. He decided to go to a nearby clinic to get it checked and to get something for the pain. After that he would decide whether to go to Dell's place.

Bill walked the mile to Dell's and as he passed a small pizza shop he thought about getting Sami something to eat. He looked in the window and saw Fatima. She was sitting with a young man and they were laughing and having a grand time. *Well, that didn't take long. What did you expect? She's beautiful and... Crap. I've got to forget about her. Why would she want anything to do with an ugly guy like me anyhow?* He turned and headed to Dell's apartment with his head down.

When he arrived, Sami was not there so he took three pain pills and sat on the couch to wait for him. He looked around and could feel Fatima's touch and a hint of jasmine in the place. She was fitting in quickly. Bill leaned his head back for just a moment.

Dreaming of the desert and of the woman he saw bathing at the spring, he smiled. Bill could feel the heat of the land and relaxed as the woman came to him and put her body next to his. She was smiling shyly at him.

He heard her voice and felt her insistent manipulations and then pain as she probed his shoulder. He opened his eyes to two pools of brimming liquid concern that looked down at him.

"What has happened, Hakim? Who has hurt you? Wake up, please."

Through his haze Fatima came into focus and he smiled and pulled her to him. She molded to his body and he heard her quiet murmurs through her tears. Then he was fully awake and pushed her away with his right hand. He turned his head from her gaze. As he looked away he saw Sami and Dell watching and he tried to rise.

Fatima looked down at him as she stumbled to her feet, the look of hurt and betrayal clear on her face. Tears flooded her eyes as she ran from the room.

Dell said, "I would kick your ass if you weren't hurt. We're going to have a long talk."

Sami said, "I am not sure if he is worthy of my sister's attentions."

"What are you two talking about? What did I do?"

"Why do you hurt my sister so?"

Dell said, "You're dumber than a box of rocks."

"What should I do? I saw her... at the restaurant. I don't want to get in her way. She has her own life and doesn't need me in it." Bill could see the anger and hurt on Dell's face. What was he supposed to do? She had lied... no, that wasn't true. Fatima had saved his life—more than once. But now she's in a new world and fooling around with... No, that wasn't true either. She needed to find someone who would care for her... love her. But she needed advice. "I'll go talk to her."

Dell looked at him and said, "Fatima was with the officer watching the house. Don't you go hurting her—more than you already have. She's a good woman!"

"I know that but... damn. I'll try." He got up stiffly, nursing his left shoulder and walked into Fatima's room.

He stopped just inside the doorway and saw her lying on the bed crying. "Fatima?"

At the sound of his voice she jumped off her bed and rubbed her face. She glanced at Bill but turned her face away.

"Fatima. I'm okay. It's only a scratch. Just a little sore."

"May I attend to your hurt?"

"It's okay. There's no need for you..." He watched as her body drooped in defeat. "Well, I could use a new bandage."

Fatima sat him on her bed and then ran to get the first-aid supplies. Bill felt her sit next to him and reveled in the caring touch he longed for. He turned to look at her but with her fingers she turned his head away. She couldn't bear to look in his eyes. Removing the old gauze bandage, she saw the damage to his upper arm. It wasn't bad but she knew he was in pain.

Bill reached in his pocket and took another pill as Fatima began to clean the wound. Her touch was like points of fire on his skin. The feeling changed to a warm healing and he began to relax.

"You are very good at taking care of me. I'm sorry I've been so rude to you, but I didn't want to get in your way."

"In my way? I don't understand."

"What I mean to say is you have done so much for me and now that you are here I want you to be happy and find a good, new life."

"But you have released me from your protection. Why would you care what happens to me? Lie down so I can cover your wound."

Bill lay back and closed his eyes and enjoyed her touch. "Fatima, I spoke too quickly... I mean, I will always protect you... You are important to me and I will never forget what you did for me in the desert. I... care for you."

"Do you take back your obligation?"

Sleepily Bill said, "Yes. But it is only until you find the one you love. Then he will take over."

His words hurt... held her close... touched her heart... brought back her tears. Fatima let her mind go blank for a moment, remembering Bill's touch. She had missed that feeling and needed it. Taking a deep breath she asked in prayer that she would be brave enough. "Hakim... I mean Bill. I don't have the words in your language so I will speak in mine."

She took another deep breath and then plunged forward, not looking at him. "You are the heat of the desert that fills me when you touch me. In my land you were my oasis, my clear cool water that gave me the nourishment I have never had. I felt complete in your arms. Hakim... I have never wished to be held by a man until I felt you next to me. I will, no... I must tell you that I am yours and will never desire another. The winds touch me in heat and comfort but only because I have found you. Do you not think of me in this way? For as long as I live there will be no other. Cast me aside and watch me wither if that is your wish. Or hold me and I will serve you and be yours in any way that you desire. Can this happen, Hakim?" She turned and looked down at him. Bill was sleeping.

A wave of anger came over her and she raised her hand to strike him, but with her hand raised she looked at his face. He had the face of a child in sleep. No worries creased his brow, but then he frowned, pursed his lips and let go with a long low rumbling flatulent noise. His mouth turned up at the corners in a smile and his face had a look of pure contentment.

The smell touched her but the heat of anger flew away. Fatima began to laugh and couldn't stop. It became uncontrollable and she ran from the room. He was perfect!

Dell had been standing near the doorway, worried about what his idiot friend might say, but when he heard Fatima's words, he turned and moved back into the living room. Fatima ran to him and her laughter caught him unaware until he realized she was happy. He held her and joined her in laughter. It had been so long since he had laughed; it sounded strange but he couldn't stop. He looked over at Sami and motioned him to come to them. He held them both in his arms and tears of joy coursed down his cheeks. Haji barked, twirled and finally leaped into the mix.

Sami asked, "Why are we so happy? Has Bill done the right thing by my sister?"

Fatima finally calmed down and answered. "He has not but I cannot hide my feelings. He is like a child when he sleeps and he has taken his protection of me back. For now it is enough."

Dell said, "Don't give up on him, Fatima."

"I cannot. I must run to the apothecary shop and get more medicine for Hakim."

Sami asked, "Is he in pain?"

"I think it was something he ate." And the laughter started again as she hurried out.

Chapter 24

Homeland Security Director Hornealius Hapholte had changed into his third *Michael Bastian* of the day. He enjoyed the feel of a freshly setup suit. **Hornealius** took his seat and said, "This is the fourth time I've been to your farm, Derik. I'm not comfortable with this arrangement."

General Walter Amines, NSA Director, smiled and put his hand on **Hornealius'** shoulder. "I've been here a number of times. It's not unusual for government officials to socialize and even become friends. We're old friends enjoying a weekend at a government colleague's farm. A bit of fishing, golf, and horseback riding is just the thing for powerful men to relax."

Hornealius said, "You do have a point, Walter, but I need to be back by 6:00. You'll never guess who wants to see me tonight."

Senator Derik Bartholomew said, "Wonder Woman."

"How did you know that?"

"I set it up, Horny. I think you deserve a little excitement after all the hard work you're doing."

"You do know how to treat your colleagues, Derik! I'll be thanking you later."

Derik said, "Let's get down to business so Horny won't be late."

General Amines smiled and said, "I still have a problem with Loretta Smithe. I don't have access to what she knows about Aisha. This trooper she's brought in has made a trip to Lebanon and stirred up a hornet's nest. He obviously found something—there's been a lot of activity, but I can't find out anything about the mission. This is going to be a problem as our agenda goes forward."

Horny said looking at Derik, "I told you this guy was trouble! We need him eliminated and his partner as well."

Derik said, "I have the situation in hand. Aisha has complete control of Loretta Smithe. And Dell Sharpton is being led around by his nose. He hasn't come close to uncovering anything concerning our operation. If he does, we'll deal with all of them."

General Amines asked, "How can an Arab terrorist be in control of one of my Section Directors?"

"Loretta has secrets you don't know about, Walter. You'll have to trust me on this. When the time is right, all of the people concerned will be disposed of. It's not a problem."

Senator Bartholomew had met with Aisha the night before. He enjoyed humiliating her to prove his control. She would eat from his left hand to see her scheme go forward. He knew how dangerous this game was but it excited him to have her—in every way possible. She was a wildcat but knew what she had to do to get her hands on the material that would terrorize the U.S. He knew it was like making love to a cobra, but Derik held a knife to her throat and she knew it. Aisha would be the first to die when the bomb went off, leaving a clear path to start the takeover of the U.S. Government.

"Horny. Have the bomb assembly ready for our Middle Eastern friends. You will deliver everything except the nuclear material when I give the word."

"You seem so sure of yourself, Derik," said Walter Amines. "Are you positive these terrorists will believe the material is active?"

"Of course. The radiation detectors are part of the deal and our techs have made the necessary adjustments. This will not be a problem. I have their leader eating from my hand."

Hornealius said, "I've seen a few minor reports about some Russian nuclear material that vanished forty years ago. This information has popped up a few times and if terrorists are able to get their hands on it, well, I don't have to tell you what could happen."

Derik said, "That rumor has been around for years. No one would be foolish enough to use it—even in research—much less give it to a group like Aisha's. Now here's what I propose we do when the bomb goes off..."

Chapter 25

Bill and Dell walked into the squad room and Captain Teasdale rushed out bellowing, "Where have you two been? You think you can just take off on your little vacations whenever you like? Well, let me tell you... Say, did you bring Haji with you?"

Bill said, "Not this time, Captain, but he really wanted to come. We'll bring him by later."

"In my office, now!"

In the office Bill said, "Captain, you know this isn't our idea. The Feds tell us what to do and we've got no choice. Dell's not happy about it either."

"Yeah, I can tell." Captain Teasdale looked over at Dell, who was sitting with a bored look on his face. "Are you guys back on duty?"

Dell answered, "Until they want us again. What can we do for you, Captain?"

What is with Dell? thought Teasdale. *He's acting almost human.* "Just check in with Wilson. I don't think we have anything pressing. Maybe you should look over the reports and see if there is anything you can do. We've had a string of robberies and one or two hate crimes but nothing out of the ordinary."

Bill said, "I could use a little ordinary right now."

"Dell, where are you keeping those two fine kids? I think I would like my son to meet that girl. She's a beauty. And the boy, Sami, seems to have taken a liking to me. You know if you need anyone to look after Haji... well, I would be glad to do it."

"The girl won't be getting anywhere near your kid but I'll think about the dog."

"Get out of my office!"

Wilson said, "Look at those two! They're getting more like one another every time I see them." He hooked his thumb at Dell and Bill sitting in the back of the unmarked car. Both of them appeared to be in a trance.

Herman said, "Yeah, it's kind of scary. Bill's been hanging out with Dell for too long. But I'll tell you one thing. Dell has saved our asses more than once, so as long as we're here surrounded by Hajjis, I like having them around, no matter how weird they are. Wilson, why don't you wake them up?"

"You mean Sergeant Wilson. Don't you, Detective?"

"You pull rank every time there's trouble."

"RHIP... Rank has its privileges. Wake them up."

"Here's a trick I learned from Bill." Herman leaned over the seat and slowly pulled both of their weapons from the holsters. He smiled over at Wilson as he shook Bill and Dell.

Bill was actually sleeping, still recovering from his wound and the painkillers he had been taking. He had been

199

dreaming of the desert and Fatima. His eyes snapped open and he saw Herman and Wilson smiling. "What's so funny?"

Herman nodded towards Dell and said, "You two could be roommates."

"Bite me." Bill checked for his weapon and said, "Hey, where's my gun?"

Herman handed him his weapon saying, "A little trick I learned from you. I didn't want to be shot when I brought you back from the dead."

Bill looked over at Dell and saw the familiar not-at-home right now look. "Come on, Dell. Time to go to work." He shook Dell and watched him stir.

Dell stood in the mist and felt fear for the first time. He knew he had nothing to worry about with these ghouls that swirled nearby but the fear came from being back in the mist. It had been a while and he didn't want to be there. He had thought his life might be turning around with his new family, but this return showed him he had a long way to go to break the cycle.

The darkness began to break up and in his mind's eye he saw a group of white and black men standing over three Arab children. The kids were tied to chairs and one of the men held a hunting knife pointed at the little girl. The children were terrified. Dell looked out the window of the green lap-sided house and saw a dark blue car parked just down the street.

"Come on back, buddy. We've got a little job to take care of." Bill slapped him lightly on the face and Dell lunged for his weapon. It wasn't there.

"Where the hell's my gun?"

Herman said, "See. I knew that was a good idea. This guy is scary."

Dell retrieved his pistol and said, "Let's go."

Wilson said, "Go! Go where? We're just watching the white house and we're not supposed to move in until we get backup."

"We're moving on the green house with the blue car parked just down from it." He pointed at the house across from where they were parked.

"The green house? Are you crazy? That's not the right house. And we're in the blue car!"

Dell got out and walked down the block to get the sun behind him and then crossed the street. He stopped to look back at the car and saw Bill getting out.

Bill said, "He's never been wrong before. Are you coming or staying?"

Herman said, "This is going to be bad." He got out of the car and went with Bill.

"Shit!" Wilson made a quick call and then followed.

They caught up to Dell, who was waiting near the back door of the house. He whispered, "There are five men—two blacks and three whites. They are holding three children and we've got to stop them before they hurt the kids."

Herman asked, "Weapons?"

"One has a knife but I don't know about the rest. Don't hurt the children! Wilson, you're in charge. Bill and I'll go straight through and you and Herman cover us."

"I can see why you drive the captain crazy. Okay, Dell. Lead the way."

Dell didn't bother trying the back door knob. He lunged forward with a kick ripping the door off the hinges and then sprinted through. Bill was right behind him. Dell ran through the kitchen into the living room and with his left hand he grabbed the wrist of the surprised looking man holding the knife. In the same motion he clubbed the man in the head with his pistol and dropped him to the floor. Bill yelled out, "Police! Get your hands in the air! Anyone makes a wrong move and you're dead." Wilson and Herman rushed into the room and spread apart with their guns leveled at the men.

One very large white man roared out and made a move at Dell, but Bill rushed him and his right arm took the man across the throat while his left hand came around to the small of his back and pressed hard. The big man did a complete flip and the air whooshed out of him as he slammed into the floor. Bill pressed his weapon to the back of his head. One of the black men made a move to reach behind him and Wilson in a steady, low, raspy voice said, "Go ahead. Make my day." The man looked at the 40 cal. semi-automatic pistol pointed at his head and held his hands high in the air.

After the men were cuffed and frisked, Bill untied the children. He said in Arabic, "You are safe now. We will let no harm come to you." The children looked at him for a moment and began to cry tears of relief. They rushed to Bill and he knelt to hug them.

Herman said, "Go ahead. Make my day? Are you serious, Wilson?"

"Well, I always wanted to say that. Besides, it worked. Didn't it?"

"Wait 'til I tell the guys at the squad. This is gonna be great!"

The men were charged with kidnapping under the hate crimes act. Bill grew in status with the Arab community and *White Snake* was met with smiles wherever he went.

Wilson's new nickname, *Dirty Harry*, spread quickly and he liked it.

For the next two weeks Dell spent every moment he could with Sami, Fatima and Haji. He actually smiled almost every day.

Bill continued to agonize over his feelings for Fatima. He visited Dell often and walked Fatima to work or the bus stop on occasion and he would catch her watching him when his head was turned. He also watched Fatima when she wasn't looking. They spoke of small things and both were careful not to bring up their feelings. Sami often went with them to buy things at the market because he no longer worked there. Dell had insisted that Sami concentrate on school. He was actually making plans for Sami to attend college and seeing a future that included them being with him as a real family.

Captain Teasdale, while still being himself at work, was becoming a frequent visitor in his off time. He invited them to his home several times. Barbara, the captain's wife, fell in love with Sami, Fatima and especially Haji. It took a few visits to overcome her dislike of Dell because of Phil's ear nearly being shot off. She blamed Dell for that. She eventually did warm to him but only because of the way he treated his new family. When she met Bill, it was a true friendship at once. And she immediately recognized what was going on between him and Fatima. It was bitter-sweet.

Dell and Bill walked into the Commissioner's office. Dell had knocked before entering and the Commissioner looked up in surprise.

"What's going on with you, Dell? That's the first time you've ever knocked. You two have a seat and grab a cigar."

They sat quietly and each took a cigar from the humidor.

"I'll get right to it. The Feds are coming for you and it sounds like you're going to be going away for a while."

"Pat, I'm going to turn that down. I'm through wandering around with the Feds. I've been thinking of putting in for a transfer and settling down," said Dell.

"That goes for me, too," said Bill.

"You guys seem to think you have a choice in this. Let me tell you. I just got off the phone with the Vice President—again—and he put it in no uncertain terms. They will lock you both up if you refuse. I've seen this before. Just get this done and I'll try to pull some strings to get them off your backs."

Loretta came bouncing through the door and gave the Commissioner a bright, beautiful smile. "How are you, Pat? I see you have my boys all ready to go. You've been a great help and I know there will be some recognition of you."

Pat O'Hara looked on at the very pretty woman in the bright yellow sundress as she twirled around to face Dell and Bill. "Are you ready to go?"

Pat said, "Can I ask you a question, little lady?"

"It's Loretta and you can ask me anything."

"What is going on? And where are you taking them?"

Loretta gave him another bright smile and turned her back on him. "Time to go. I have a car waiting outside."

Dell said, "I'd like you to answer the Commissioner's question."

"No can do, Dell. You know what's at stake here. Heck, I don't even know everything, but we've got to leave now."

"I need to call my house."

"All taken care of. The agency sent a man over to inform your little friends that you won't be home for a few days. If you want, we'll have someone keep an eye on them."

Bill said, "Keep your people away from them. We'll get someone to check on them as soon as I talk to them."

"Aren't they both at school right now? Give them a call but they've already been notified... Okay, but make it quick."

Dell dialed Fatima's cell but it went straight to voicemail. He left a quick message and nodded to Bill as he rose from his seat. "Like Bill said, keep your people away from them."

"Whatever you say, sugar. Come on, you two. We have things to talk about."

Back at Loretta's secure location, William came in with two glasses of Jameson, a glass of Scotch and a cup of Earl Grey tea. He set the libations on the coffee table and asked, "How are Sami, Fatima and Haji? I'm sorry I haven't been able to come by."

Dell answered, "They're adjusting well. Thanks for asking."

"I can see that they have had a big effect on you... and Bill. How are you, Bill?"

"I'm doing okay. I never got to thank you for what you did out in the corn. What have you been up to?"

Loretta waltzed into the room and said, "That's one of the things we're going to talk about. The men you took out had nothing to do with our operation. I had a lot of explaining to do to keep you out of hot water." All three men just stared. She said, "Well, isn't this a happy little group."

William said, "We did what we had to do and Bill took a bullet doing it."

Loretta said, "Funny thing about that bullet. It came from..." She looked at Dell and changed the subject quickly. "We have another lead on the *Dirty Bomb* terrorists. It seems the books Dell picked up in Lebanon had some very good information in them. Our guys have cracked a deeper code and this situation is real. We've found out that they do have the material and it's Uranium 238. They have at least fifty pounds of it. We've been tracking—or trying to track—Plutonium, so this is a big event. The good news is much of it is degraded, we think. It can't cause major harm but it would be a massive headache for the government. The bad news is we think they have everything ready to assemble."

Dell asked, "How do you know this stuff is degraded? And if you know it's no good, wouldn't the terrorists know it too?"

"It all depends on the equipment they have to test it. Most of the reports I get say it will cause a lot of problems and terror but probably won't be a health risk."

"Do they have any people who know how to handle that stuff? All it takes is one man to know the quality of the material."

Loretta smiled and said, "We have no knowledge of them having an expert."

Dell gave her a hard look and said, "This whole thing is starting to smell. I feel like I'm being led around by my nose. My senses say that they have the real thing and are going to use it. What is it you're not telling us?"

"I've told you all I know..."

"You never tell everything you know, Loretta."

She said, "Let's just get on with this. You have an assignment."

Dell looked up at Loretta and nodded.

Bill asked, "So where are we going?"

Loretta looked at William and said, "Let's hear what William has to say."

"I've been assigned to research this and I've come up with a few places they could store and work on this bomb without being detected. They all deal with underground tunnels."

Bill let out a groan and then said, "I knew this was a bad idea. Thanks a lot, Dell. It's always been one of my dreams to die a mile underground."

William smiled. "It's more like two miles under or into the side of a mountain. But look on the bright side, Bill. I'll be there with you." He blew Bill a kiss. Bill came back with the famous Jersey salute. "We've had a couple of hits on our search and I've narrowed it down to two possibilities. One is an abandoned mine and the other location was built 20 years ago and made ready for storage but hasn't been used since."

"William, why don't you take these two downstairs and show them what you've found?"

Dell said, "Hey, William, how about taking us to get something to eat first?"

Loretta said, "I can have anything you want brought in."

"No. I'd like to go to Ming's on H Street. Nothing like good Chinese when it's fresh. What about you, Bill?"

Bill had heard this line about food before and he knew Dell needed to talk in private. It was starting to dawn on him that something might not be right. "You got it. I love Chinese and I heard Ming's is the best in town." He stood and said, "Let's do it, William. Time I got to know you socially."

On the ride to H Street Dell pulled out his new titanium phone and showed it to William. He pointed at it and then at William. William nodded and pulled his out. It was exactly like Dell's. Dell took it, then motioned for Bill to give him his cell.

Dell said, "You ever been to Ming's?"

William said, "No. But I do enjoy Chinese food. What's their specialty?"

"The Cashew Chicken is great."

Bill said, "Well, hurry up, you're making me hungry."

William said, "What's the idea with the..." Dell put his finger to his lips and William finished. "... with the cashews? Do they roast them in oyster sauce?"

"Now, how did you know that? It's an old family secret—at least that's what Wong told me."

"I've been all over China and it's a well-known secret."

Bill asked, "Is there any place you haven't been?"

"Kachin."

"Oh, I see." Bill punched Dell, raised his hands and shoulders.

"It's in northern Burma." Dell could see the do-what look and said, "Near Thailand."

"I know where that is."

"Good for you."

As they entered Ming's, Dell talked to Mr. Wong and had him take the cell phones into the kitchen.

"That will keep them busy translating what the cooks are saying. Let's get a table."

Ming's was near capacity and filled with laughter and noise. The sports bar area had a ball game on and the chatter was loud, spiking with the action on the screens.

Dell asked Bill, "Do you trust William?"

"Yeah, I do. As much as I didn't like him at first, I see he's a man of his word."

William said, "What's this all about, Dell?"

"How well do you know Loretta and this group she's running?"

William took a moment to answer. He had come to trust these two men but there was only so much he could tell them. Perhaps it was time to bring them in a bit deeper. The local Arab communities trusted them and Mossad had confirmed all that had happened in Lebanon. Dell and Bill were the only people he had come to trust completely in a long time and it felt good. He would give them enough to find out what Dell had in mind and then decide if more could be given out.

"What I tell you is not to be let out." He looked at Bill when he said that.

Bill said, "What? Hey, I'm not the one who keeps secrets from his partner, but I don't go around shooting my mouth off either."

"You're right, Bill. You are someone I trust. And that thing about Fatima... was only to protect everyone concerned."

"Shit." Bill gave Dell a hard look. "Okay, I admit it; I'm pretty sure I didn't handle it well."

Dell said, "You need to get over it."

William broke in. "Only a few people know about Fatima and Sami and it's going to stay that way. They have no history and that's the best way to keep them safe. Fatima's too pretty to leave dangling for long. She did what she had to do."

"Yeah, Yeah. I know that. All I want is for her to be... What are we talking about Fatima for?"

"Seriously, Bill. I've been all over the world and it's the same no matter where you go. It's a very hard life for beautiful girls who don't want to become wives at twelve or slaves or whores. Fatima is one of a kind! Don't break her heart."

"Yeah, yeah. Can we talk about something else? Besides. We're getting along now and I know that... never mind. "

William said, "I don't belong to Loretta's group. I'm on loan to her. I'm also keeping an eye on her."

Dell asked, "So who do you work for?" After the blank look William gave him, Dell continued. "I don't think she's all she claims to be. I have reason to believe she is playing both sides of this game."

Bill snapped his fingers and said, "The woman in Beirut. That's why you gave me that dirty look."

Dell explained all that had taken place and also said, "She's just not on the level about this dirty bomb business. She speaks Arabic like she was born in Egypt."

William said, "So do you. She spent several years in Egypt with the CIA. She was born in the States but has been a person of interest for a while. Loretta keeps making big progress on anything that she's assigned to so I'm only keeping an eye on her for... security reasons. I'm here to help her and to get the feel of her."

Bill piped up, "Dell's got a pretty good feel of her." Then he started laughing and couldn't stop. William joined in while Dell glowered.

He finally chuckled and said, "The things we do for our country." This brought more laughter.

William said, "So all you have is a hunch? Why did you want to get away from the house?"

"I'm sure that everything she gives us is bugged and wired for tracking. The guy I was after in Beirut was ambushed by people Sami thought were on my side. That is until they tried to kill us. Before that, Sami said there was a reward out for us and no one should have known we were there unless the Mossad let it out."

"That didn't happen. Believe me. I've had my phone checked and it's safe."

"You might want to check it again."

After Dell paid for the meal Mr. Wong brought out the phones and said his kitchen staff was very unhappy with their phones. He placed all three on the counter very carefully.

Bill looked at them and they were identical. He whispered to Dell, "How do we know which one belongs to who?"

William said, "Pick one up and press a button."

Bill reached out and grabbed a phone and an electrical charge ran through him. "Damnation! What the hell was that?" He dropped the cell phone to the floor.

"It's keyed to the owner." William leaned down and picked up the phone.

Dell took his phone, which left only one on the counter.

Bill gently reached out and touched his phone twice before picking it up. "So how do you know which cell is yours?"

Dell said, "It's marked. Didn't you read the manual?"

"What manual? It was in that box with the money and that sweet pistol you wouldn't let me keep!"

"It was in the paperwork we had to read the first time we came to Washington."

"You read that crap?"

Dell walked out of the restaurant and got in the car.

Dell, Bill and William went over all the information about the possible locations of the terrorists they were looking for and which of the two possible underground locations they might be in.

Bill said, "Here's what I don't understand. Even if they can make this bomb a mile underground or in the middle of a mountain, how are they supposed to get it to where they can use it? I mean, there isn't any way for them to move radioactive stuff across the U.S. without a detector going off, is there?"

Dell said, "He has a valid point."

William said, "It doesn't have to be big. It would probably fit in the back of a pickup."

Bill asked, "How are they going to get it airborne? Use a balloon or a rocket or something?"

William said, "Not necessarily. If it explodes in the top of a tall building, it would have a major effect and there are ways of transporting that kind of material without being detected."

Loretta came bouncing in and said, "You're fed, informed and now you're ready."

Dell said, "When do we leave?"

"Not for a couple of days. I have to make arrangements."

William said, "It will take me another couple of days to do more surveillance and check in with another group."

"No checking in, William. This is my operation and that's the last word about that."

Dell said, "Well, we're going home. Call us when you need us."

"Dell, you're not going to stay with me for a day or two?"

"Sorry. I've got things to do and we're still officially on duty with the State. Bill and I have to be at work at 0700. Maybe next time."

As they walked out the door Loretta called out, "Make sure you have your cells with you at all times."

Bill slowed but Dell nudged him out the door. "I was just going to ask about the manual for this crazy phone."

"Forget it. I'll show you how to tell which one is yours."

The next morning Dell went to see the Commissioner and Bill went to the squad room.

Commissioner O'Hara looked up from a large pile of paperwork when he heard a knock on his door. "Damn it, Sharpton, stop knocking, It's too much of a shock. Com'on in and have a seat. Now, what can I do for you?"

"Pat. I need a favor."

"This is a first. You name it."

"Bill and I are going to be leaving soon and I need someone to keep an eye on my kids."

"Don't you have anyone to look after them?"

"I mean protect them."

"What's going on, Dell? Where are you going?"

"You know I can't tell you that, but something is not right and... here." Dell handed the Commissioner a sealed shipping envelope. "If anything happens to me I would like you to see that Fatima and Sami are taken care of. Can you do that without asking too many questions?"

Commissioner O'Hara sat back and studied Dell for a few moments. He couldn't believe the change in him. Dell was being polite. That put a scare in him. "Dell, you need to get your head on straight. Don't go out there with those Feds being Mr. Happy. You gotta go out there with the old Dell. That's what's kept you alive for so long. That and Bill. I'll take care of everything from this end and I'll make sure those kids are looked after. Get that out of your mind. What about Bill? Is he still screwed up from your last trip?"

"Yeah. He's coming around but he still has a lot to work out."

"Don't let him come around 'til this is over. If you're walking into some kind of trap, you'll want him the way he is now. Remember one thing: if you need any help, give me a call. To hell with the VP or anybody else that tells me to back off one more time."

"Thanks, Pat. I won't forget this." He handed the Commissioner a notepad.

"That's a number you can text me at but only if it's an emergency."

As soon as Dell left the office, the Commissioner told Gina to get Bill Anders to his office ASAP.

When Bill arrived, the Commissioner chewed him up one side and down the other and told him that if he didn't get it together he'd be walking a beat on Highway 109 for the rest of his career. He didn't give Bill a chance to speak but kept at him for fifteen minutes.

Bill finally leaped to his feet and said, "You can kiss my ass, Pat. Nobody is going to take my job away from me. I have a family to support." Bill slammed the door as he left and slammed the outer door, too.

Pat O'Hara smiled, knowing he had done just what Bill needed to keep him in a mood that would keep him and Dell alive.

Back in the squad room Bill stomped up to Dell's desk and said, "Do you believe what that son of a... hello, Fatima. What are you doing here?" Bill looked around the room and every eye was on her.

"Mr. Dell invited me to see where you work and meet the other officers. How are you, Hakim?"

Bill winced and glanced around. Yeah, everyone heard. Now he had another problem. "I don't think it's such a good idea, you being here. Why don't you let me take you home."

Captain Teasdale came to the door of his office and yelled, "Sharpton, Anders, get your asses in... Oh, hello, Fatima. I didn't see you there. How's Haji... and Sami?"

Fatima asked Dell in Arabic, "Why would Mr. Phil speak so rudely to you and Hakim?"

"It's the way with men who work together. He meant no offense."

Fatima said, "I am very well, Mr. Phil. I have come to see where my brother and my protector work with their friends."

Bill winced at taking another hit. But hearing her say that made him smile.

212

"I need to speak to your brother and... protector a moment. Would you two please step into my office?"

Dell said, "Be right there, Captain. Fatima, just have a seat and we'll be right back. Maybe the guys will show you around." There were chairs and trash cans hitting the floor as everyone in the room rushed toward Fatima.

Bill loosened his pistol in his shoulder holster and the crowd slowed. He gave them the *evil eye*.

"What can we do for you, Captain?"

"You two think you can get away with anything. I'll have you know that I can't operate this section undermanned. I ought to..." He stopped when he heard Fatima's tinkling laughter filter into the office. He looked out the glass and saw everyone walking with her on a tour of the squad room. They were at the bulletin board with photos of the squad members. "That is one fine young lady. How am I supposed to yell at you with her around?"

"Sorry, Captain. I won't ask her to come again."

"You'll do no such thing. The only thing that would make it better is if you brought Sami and Haji with her." Captain Teasdale had a pained look on his face but took a breath and said, "Oh, crap. Look, guys, I understand that you're on some special assignment, but it's hurting us here."

Dell said, "We can't do anything about the other thing but we'll give you all we can when we are here. What do you need?"

"You're still scaring me, Sharpton—being so nice... Now, if you could get Bill to... Anders! Are you listening to me?"

Bill was turned around watching every move the guys made around Fatima. He didn't like the way she seemed to be enjoying herself, but wasn't that what he wanted? For her to be happy? He had no right to expect her to feel...

"Anders! What the hell's wrong with you?"

"Are you talking to me, Captain?"

Dell gave him the shut-your-mouth look and Bill turned back to hear what the captain was saying.

"I got a tip about another jewelry store robbery but I don't have anyone with your pull in the community to get any information out of the Arabs. Nobody can speak to them the way you and Hakim can." Captain Teasdale smiled at Bill as he said the last part.

"I think I liked *White Snake* better."

Dell said, "You need more people that can speak Arabic in here. What about letting Fatima give some classes to the guys?"

Bill jumped up and said, "The hell she will! I'm not letting her spend any more time around these guys. Look at them out there!" Bill pointed to the group clustered around Fatima.

Captain Teasdale said, "I think that's a great idea. I might even take a few lessons from her."

"The hell you will."

"Anders, what did you just say to me?"

Dell stepped in and said, "What he was trying to say is that would be a great idea. I think Sami could even help out. Of course, they would have to get paid."

"I don't see a problem with that. I'll run it by the Commissioner right now. You two take Herman and Wilson with you and get me a bust on this robbery."

Dell grabbed Bill's arm and led him out of the office.

"Are you crazy, Dell? You're gonna let our kids hang out with this bunch?"

"Fatima's not your kid. You trust these guys, right? We'll talk later. Wilson, Herman. You two ready to roll?"

Dell said, "Johnny, take Fatima home and make sure she's okay."

"But Mr. Dell, I want to see more pictures of Hakim... I mean Mr. Bill."

Bill lowered his shoulders, turned red and walked out of the room. The men all grinned but withheld comments because Fatima was there.

When they arrived at the jewelry store Bill dragged Dell off to the side while Wilson and Herman went inside to interview the owner.

"What is wrong with you? I'm not letting her hang out at headquarters. That's final."

"First thing, Fatima's not yours to order around. You washed your hands of everything."

"I took my protection back."

"You hurt her every time you come around... You know how she feels about you. Listen. Think about it. What better place than police headquarters is there to protect them while we're gone?"

"Yeah, but I don't want those guys hanging all over her. And... I don't know how she feels about me."

Dell grabbed Bill's coat sleeve and pulled him close. His whisper had venom in it. "Get this straight. She did what she had to do and I'm the one that made her keep the secret—to protect all of us. We're going to get this settled and you're going to stop hurting her! She cares a lot about you."

Dell took a deep breath. "Bill. You're like a brother to me and I know I hurt you but stop this shit. Fatima is not as strong as she seems. You are tearing her apart and I'm going to throw you out of her life or kick your ass if you don't wise up." He took another breath and said, "She's old enough to take care of herself and besides Sami will be there."

"Okay, but I'll have to have a talk with her first."

"If you hurt her again I'll kick your ass!"

"Come on, Dell. I care about her. Look, I know I've been stupid. It's just that I've been... I wouldn't... I'll try not to hurt her."

Dell went into the jewelry store with Herman and Wilson while Bill went to a local restaurant and spoke to the owner and some of the kitchen staff. By now most of the Arab community knew that the *White Snake* spoke very good Arabic.

Bill returned and called the guys outside. He said, "This is in retaliation for Mr. Bernstein's store getting robbed by some Arab thugs last month."

Herman said, "Mr. Mansoor said these guys were polite and didn't break the place up."

Dell asked, "Jewish kids did this?"

Bill said, "That's what it sounds like to me. Even got an address on one of them. One of the local kids followed them down to 14th Street."

Wilson said, "Let's go."

Bill said, "I think we need to get back to the station. Herman, you and Wilson can deal with this, right?"

Dell said, "We're not going anywhere 'til this is over."

They parked a few blocks away from the address and casually walked down the street. It was a decent neighborhood and predominantly Jewish. Many of the signs were in Hebrew and it had a nice feel to it.

As they passed a tailor's shop, an older man stepped out with a worried look on his face. "Gentlemen, won't you please come into my store? I have something I wish to discuss with you."

Wilson looked at Dell who nodded in assent. Herman stayed outside to keep an eye on the address where the suspect might be.

"Gentlemen, please have a seat." They took seats around a small table in the rear of the store and the man brought out coffee to drink. He poured and then took a seat. After everyone had sipped the coffee he said, "So you are here to arrest someone?"

Wilson said, "We're looking into a robbery that happened yesterday."

"And you have a lead?"

"We do."

"Let me come to the point. I can help you with this problem but isn't there some way we could work this out without an arrest?"

Wilson said, "I can't see that happening. A store was robbed and valuable items were taken."

"No harm was done to the store or the owner; isn't that correct?"

"Come to your point, Mr..."

"Cohen. My name is Ben Cohen. The point I'm trying to make is: I know who was involved and I know the crazy reason for what happened."

Dell asked, "What is it we can do for you, Mr. Cohen?"

"They are stupid kids—only trying to... I think to even the score is how you say it. But we don't blame the Arabs for what happened to Bernstein. We also know *Desert Rider* and the *White Snake* to be respected in all our communities. Can we not come to an arrangement?"

Wilson said, "If you're offering a bribe, I will haul..."

Dell put his hand on Wilson's shoulder and stopped him. "I think Mr. Cohen is trying to find a way out without punishing these young men."

"Exactly. I certainly meant no offense."

Dell said, "It's not going to happen. We have to arrest the men and they will be charged. It will be up to the DA to decide what they will be charged with. Now, if the owner of the store decides he wants to cooperate, maybe the charges could be lowered. If there's any bribing going on, the DA will know and the men will be charged to the full extent of the law."

"I understand. A committee is going to return the item this evening with our complete apology. These are good kids who have done a stupid thing."

Wilson said, "Turn them and the item over to us and it will be up to the DA and Mr. Mansoor, the store owner, as to how far this goes."

Mr. Cohen said, "Very well. Will you wait here for a moment?"

Wilson said, "We'll wait."

Mr. Cohen made a call and then left. Bill and the others joined Herman on the street. Within a few minutes two old men led three young men out of the apartment building.

Herman said, "This is working out pretty easy. I kind of like having you two around."

As the men walked up Herman nudged Wilson and said, "Aren't you going to say it?"

"Say what?"

"You know, 'Go ahead make my day.'" Herman started chuckling and couldn't stop.

They led the three young men to the car and Dell and Bill decided to walk back to Dell's place. It was only a few miles away.

Bill hadn't said a word for more than a half hour. His mind was on Fatima and all those men back at the station. He wondered if she was enjoying herself. He was also thinking about what Dell had said.

It was around five o'clock when they arrived and Haji was whining with excitement. Sami was all smiles as he hugged Dell and then Bill.

Fatima stepped out of her room and when she saw them she ran to Dell with a hug. She turned her bright smile on Bill and said, "Oh, Hakim! I enjoyed all the pictures of you at your station. You have very nice friends there. They were all so nice and polite. Did you know that Sami and I have an evening job there now? That is, if it is all right with you and Mr. Dell."

Bill looked at her and saw pure happiness and excitement. It melted away all his bad notions. "I'm very happy to see you smile." He looked at Dell and then back at her. "We are both happy for you and Sami. Yes, it will be good for you to teach some of the men Arabic."

Fatima said, "Oh, it will be a great way to know more about what you..." She saw the strained and hurt look in Bill's eyes and tears sprang to her own. She turned and ran to her room.

Dell turned on Bill who said, "What? I didn't say anything."

Haji growled and turned away from Bill and ran to Fatima's room.

Sami said, "You call yourself her protector but you can't protect Fatima from you! Perhaps it would be better to give up your protection and not come here again."

Bill felt Sami's barb like a jab to his heart and the thought of not coming to see them was almost more than he could take. His shoulders slumped as he crossed the room and fell back on the couch. Dell said nothing.

Bill motioned for Sami to come and sit. He put his arm around Sami's shoulders and hugged him. "I've been a jackass about all this. I'm sorry." He saw the confusion on Sami's face and switched to Arabic. "My donkey is smarter than I. I have been wrong about so many things. You and Fatima have saved my life and made it better. I am in your debt. I will do what you decide, but know this, Sami, my brother; I will atone for my behavior. I speak these words in the language of your faith. I love you as my brother. You are much more of a man than I am in many ways. I want to protect Fatima and I have no wish to hurt her. I will become a brother you can be proud of if you will have me."

Sami stood up and faced Bill. "Words come easy to you, Hakim, and you speak almost like a man now, but words have no meaning without actions. It is not to me that you should speak these words of atonement. My sister is finally able to walk without fear of being taken away. She is in a new place where she smiles and feels safe. But it is not this place that controls her happiness or her tears. It is you, Hakim. I will not accept your offer of brotherhood unless you can remove Fatima's tears. My brother, Dell, and I have spoken of this and he agrees. You were treated badly but it was something that had to be done—that is finished. No more deceit will pass my lips to you. I forced Fatima to keep her secret. I didn't trust you after I saw you with her in the desert. I thought the *White Snake* only wanted to defile my sister and had tricked her, but I was wrong. You are an honorable man."

Bill looked at this man-child and a wall collapsed between them. Here was a child from which Bill could take lessons in manhood. With his right hand he kissed his fingers and touched his heart and then placed his right hand upon Sami's heart. Sami came to him as a child and hugged his new brother.

Bill said, "I will speak to Fatima with your permission."

Sami said, "A protector need not ask but you have my blessings."

Bill entered Fatima's room and Haji growled. He bent down and offered his hand to Haji who sniffed his hand and then ran from the room.

Hearing Fatima's muffled tears made Bill want to gather her in his arms, but instead he carefully touched her shoulder. She sprang up in surprise, working in vain to wipe away tears that wouldn't stop flowing.

Holding her small wrist in his left hand, Bill gently wiped a few tears from her face and brought them to his lips. Their salty taste told him just how wrong he had been. He released her wrist and said in Arabic, "I have been a fool, Fatima. I let the past cloud my eyes and my heart. In truth, I cared for the girl that saved my life in the desert. I had grown used to her looks and they pleased me because I enjoyed all that she was—especially her heart. When I saw the real you in the desert, I thought you were an angel in a dream, but when I first saw and heard you as you are now and came to see that the angel was no dream but real, well, all of the hurt of my past came upon me as a shadow covers the light."

Bill sat down beside Fatima and stared at the rug-covered floor. "I have misjudged and treated you badly because of things that have happened in my past. I was wrong to let that happen. If you wish me to leave then I will go and leave you in peace."

Fatima looked hard at Bill to determine if this was something her brothers had made him say. She saw the veil of tears in his eyes and she nearly leaped to him but she remembered the hurt he had caused her. Her anger rose but the memory of his touch in the desert drew the flame of anger down and drowned it out. She reached out to his right hand and wiped her tears from his fingertips. Then she moved her hand to his eyes and let his tears mingle with her own. She brought her fingers to her lips and kissed the tears, letting the salty taste seal the cracks in her soul. Cracks that were not only from her time with Bill but for the hard decisions she was forced to make all her life. She could feel the flame of hope alight in her soul.

She said, "I will speak in English so I will not deceive you. I do not wish you to go, Hakim... Mr. Bill. I wanted to speak the truth in the desert but you only saw me as an ugly child." Bill looked up at her and started to protest but she held back his words with her fingertips. "It is true. You spoke in your fevered state and you spoke to Mr. Dell in English when you didn't know I could understand. I was wrong to hold the truth from you but my only concern was for Sami. I hope you can understand now. I do not expect anything from you except your protection. I place no restrictions on you, Mr. Bill. My feelings will not cause you pain. I will not speak of them unless I am asked by you." Fatima looked at the floor, not able to bring her eyes up to him.

"I will be like your sister and try to make you happy." She so wanted to tell Bill of her love for him, but didn't think she could take the possible rejection. Bill was a simple man in many ways and she knew she could draw the words from him but she wouldn't allow this. Bill must see her as she truly was and his love must come from his heart—not from her need. It would break her if he later questioned his words. She would remain silent—unless he demanded the truth. Her heart wanted to break or fly in joy but it was not up to her which direction it would take. Bill owned her heart and she would have it no other way.

Bill looked into the dark shimmering pools of her eyes that refused to look directly at him and there he saw true love. The wall broke between them and he knew he wanted more, but she was so young. Why would this beautiful girl want him? He knew in his heart he wanted more but didn't want to be the one to say it. Could he be the one to make her happy?

He spoke in Arabic. "I will speak and you will hear my truth. The first time I saw you, I only saw a child with impairments. I learned quickly that even as a child you were special and I put my trust in you. But as we traveled the desert you became a child no longer. I saw someone who took care of me, protected me and saved my life. No one had ever cared for me so. You were in my dreams in perfect form, but I know now it was not a dream. Your heat and softness put me in a place I never thought I would find."

Fatima blushed and turned her head away in embarrassment.

Bill gently turned her head back to him. "I do not say this to cause you embarrassment. I want you to know the truth. When I look at you, I think that I..."

Fatima put her hand to Bill's lips and said, "Don't say the words that will tear my heart if you take them back. I do not wish them to pass your lips... unless they come to me forever. I do want you to protect me and show me how to live in this new world. We will talk later of this, but Mr. Bill, think on what you would say to me and know that my heart is fragile. Ask no more of me for a while."

"I'll only ask one thing of you. Call me Bill, or Hakim, but not Mr. Bill."

To Fatima, this was as close to an admission of love as she could expect from Bill right now. With a quick move she stood, pressed herself to him and kissed his lips. It was a soft, gentle, heated kiss. "Do not think of me as a child. And Bill. Do not tell Sami of what I just did. That is only for you to know. Come, let's go and show my brothers we are well."

Bill followed her to the living room with the essence of Fatima on his lips. It was a taste he would never forget.

Fatima led a beaming Bill to stand in front of Sami and Dell.

Dell saw that familiar total grin on Bill's face. He looked like his old self and it made Dell smile. "I guess you two have worked things out. Should we celebrate?"

Fatima gave both of them a direct look and both saw the touch of sadness. "Bill and I have decided... that Bill will continue as my protector and he will show me how to live in this new world. We will be best of friends." Her voice trailed off and her eyes dropped but she held her head high.

Sami said, "Is that all? You will be friends?"

"It is enough."

Bill watched Sami and saw the anger but didn't understand it. This was Fatima's idea. He wanted more than friendship but knew it was silly to think a beautiful woman like Fatima would think of him as... as someone she loved more than a friend.

Dell stood and said, "Com'on, Bill. We've got to report in." He knew there was much more in Fatima's words and he also knew what was in Bill's mind. It was a step in the right direction.

Chapter 26

A week later Bill and Dell walked into the squad room and heard laughter. Dell said, "This place is getting to be like a damn circus."

Captain Teasdale sat in his office with the door thrown open bending over and twirling his right hand around in circles. Haji stood on his hind legs dancing around under Teasdale's hand. Captain Teasdale was laughing and slapping his leg with his other hand.

Off in a corner of the big room Fatima had a blackboard set up teaching Arabic to five policemen and a young man Dell didn't recognize.

"Sharpton! Anders! Get in here now."

Dell and Bill walked into the captain's office and Teasdale said, "Watch this." He brought his hands together and Haji sat up with his front paws together. "Look! Haji's praying." Teasdale then moved his index finger in a circle and then swung his arm around. Haji stood, turned in a circle and then did a backflip. "Have you ever seen anything like that? Haji is the smartest dog I've ever seen."

"At least you'll have a new career after the Commissioner sees this circus."

Captain Teasdale did his imitation of a ripe tomato and said, "Sit down. I see the old Dell is back. I was just getting over the shock of seeing you smile once in a while."

Dell just stood giving Captain Teasdale an I-don't-give-a-crap look. The tomato went to fire-engine red.

Bill was smiling with his—*Bill Anders* smile and said, "Haji really likes you, Captain. Say, who's the kid over there with the boys and Fatima?"

Teasdale took a deep breath as Dell and Bill took a seat. "That's my son, Philbert." He leaned over the desk and said in a conspirator's tone, "I think he's got the hots for Fatima. I mean, he took one look at her and it was all over."

Bill started to jump up but Dell put his hand on Bill's arm. Dell asked, "What do you mean it was all over?"

Captain Teasdale straightened up and puffed up like a frog and said, "I think he's in love! And I've got to say that I totally approve." His voice dropped to a whisper and he said, "You know, I didn't think much of Arabs until I met Sami and Fatima. Now I think they are all right. Why, in a couple of months Philbert could get her trained to be just like a normal American. He's taking her ice-skating tonight after the lessons."

That was all Bill could take. He leaped out of his seat and yelled, "Overmydeadfuckinbodyheis!"

"What did you just say, Anders?"

Dell stood up and as he steered Bill from the office he said, "Bill said that's a great idea."

"That's not what it sounded like."

Everyone heard Bill's outburst and turned to see Dell leading him out of the office. Bill was shooting daggers at young Philbert and Fatima.

Fatima knew why and smiled inwardly. She said, "That's the end of the lesson. I'll be back on Tuesday. You are all doing a wonderful job!"

She walked over to Bill's desk and could see the heat rising from the top of his head. "Mr. Dell. Mr... Bill. Is everything okay?"

Bill whirled on her but that beautiful bright smile and those eyes sapped the heat from him. All he could say was, "I heard you're going ice-skating."

She hopped in her excitement. "Yes! I have seen it on TV but can you imagine? Actually walking upon ice! I am so excited." She saw the distress on Bill's face and she leaned in and whispered, "With your permission, of course."

Bill's anger was completely drained and he smiled and said, "You don't need my permission to have fun. Of course it's okay. I should have thought of it."

Still in a whisper, Fatima said, "I would much rather go with you, but Philbert seems so lonely and he says he is an expert skater. It's his way of paying me back for the language lessons."

Philbert Teasdale stepped up beside Fatima and put his arm around her waist and said, "Are you ready, Fatima? I can't get over how much I like your name."

At Philbert's touch Fatima jerked and tried to break the hold without being rude, but Philbert held on until a hand squeezed his wrist and spun him around. Sami stood looking up at him with a bright smile on his face. "Hi, Phil. Are we all ready to go? I'm so excited about walking upon ice!"

Philbert rubbed his wrist and said, "Oh, Sami. I didn't know you were going too."

Sami said, "Some traditions will never change, no matter where we live. An unmarried woman must be chaperoned."

Dell smiled and said, "I agree with that."

"Me, too," said Bill.

Fatima said, "I hope you don't mind, Mr. Philbert. I knew Sami would want to come."

"No... no. It's okay, I guess." He smiled and said, "Well, let's get to it!" He reached for Fatima's hand but she deftly moved from his reach.

Sami leaned in towards Bill and whispered, "Some traditions go away quickly in a new place." And then he hurried to place himself between Philbert and Fatima.

"What did he mean by that?"

Dell said, "You're a log shy of a load, Bill."

"Now, what the hell does that mean? Why don't people just say what they mean?" Bill rose and followed Dell out of the squad room.

Chapter 27

Loretta sat showing a blank expression but inside she was full of rage, fear and most of all helplessness. Aisha sat across from her as the traditional coffee and greetings were exchanged in accordance with the way of Arab men.

"I believe it is only proper we speak as men as we lead men in their work. Do you not agree?"

Loretta bowed her head slightly. "As you wish, Effendi. You are the master of me for the moment."

"Oh. It is more than a moment, Little One. Until the day I release you, you are mine to command."

"May I please see my son and daughter?"

"Perhaps. If this meeting goes as I have planned." Aisha watched a light tremor pass across Loretta's face and then disappear. She smiled inside knowing she had the agent of the United States in a cage where there was no escape. "Are you controlling this Seer of yours?"

"I have my entire team looking into false leads. He is no threat to you."

"One like him is always a threat. The one who follows and keeps him safe is strong again. Why is this?"

"Bill Anders is no threat. He is completely oblivious to what is going on around him. I have complete control."

"It is not you that controls him. There is someone else. This person has great influence on him and the Seer. Who is it?"

"You are mistaken. I control them both."

With the speed of a cobra's strike, Aisha reached across the small table and slapped Loretta so hard that blood seeped from her lips. She emitted a flash of anger, but then Loretta's expression blanked.

Aisha said, "You seem to have lost your regard for your children. Perhaps another demonstration would bring you back to reality."

"No." Loretta pictured the beating her six-year-old son and five-year-old daughter had endured three times before when she did not satisfy this bitch. "There is... a girl... and a boy who the agents protect. They are meaningless."

Aisha raised her voice and the men behind her took small steps—ready for action. "Why was I not told of this immediately?"

"They... they have only recently come into their lives. They helped the agents in Lebanon and the agents brought them to the States as a gift for saving their lives. I swear that they are not important. Only a small amusement until they are placed with an Arab family to raise them."

Aisha motioned for one of the men to come close and whispered in his ear. He left and another man took his place.

"Since you are cooperating so well I have decided to let you speak with your children." She snapped her fingers and a man entered carrying a laptop. He placed it in front of Aisha and she turned the screen to face Loretta.

Loretta could see Sam and Kiri sitting quietly looking to their left with terror in their eyes. Loretta's training quickly took in everything in the background but there was only a blank wall.

The children's vision switched to look directly at Loretta and they brightened. "Mommy!"

"Hi, Sam. Hi, Kiri! Are you okay?"

Kiri cried out, "They hurt us when we're not good, Mommy."

Loretta saw Sam tug on Kiri's shirt sleeve telling her to be quiet. Good boy. Loretta brought her right hand to her face and rubbed her nose. This was part of a game she had played with her children so they could talk, even in a crowded room. It meant I know the truth. "Darlings. I want you to be good. Mommy will come get you soon."

Kiri sniffed and with her left hand rubbed her ear, which meant please hurry. She said, "We will be good, but Mommy... we miss you!"

"I miss..." An arm came into view as it lashed a rod across the children's legs. They screamed in pain and the screen went blank. Loretta was out of her chair and her claw-like nails speared at Aisha. A bodyguard caught her wrist in a steel grip and elbowed her in the face. Loretta was dazed and slumped back into the chair.

With another lightning fast move, Aisha lashed out with a crop and smashed the man across the face. "Fool! No visible marks! We can have no suspicion." She looked at Loretta and said, "I am sorry for that."

Loretta said, "I will cooperate but if you harm my children I will hunt you down and tear your heart from your chest—you and all your men."

"You will die trying. Now, do you understand that this Seer and his dog are not to come near my people? If they do... well, I don't have to tell you what I will personally do to your beautiful children."

"I understand."

"Then get out of my sight, you infidel whore. When I summon you, come running like a bitch in heat!"

A black cloth bag was put over Loretta's head and she was roughly led out. She smiled to herself. She had finally faced the fact that these animals would kill both her children and her before they fulfilled any promises. She had successfully planted one of the latest tracking and listening devices that was available only to Special Programs. It was made almost entirely of hardened plastic and was inactive except for a few nano-seconds when it sent a microburst to one specific receiver. It was undetectable, except by equipment made specifically for the device and then it could only be detected when it sent the microburst of information.

Her decision to plant the device came only after she decided she and her children were not as important as the safety of the country that had given her so much.

Now she had to find a way to protect Sami and Fatima without getting Dell and Bill killed.

Loretta had self-trained from early childhood to have as many personalities as she needed. The agency had continued her training in this regard and now she was considered to be one of the best. Even the groups that used her knew nothing of her children.

Her only escape had been her four years at college. She fell in love, had two children only nine months apart. They were the loves of her life and to keep them safe she made a deal with her professor/lover that she would raise them by herself and never reveal to anyone the identity of their father. This suited the busy, self-absorbed professor perfectly as he wanted nothing to do with the children.

From an early age she knew she would be a spy, and her parents had drummed into her that in such a life there could be no attachments. Only one other person knew of her children. Her ex-lover, Senator Derik Bartholomew.

Derik had been a professor of Psychology at the University of Alabama for several years with a background in combat stress in which he earned his PhD. Later he was chosen to head up the Clandestine Operation of the NSA about the same time Loretta returned to her duties at the CIA. He handpicked her to come over to the NSA when she was ready and kept her secret safe. Their love affair never picked up again but Derik groomed her to be head of an operational group.

Now he was a Senator with rank and power and they never spoke to one another, nor did he ever show any interest in the children. Loretta was in a position now where he could not track her—or so she thought.

Chapter 28

Bill and Fatima sat facing Sami, who stood with his hands on his hips.

"I think it is time to bring this matter out in the open."

Bill asked, "What matter, Sami?"

"I prefer you do not speak until I am finished." Sami glowered over both of them and even with his diminutive size he seemed a tower of strength. "You have brought shame to our family. You spied on Philbert and Fatima while they innocently enjoyed walking upon the ice."

Bill said, "Skating." The look Sami gave him made him wish he hadn't said anything.

"You had Philbert's car towed to Hoboken—where it was damaged. And worst of all, you allowed Philbert to see you at the arena and witness his car being towed away. The result is that we have been humiliated and you have been threatened by your captain! He has declared that you will count syringes on garbage barges if you interfere with his son again."

Fatima said, "I didn't know that."

Sami snapped at her. "This is your fault! Your education should not include how to compromise men! I lie awake at night worrying what you might do next. It is like the time you... you... lay with this one in the desert. Is it your wish to see Mr. Bill fail in his duties?"

"No! Never! I would never do anything to hurt Bill!"

"You will address him as Mr. Bill! He is your protector and seems to want no more than that. He is not your..."

Fatima started to speak but Sami slashed his right hand across his body in a gesture that said Fatima was to say no more.

Bill looked over at Dell for help but Dell simply waved his hand towards Sami.

"Look, Sami. I'm sorry about that. I guess I was trying too hard to protect Fatima and..."

"You acted in jealousy. A true protector would never cause embarrassment."

Bill's face turned red in anger at being interrupted by a child. This kid needed a lesson in manners. He started to snap at him but then thought about the times Sami had protected him and Dell in the desert. He was much more of a man than his youth portrayed.

Bill had thought about nothing except Fatima since she kissed him and told him not to say something he might want to take back. He knew the truth. He was jealous and had acted like a schoolboy.

"What do you want from me, Sami?"

Sami took a step towards Bill and put his arms around Bill's neck. "It is time you faced the truth. Fatima is more than someone you are protecting. Everyone knows this except you. I consider you my brother and I don't want to see Fatima suffer... or you."

Bill wrapped his arms around Sami and kissed his cheek. He then rose and motioned for Dell to follow him into Dell's bedroom.

After about ten minutes he came out and stood before Sami, never looking at Fatima. "My brother. I am here to ask permission to see your sister in a familiar way. I give my oath I will bring no shame to your house." Bill made himself look only at Sami, just like Dell had told him.

"You have it, Hakim."

Bill finally looked at Fatima and saw her tears and smile and knew then he never wanted to be without her, but he would wait to tell her. He never wanted her to fear his word might be taken away.

The apartment door opened and William came in. He took the situation in and knew what had transpired. "Well, it's about bloody time." He pulled Fatima from her seat and swung her around and hugged her and then Sami.

Fatima said, "Mr. William! It's so good to see you! Where have you been?"

"Doing a bit of spelunking. I think I will take Bill with me next time—very cozy."

Bill said, "I can hardly wait."

"First thing we must do is see that you are properly fitted. I know just the place."

Dell asked, "When do we leave?"

"Your chariot awaits."

Bill said, "Damn." He took Fatima by the hand and led her to her bedroom. A few minutes later they came out and both were blushing and smiling.

Bill lifted Sami, hugged him and said, "You're a good man."

On the drive down to Washington, William briefed Dell and Bill. "I didn't find anything solid, but there was evidence of recent activity at a few sites. Loretta said to pick you two up and do a thorough check."

Bill said, "I don't know anything about caves or holes in the ground. Why don't they send the experts in?"

"Why, Bill, we are the experts, actually. At least we are the only ones with knowledge of what we're looking for." William glanced at Dell who was in his not-at-home mode.

"When did that start back up?"

Bill looked at Dell and said, "I don't know. Haven't seen him like that in a long time. Maybe he just needs some alone time with Loretta."

William took out a pad of paper and wrote, *Just between you and me. Loretta's been acting a bit hinky lately.*

Bill said, "What does... Ouch!" He rubbed his shoulder where William had elbowed him.

Dell felt the tug of someone pulling him back and he shrugged. The mist began to clear and he saw two children: a boy and a girl with cuts and bruises on their faces and legs. They were tied to chairs and frightened. Then Loretta appeared behind them. She was in tears struggling to reach them, but a clear wall was between them, blocking her efforts to rescue them. He turned his head and saw two people held to the ground. They were being beaten by an Arab he recognized from Lebanon. The dark hairy woman was their beside them.

"Come on, buddy. Time to rise and shine. We're here."

Dell's vision cleared and he looked at Bill who, like always, was holding his gun. "Stop taking my weapon!"

"Sorry, Dell. Not gonna happen. We've got to talk to Loretta. I don't like this searching caves and stuff. Maybe you could talk her into letting me stay and look after Sami and Fatima."

"If I go, you go."

"Thanks, buddy."

They walked into the living room where Loretta was seated with her back to them. She turned at their approach and Dell and William both saw the frightened look on her face. It was there for only an instant and vanished just as quickly.

Loretta put on her brightest smile and said, "There you are! Oh, Bill, you look so happy. Are things working out with you and that beautiful young woman?"

"I hope so. How are you, Loretta?"

"Me? I'm always happy but I do get a little pick-me-up when Dell is here. Can I get you boys a drink?"

William said, "Tea would hit the spot. What say, gentlemen?"

Dell said, "That's fine by me."

Bill said, "Coffee, milk or Scotch. Whichever is easiest."

Loretta said, "Dell. Are you feeling well? I've never known you to turn down a Jameson."

Dell could feel the tension in her voice more than he could hear it. Something was very wrong. "I need to have a word with you—alone."

"I don't think we have time right now."

"Then make time."

"Very well. You boys make yourselves at home while I take care of this one," she said with a laugh.

Bill leaned over to Dell and whispered, "Pictures, Dell. Pictures."

As Dell followed Loretta, William asked Bill. "So how's the shoulder wound Dell put in you?" Dell heard and winced. Now he would have to tell Bill the truth.

"What do you mean? I got shot by the terrorist."

"Righto, old chap. My mistake. Let me get you a Scotch."

Chapter 29

Loretta turned and came to Dell with a sultry look. Dell shoved her to the floor and pulled his pistol, aiming at Loretta's head.

"What is it, Dell? One of my main rules is you never pull a gun on the boss!"

Dell stood over her and pressed the barrel of his .45 caliber Taurus OSS to Loretta's forehead.

Loretta could see that the safety was off and Dell's finger had pressure on the trigger.

Dell said, "I want to know what's going on. You're playing all of us and I better start getting some answers now!"

"What are you talking about? No one is playing you... We're on the same team."

"Which team is that? The one where we're sent on wild goose chases or the one where you are collaborating with terrorists?"

"You're crazy, Dell. I don't know what you're talking about." Loretta couldn't hold Dell's gaze and looked down and to the left. She didn't make any sudden moves because she knew she would be dead if she did.

"You know, for someone who's in charge, you're not too damn bright. Do you remember why you brought me into this big pile of crap? I see things no one else sees."

"Can I get up?"

Dell took a step back but his pistol never wavered from its target.

"Why don't you tell me what it is you see before we both end up dead? I'm not collaborating with the enemy! I'm trying to stop a cell from bringing havoc to the United States."

"So you haven't talked to the Arab woman in charge of setting the bomb off? You know, the one that has a young boy and girl that look a lot like you. And they're tied to chairs?"

Shock took her as Loretta fell back onto a cushioned chair. Her secret was out, finally. She felt the dam of emotions burst and she collapsed in tears. She quickly stood and choked out, "Don't shoot. I have to turn off the alarm." She hurried over to her armoire and pressed a button to stop the timer. Another ten seconds and an armed team would have come in. Turning back to Dell, Loretta held up her hands and returned to the chair.

Looking at the carpeted floor she said, "They are my children and they're being held hostage by that woman. Her name is Aisha."

"Why didn't you tell me?"

"If they even suspected I told anyone, Sam and Kiri would be dead. No one knows about them. I've kept them off any records since they were born. The only person who knows I am their mother is their father, and he wouldn't tell."

"How do you know he wouldn't tell?"

"Because he's a U.S. Senator and he's married. It would ruin his career."

"So you've turned traitor for your children?"

"It's not like that, Dell. I'm not a traitor... but they have my children!"

Dell said, "There's more to it than you're telling me. These people have the bomb and they're going to use it."

"They don't have any nuclear material. All they have is depleted uranium."

"Out with it, Loretta!"

"I swear I just found out about a plot involving a group of idiots trying to make the U.S. strong again and finally giving the U.S. a reason to devastate the Middle East. I'm doing all I can to stop this without killing my children... I swear!"

Loretta's tears were real. Dell knew this was no act, but she was endangering the very people they were trying to protect. War in the Middle East would put an end to the life he knew growing up and kill many innocent people. The U.S. and the world only wanted to protect the oil—and the power it afforded them.

Loretta looked up at Dell and pleaded, "I'll tell you everything, but you have to promise not to expose the plot yet. I want my children back."

"I'm not making any promises. If that bomb goes off, it will cause the death of millions around the world."

"I know that. Please, Dell. Put the gun away and listen. I'll tell you everything... and then you can decide. Who's watching Fatima and Sami?"

Terror came over Dell. It wasn't a vision but he knew the feeling. Yanking out his phone he checked it. There was no signal.

Loretta jumped up, pulled at his sleeve and guided him to her armoire where she presented him with a secure phone.

Neither Fatima nor Sami answered their phones. Dell called the Commissioner.

"Pat?"

"For Christ sake, Dell. This is my private..."

"Listen, Pat. I'm calling in another favor. I need men sent over to my apartment right now! I think Fatima and Sami are in danger."

"They'll be there in ten minutes, but I'll have two squad cars there in one minute. We'll pick them up and move them to a safe location. I'll call you. I've got your back." Commissioner O'Hara ended the call and then dialed the Terrorist Task Force Headquarters.

"Put Captain Teasdale on the phone. This is Pat O'Hara."

"He's on another line."

O'Hara screamed, "Well, get him on this line and I mean right now!"

"Hello, Commissioner. What..."

"Colin. I want two squad cars at Sharpton's apartment now! I want your entire team there in ten minutes or less."

"You know I don't like to be called Col—"

"Listen, asshole! Fatima and Sami are in danger. Do it. Do it now!"

"What about Haji?"

"What?"

"Is Haji there?"

"Yes, you..." O'Hara took a deep breath. "Phil, I wouldn't be telling you to do this if it weren't important. There's no time to explain."

"Yes, sir!" Captain Teasdale threw the phone down but didn't disconnect it. Pat could hear him shouting. "Wilson! Get two squad cars over to Dell's place! Right Fuckin Now! Haji's in danger! Everyone! Full gear! We're pulling out in two minutes. Anyone left behind is fired! Commissioner's orders. We've got to save Haji... and Sami and Fatima."

O'Hara heard chairs crashing and people yelling. He smiled and hung up. Then he picked up his belt holster, pistol and five extra clips and rushed out the door.

O'Hara lived only a few miles away and arrived at Dell's street just as men were shoving Sami and Fatima into a black Ford van with government plates. Then it pulled away, smoking the tires. He quickly wrote the plate number down and got out of his vehicle, viewing two bullet-riddled patrol cars. There were rifle casings everywhere. He ran over to see four of his men lying in pools of blood. He checked for vital signs but all four policemen were dead.

Commissioner O'Hara pulled out his phone and with steady hands dialed dispatch to send EMS and a Crime Scene team. Then he gave a description of the vehicle and plate number, instructing the dispatcher to coordinate with the locals to check every black van crossing the bridges into New York City. He didn't give it much hope but it had to be done.

237

He could hear neighbors and gawkers rushing out to see what had happened and heard the sirens in the distance.

Holding up his pistol and shield he said in a commanding voice, "No one comes near the patrol cars. I want everyone over there," pointing to a tiny park beside the apartment building. "There will be an assault team here in a few moments and you don't want to be out in the open when they arrive. Now move!" The fifteen people that came to look now rushed to where Commissioner O'Hara directed them to go.

He put his pistol away, made his way over to the park, pulled out a notepad and began taking names. He didn't want to be standing near the bullet-riddled patrol cars when Teasdale and his men arrived either.

A big black armored van bounced over the curb and onto the small lawn in front of Dell's apartment. Men in full gear poured out. Two rushing to the patrol cars, others taking the apartment building by storm and three securing the perimeter. It was a well-practiced effort, except for Captain Teasdale yelling at the top of his lungs into his radio, "Find Haji! Find Haji!"

Pat walked over to Teasdale standing spread-legged on the sidewalk with a wild look in his eyes. O'Hara said, "We're too late, Phil."

Captain Teasdale ducked, spun and raised his weapon but the Commissioner blocked and removed the weapon from his hand.

"What the hell! Don't ever sneak up... Oh, it's you, Commissioner."

"We're too late, Phil. They've got the kids."

"What about Haji?"

"I don't know... Did you hear what I just said, Phil? They have the kids."

The crazed look left Captain Teasdale's eyes and he asked, "Do you have a description of the get-away vehicle?" Pat handed him the note pad and Teasdale yelled, "Herman! Get this on the radio." Herman rushed to grab the notebook and ran to the van. After a moment Teasdale leaned in close to O'Hara and asked, "Say, Pat. Do you think I could have my gun back now?"

Handing his pistol back, O'Hara said, "Don't shoot anyone."

The radio squawked, "All clear, Captain. There's no one in the apartment—including the dog."

Phil Teasdale said to no one in particular, "I'm gonna kill somebody. If they hurt Haji I'm going to tear their..."

"Teasdale! Settle down and get one of the men to interview those people over there. Someone must have seen something. Can you do that, Phil? I've got to tell Dell and Bill what has happened."

"Oh, shit... Del and Bill! Tell them we'll get Haji back...! And the kids. I'll handle it from here." He called two of the men securing the perimeter and told them to start the interviews and get transportation back to headquarters for anyone who saw anything. He could hear the wails of many sirens coming their way. "Commissioner. Did the patrolmen make it?"

"All four of them are dead, Phil. It's bad."

The black van drove two blocks and turned into an alley, then through a rollup door and came to a halt inside an auto-repair shop. Fatima and Sami had their mouths taped, hands tied and bags over their heads. Haji was secured with a choke collar and had been given a drug to knock him out.

Hamdhi said, "Why are we taking children as hostages? We don't need hostages with what we are doing. And why the dog? Will he report to the police?"

"You ask too many questions. We do what we do because we are told to do it."

"But, Atif, I don't want to kill children. They appear to be Arab. I will kill the dog now if that is needed, but children?"

Atif stepped over to Hamdhi, put his arm around his shoulder and said, "You are my brother and I tell you the truth. If you don't stop asking all these questions you will not make it to the celebration. I will tell you one more time, Hamdhi. These are the children of the Seer and his partner. The dog too. We have to get the Seer's mind away from the bomb. He may lead the infidels to it before we can set it off. We are not to kill the children—only hold them and take them wherever we are told. I tell you this one last time: shut up or you will get us both killed. Aisha may be a mere woman but she has the heart of a wolf, fangs of a cobra and the compassion of a stone. Do this for me, brother."

Hamdhi nodded and they loaded Sami, Fatima and Haji into a light blue Dodge Charger with a false bottom in the rear seat. It would be a short drive to Monmouth Executive Airport, only eight miles away. Hamdhi looked at Atif who smiled and answered the unspoken question. "I do not know where we are going. Just far enough away to get the Seer and his partner away from the bomb. Aisha told Achmed that the bomb is assembled and the *material* is now in this country. It won't be long now, brother!"

They took their time and had no trouble getting to the airport. Soon their cargo was loaded and they were airborne.

Chapter 30

Loretta told Dell everything that had happened including how she had met her children's father. She was barely in control of her emotions.

Dell pressed hard to be sure it was all she had. He finally said, "Why are you giving me all this now? I don't think a gun to your head would frighten you—so why now?"

"I finally decided that I wouldn't let these terrorists use my children to hold me hostage. I've also been made aware of a new wrinkle in this dirty bomb plan. And it scares me." She paused a moment to gauge Dell's reaction to all she had said. His look told her he wouldn't stop until he had everything.

"Here's what I found out. Russians were developing a suitcase nuclear bomb back in the 70's. Something happened at a test site in Siberia and the suitcase was lost. They lost all contact with the team and the enriched yellow-cake Uranium 238 could not be detected. The Soviets didn't want the embarrassment so they reported that the bomb was disposed of deep in the earth beneath Siberia.

"What a few in our government now think is that the yellow-cake was stolen and shielded in a way that none of our sensors could detect. They believe the Shah of Iran was the recipient of this material."

Dell gave Loretta a hard look. "What the heck would the Shah of Iran want with Uranium? He was always friendly with the U.S."

"We believe he wanted it for the day his people turned on him, but it didn't work out that way. It is now believed that the Iranian government has it and wants it gone. There would be no way to use the material in any of their research. It has markers we and the Russians would recognize right away."

Dell said, "So they gave it to terrorists? That's crazy!"

"It's crazy until you hear about the deal France, Germany and a few other countries in Europe made with Iran. It involves a terror free zone and a secret pact not to use nukes on the Middle East or Europe. It gets even worse. The team just found out the Iranians have arranged for an Arab cell to detonate a dirty bomb on U.S. soil using this material. They are hoping the U.S. and Russia might turn on one another in the aftermath. What I now think is that the terrorists we've been chasing are the recipients of that material."

Loretta knew her children's lives hung in the balance. It was a relief to get this out and Dell was the one person who might believe and help her. She knew now that she had to stop these people from setting in motion something that could change the world forever.

"Dell, I swear that I haven't compromised the security of the U.S. Yes, I've led you away from these people and I did it thinking I would keep my children safe. But they're not. I knew in my heart that you were the one person who would see through what I was doing without giving it away. I need your help. I need you to stop this and save my children and probably yours too."

Dell put his weapon down and sat on the bed. He had cared about very little most of his life. He was dragging along through life hoping he would get into a situation that would end his miserable existence. But Sami and Fatima had changed all that. Before, the only thing that stopped him was Bill. He didn't deserve to be a part of this but he wouldn't leave Dell's side. Now all three meant too much to him to continue the way he had before.

He looked at Loretta and saw a way to change his life for the better. She had given him a reason. He couldn't understand how she could carry the threat to her children without breaking and now he saw she was at her wits' end.

"We'll get them back. And if these terrorists try to harm Sami and Fatima, I will kill them all."

Loretta moved to him and held him tight as she cried. She couldn't stop. She felt Dell's arms go around her and the tears streamed from her eyes as she huffed for breath.

He said, "I've got to talk to Bill. Stay here for a while, get your nerves settled, and then we'll get started."

Dell entered the room and saw that William was gone. Bill sat looking at the southern scene and was smiling.

Bill turned at the sound of Dell's approach and said, "I want to take Fatima and Sami there." He pointed out the window. "It looks peaceful."

"Bill, I've got something to tell you. I'm the one who shot you. I hit the terrorist but the round went through him and hit you too."

Bill said, "I know. I guess I've known for a while. It doesn't matter. That shot helped me. It made me realize that I'm pretty sure I love Fatima. And I think she loves me. What am I going to do? She's so beautiful and I'm... I'm not the smartest guy in the world. I don't know if I can make her happy. What can I do?"

Dell was amazed that Bill took the news so well. He had dreaded telling Bill that he had shot him. "What you need to do is tell her. I know I've walked around like some black cloud, but I've known for a while that she loves you. You are the only person that makes her happy. You really don't know what you do to people. You're like a magnet. People are naturally drawn to you. Fatima loves you. Now, here's what we're going to do. I'm taking you back and you're going to tell her how you feel. Stop guessing. You've known the answer for a long time but won't admit it."

Dell turned to see Loretta smiling at them. She ran to Bill and hugged him. "I'm so happy for you and Fatima." She looked at Dell and said, "Go! I'll get William and we'll meet you at your place. Now, go."

Chapter 31

Aisha held a pistol to the head of Abdul Baari and pressed it hard against his temple. "Your man was the one who lost the case with the information on our cells and the code books that could set our Jihad back many years! You are responsible for the loss of fifty million dollars in diamonds! And now you question what I do with the infidel senator? I should kill you and your entire gang of idiots!"

Abdul knew his life hung in the balance on how he responded to this tiger of the desert. Why hadn't he listened to his lieutenant? Benhjim had warned him not to question Aisha's methods. Abdul was disgusted when he heard that she was acting like a lapdog for the American, but he should have kept his mouth shut.

"My man is dead and we have taken steps to prevent any further harm to our cause. I apologize for anything I may have said about your... methods, Aisha. Forgive me!" He kissed his fingers and touched his heart. "You are a great leader and your word is law. Tell me what I am to do and it will be done."

Aisha smiled, knowing that she held these men tight in her grip. The day might come when they turned on her, but she would be in paradise before that day came. Her plan was perfect. The stupid American Senator thought he could trick her with his depleted uranium—what a fool. Derik Bartholomew had no inkling that she now possessed the actual product via her friends in Iran. All she needed from him was a delivery device and she was promised that in a week. Then she would kill the infidel with her own hands. She smiled at the thought of destroying so many Americans and causing a world war between the Russians and Americans. Soon, very soon, the Arab world would descend on the weakened West and use infidel blood to nourish the new land of Islam.

Aisha laid out Abdul's part of the plan and then warned, "Fail me again and I will wipe your family from the Earth!"

Chapter 32

Dell pulled out of the drive in Arlington Heights heading for the highway. It was the first time he had driven when Bill was with him.

Dell's phone rang.

"What...? Hi Pat. What's...?"

Dell slammed on the brakes and slid the car to the curb. "What?"

Dell screamed, "When...? What about the squad and the men you were sending...?"

"We'll be there in an hour."

Bill said, "There's no way to get to Brick Town in an..." Dell accelerated throwing Bill back in his seat. Dell never let up off the gas pedal. "Well, maybe we can," said Bill. "What's going on?"

"They have them!"

"Have who?"

"The bad guys have Sami and Fatima!"

Bill's mind became a red rage. "No! Fuck no!" Bill pulled his pistol and waved it around. "I'm going to kill them all. Where did they take them?"

"I don't know, but I'll find out."

"I thought you had people watching Fatima... and Sami."

"The Commissioner sent two squad cars and the Task Force was on its way. The patrolmen got there as it was going down."

"And those fucks couldn't stop them?"

"The cops are all dead. Pat saw the van pulling away but couldn't pursue. He had to check on the men."

"The cops are dead...? How many?"

"Four."

"Oh, crap. What about Fatima and Sami?"

"No word yet, but Pat said they were alive when they were put in the van. They took Haji, too."

"Get us there, Dell."

Dell said, "It's gonna be all right, Bill. We'll get them back. And you're right. We're going to kill them all."

Both men were lost in their thoughts as Dell raced up the highway.

Chapter 33

Senator Derik Bartholomew met Aisha and two of her men at his farm two hours north of New York City.

"Are the children all right?"

Aisha said, "Of course. I promised you no harm would come to them. My plan is working perfectly. The NSA whore is under complete control."

"Aisha. I must tell you. You've been most patient for someone in your line of work."

Aisha smiled and motioned for her men to wait outside. "Did you bring the material?"

"Yes. It's all here. Don't remove it from the container until you are ready. The radiation level would set off all kinds of alarms on the east coast. Now you have the delivery device and the material. Where will you detonate it?"

Aisha moved close and rubbed Derik's already hard cock as she kissed him. "It will be one of the cities you have designated. Don't worry. Your plan will go just as I promised." She unbuckled his belt as she kissed him with more urgency.

The Senator couldn't get over how she responded to him. He completely forgot about finding out where the bomb would go off. He broke their kiss, reached down to the hem of her dress and lifted it off. She was nude underneath and, as always, looked incredible. He lifted her off the floor and spun her until her crotch was inches from his lips. He felt her mouth take him in and he gasped. Then, his mouth latched on her essence and they both moaned. He tried to step back to the couch but his pants were tangled around his ankles. He fell back, hitting the floor with a bang, but neither lost contact.

Aisha was a hungry beast as she ground her hips into Derik's face and took all of him into her mouth. He tried once to break the connection but she held on tightly using her lips and tongue to bring him to climax. Hers followed shortly and she flooded his face with her wetness.

They finally made it to the bed and she worked her magic and brought him to the edge again. She stopped long enough to put a condom on him and went back to work.

Derik thrust deep into her and felt his muscles tightening again in release. She moaned in his ear and that took him over the edge.

A few minutes later he kissed her forehead and said, "I can't believe how you make me feel. I never knew Arab women were so adept. I'm going to hate to see you leave."

Aisha said, "We leaders do what we must to see a program through. Isn't that right, Senator?"

"Exactly right."

She said, "Now I'll show you another side of an Arab woman you've never seen before." Aisha turned him over on his stomach and kissed down his back to the cheeks of his butt. She then spread his cheeks and touched him.

Derik arched his back, smiled and said, "I think I'm going to enjoy this." He felt her thumb massage him and then slip inside. He never felt the prick of the needle. Derik Bartholomew, Senator from Wyoming was dead in ten seconds.

Aisha cleaned all the evidence of her presence from his face, crotch and body. She slipped the condom into a plastic bag and put it in her pocket.

After she dressed, she called the two men in. "Load the material. Then take his body to the old well and then seal it. I will meet you at the house. We will leave for the warehouse in two hours. It is time for the infidels to pay!"

Chapter 34

As Dell came to a sliding stop at his apartment building, he looked over at a disturbing sight. Bill looked to be sleeping but his hands were twitching and Dell could hear him grinding his teeth. Even in Dell's state of distress he recognized a bomb about to explode. He gently reached over and pulled Bill's pistol from the holster and then exited the car.

Bill felt the soft slap but ignored the touch. All he could see in his mind was Fatima tied and being tortured by men that leered at her and called her a whore. Bill wanted the men dead, all of them.

One of the terrorists looked at him and slapped him hard across the face. Bill went for his gun but it wasn't there. He leaped at the man and hit him hard in the body, pummeled him and then wrestled him to the ground. The man was calling to him but Bill only heard the word whore. His hands went to the throat of the man that had hurt Fatima and he squeezed. A powerful blow to the face dazed him and he rolled onto his back. Then Bill felt the man wrap his arm around his neck.

It was getting dark as he was overwhelmed by the terrorist.

Then Bill heard, "It's me, Bill. It's Dell. No one is trying to hurt you."

"Dell...? They have her! They're hurting Fatima! I have to kill them!" He struck out at his attacker.

"It's me, Bill. I won't let them hurt her. Come on back, buddy. I need you with me. You're my only hope, Bill. We can do this together."

After a moment Pat O'Hara said, "I think he's coming around, Dell. Let him go. We'll take him down if he goes crazy again."

Bill focused on the conversation and looked up at the men of the Task Force looking down at him. "What's going on? Why am I on the ground? Where's Dell?"

"I'm here."

Bill turned his head and saw the concerned look on Dell's face and the blood. He felt the pain in his face and reached up. He pulled his hand away and it was covered in blood. He tried to get up, but Dell pressed his shoulders to the grass.

"Let me up, Dell. You're hurt. Who did that to you?"

Dell helped Bill stand and the men moved in closer, but Dell said, "Give us some room. I've got this."

Bill said, "What happened?"

Dell said, "You kicked my ass. Remind me to stand a little farther away when I wake you up next time."

"Dell, I would never hit you."

Pat said, "You two are crazy. What's wrong with him?"

Dell held up his hand and guided Bill away from the others. "Bill. I'm going to make you a promise and you know I never back out of a promise. We're going to get Fatima back!"

When Bill heard Fatima's name, he reached for his gun but it was missing. He looked around but Dell shook him saying, "I have your gun. Now I understand why you take mine all the time."

Bill focused on Dell and tears flowed from his eyes. "They have her, Dell! They have Sami too. We have to get them back." He tried to jerk away but Dell pulled him into his arms. That startled Bill. Dell had never hugged him in their entire career together. Through his tears he whispered. "Has something happened? Is Fatima okay?"

"They haven't hurt her or Sami. I would know if they had. I need you to watch my back, Bill. I'm going to find them and we're going to kill them all! Can you do that for me? You have to keep it together until we find them."

Bill took a deep breath and pushed away from Dell. He wiped his eyes and said, "Yes. I can do that. I guess I went a little crazy."

"You went more than a little crazy. You scared the crap out of me. It's good to have you back."

"What are we going to do?"

"Loretta's helping to find them..."

"Loretta? I thought you didn't trust her."

"I do now. They have her two children."

"I didn't know she had kids."

"Nobody did. She has a boy and a girl that the terrorists have had for several months. They're still alive and that's why I know Fatima and Sami are okay. One thing, Bill. You can't tell anyone about Loretta's children. It could put them all in danger."

"Whatever you say, Dell. I'm with you."

Commissioner O'Hara filled them in on all that had happened and then drove Bill and Dell to the getaway van that had been located. Crime Scene people were all over it but found few clues.

On the drive back to Dell's apartment Pat said, "I don't care where you find these people or which agency thinks they're in charge. I want to know. The New Jersey State Police will back you up one hundred percent. It's taking all I can do to keep Teasdale from running amok. I'm turning his ass loose when you find them and I'm getting out of his way. Those idiots should have never messed with the dog."

Bill woke in the NSA's Arlington house and he felt much better. He walked out of the bedroom and William leaped to his feet to give Bill a hug.

"You look much better, Bill. We thought you were going to have a heart attack."

"Are you the one that drugged me?"

"Now, Bill. I only did it so you could get some rest. Don't get angry."

"Thank you, William. I needed to sleep. I feel much better now." Bill turned to Dell and asked, "Have you found them?"

"No. But we know where they were a few hours ago. I think this is all coming to a head in a day—at the most."

"Well, shouldn't you be... doing what it is you do?"

"Believe me, Bill. I've tried but I'm getting nothing. William has a few leads that he has his people following up on, but so far nothing."

Bill slumped into a chair next to Dell and William brought him a tray of tea and crumpets.

Bill smiled at William and asked, "Are you really English?"

"Need to know, old chap. Someday I'll tell you the truth about everything."

William answered his phone on the first ring. "Agent Dubose... Where...? Is this credible...?" After finishing the call, William announced, "We tagged a guy that spent time with one of the terrorists. Apparently he liked doing drugs—hashish, opium and the like. He enjoyed boasting that he was preparing for Paradise."

Dell asked, "Where is he?"

William looked over at Bill and said, "We lost contact with the informant."

"You did what?"

"Now, Bill. The good news is he lives in the Hoboken area, where you're so well known, *White Snake*. I have a description, but as you well know, the Arab community is very hush-hush when it comes to one of their own."

Bill said, "Get me up there! I'll make sure those sonsabitches tell me where he's at!"

"My thoughts exactly. But Bill dear, please try not to kill anyone until we know about the bad guy."

Dell stood up and said, "Leave that part to me. Bill's got my back and we know what's at stake. Right, Bill?"

"What...?" Bill looked at William, Dell and Loretta. The fear in Loretta's eyes stopped him. "I got your back, but those... those..."

"Those people are your friends, Bill. They'll help us," said Dell.

Chapter 35

Two hours later Dell, Bill and William were parked two blocks from the halal restaurant that Bill and Dell frequented. Bill could barely contain his anger and anxiety. His every thought was of Fatima.

Small groups of local people joined them in their walk to the restaurant. The crowd was silent.

Bill leaned over to Dell and said, "What's going on? It's too quiet."

"I think they've heard about Sami and Fatima."

"If they know something I'm going to beat it out of them."

Dell stopped and said, "Keep in mind that these people like you. All Arabs are not terrorists. You of all people should know that."

Bill lowered his head as they continued. "Yeah... Well... You're right. I'll keep it together. Thanks, Dell."

The crowd had grown to several hundred people when the three men entered the restaurant. Hamdi, the owner, rushed to the front of the shop as they entered and took Dell and Bill by their arms. He motioned with his head for William to have a seat. He instructed his daughter to serve William some English tea and whatever else he required.

Hamdi led Bill and Dell to his office in the rear of the restaurant. As soon as he closed the door, Hamdi turned to them and placed his right hand over his heart and said, "I have heard—we've all heard what has taken place. The community is outraged at this act of terror. We want you to know that these animals are not Muslims. We have great sorrow. May Allah punish those that would do harm to your future wife, *White Snake.* And to your children, *Desert Rider.*"

Bill said, "My future wife?"

"We all know, Mr. Bill. We only await the announcement. It pleases your many friends."

Bill looked at Dell and saw his smile and asked in English, "Have you been talking?"

"You're the only blind person here, Bill."

Bill asked Hamdi, "Why have all the people followed us here?"

"To help avenge this terrible wrong. The entire community has brought to me information that will help. We have done even more."

Dell said, "What have you done?"

Hamdi held up his hand and then left the room. A short time later he and two other men dragged in a man who had obviously been beaten. "This one has information about those that have our people. Speak, Abdul, or suffer our wrath once again."

The man looked up at Dell and Bill. His face was covered in bruises and his nose bled. "Why should I speak to infidels? I will not betray freedom fighters to these dogs."

Bill's gun was out and pressed against the temple of the man before Dell could react. "I'll kill you if you don't speak."

"I have no fear of death! Take my life, for I will not speak!"

Hamdi reached out and touched Bill's shoulder. "Put away your gun, my friend. He will—how do you say—sing like a bird." Hamdi bent down and whispered to the man.

The man jerked up and said, "No! You would never do that to another Muslim. It is forbidden!"

"It is no less than the ones you protect would do. I promise you will never see Paradise."

"I have told you everything I know."

Hamdi said, "Yes, I know. I only wanted my friends to see your face. Take him away."

Bill said, "Wait! I want..."

Dell touched Bill's arm and said, "Let's hear what Hamdi has to say."

The man was dragged out of the room yelling curses until a soft thud was heard and then he was silent.

Hamdi said, "If you will allow, the community will deal with this man. He's not a terrorist but has let his life slip into the gutter in the last few years. His wife and children were killed in a car accident while he was out of town on business. The Mosque buried the children and wife in accordance with Islam and he was not able to attend." Hamdi opened his palms out in an expression of prayer. "I blame myself for his downfall. I was too busy to take the proper care of my friend. He fell in with bad people but he is only a drug user and a drunk."

Dell said, "We are wasting time, Hamdi. Tell us what you found out. I will try to make arrangements for this man to be handled by you if the information is good. I want you..."

Bill put his hand on Dell's arm and then stepped up to Hamdi. In Arabic he said, "He is yours if his words are true. If you lead us astray my wrath will be terrible."

Hamdi looked into Bill's eyes and saw tears. He knew they were tears of rage but even more, tears of love for his lady. "On my honor I tell you the truth, *White Snake*. You and *Desert Rider* are my friends. And we have all grown to love Fatima and Sami." He chuckled and said, "We're also a little afraid of your captain. If you do not return the dog to him, we're afraid he will destroy our area."

Dell asked, "Is that why you are helping us?"

"I tell you the truth... Come, my friends. Follow me."

Hamdi led Bill and Dell into the open restaurant and it was filled with the Arab people from the community. William sat among them calmly drinking his tea. Hamdi said, "*Desert Rider* has asked me why we are helping and I wish for all to hear my answer."

Hamdi was a showman who enjoyed controlling a crowd. It was one of the reasons he was so successful. Another reason was his honesty. He spoke now not with a showman's voice but that of a patriot.

"Most of you in this room are *True Believers* and many have come to this country from places that would not allow us freedom. Our families have lived in fear for years but we came here and found the fear was gone.

"Yes, I am an Arab and proud of my heritage. I tell you something else. I am an American! I will fight for this country that has allowed me to work and make a good place for my family. I will stand against any who would try to kill this country I love. Even with all its problems, my life here doesn't compare to the terrible life I had before I came."

Hamdi talked for twenty minutes and then the Arab men in the restaurant all pledged their loyalty to the great country that allowed them to live in freedom. Hamdi took Dell, Bill and William back to his office and gave them all the information that Habdhi, his friend, had given him. "We had to make a show to protect him. Will you allow me to handle this in my own way?"

William said, "You are placing yourself in great danger, Hamdi. We will honor your request and help you when the time comes."

Chapter 36

The three men met Loretta back at Dell's apartment. Bill's frenzy was returning. He could smell Fatima's aroma and saw her things and he began to pace. Knowing he must not lose it, he found ways to occupy his mind. He thought of the desert and the girl at the spring.

Loretta said, "The threat is out. Every agency that has an interest is involved but all responses come through my people. We can't let this get out of hand or... the boy and girl will be put in more danger." She looked at Dell, imploring him not to tell William about her children. Then she said, "I have a helicopter standing by to take us to the airport and then we'll go to the warehouse Hamdi told you about. I want to keep this as quiet as possible. Do you agree, William?"

"You're the boss, Loretta. If we locate them I will have to make a report but I'll make sure you're in charge."

"Thank you."

As they left the apartment, Dell held Loretta back for a moment. He took her in his arms and kissed her.

They flew into a small air strip just outside Springfield, Missouri. A team was already scouring the empty warehouse and had hot readings of something radioactive that had been there only a short time before.

Dell went through a stack of burnt cargo tags. One read TOMMY'S MOVING, INC.—IF YOU HAVEN'T PLAYED IN—the rest of the tag was too damaged to read. He sat in a chair trying not to let his despair take over. Dell felt the pull of the void. Welcoming it, he eased himself into the mist and saw a giant automobile standing vertically in the ground. Four small people stood on top of the vehicle. A bright light slammed him back to reality.

Dell ran and gathered William, Loretta and Bill and said, "The bomb's in Peoria! And so are the kids!"

Loretta was on her phone ordering a new flight plan as they moved out of the building to the waiting black SUV.

Dell made a call to Commissioner O'Hara to give him the location of the building in Peoria. Dell said, "I think I'm going to need backup on this, Pat. There's going to be way too many people there that don't know me."

"I'll be there in two hours and I'm bringing Maddog Teasdale along. Nobody will get in his way. I won't give him his gun 'til it's needed."

"Thanks, Pat."

William's and Loretta's phones chimed at the same time. Loretta checked her message and said, "There was a momentary hit on a radiation detector just off I-74 in... Peoria, Illinois." She looked at Dell and asked, "Do you know where the bomb is?"

"It's in the CAR building but I don't have an address. All I know is that it's in Peoria."

William had a Google map up on his phone and he said, "The CAR building is at 15023 West War Memorial Drive. It's only three blocks from I-74. If they detonate the bomb, vehicles will drag the particles in every direction." He sent out a text giving the location.

Bill finally started paying attention, and with a fevered look he said, "Dell, is Fatima there?"

"Fatima, Sami and two other hostages are there." He could see the frantic look on Bill's face and asked, "Bill, do you trust me?"

"With my life."

"With Fatima's life?"

Bill gave Dell a hard look but finally answered, "Yes."

"Then give me your weapon." He watched Bill's face turn red. "I promise to give it back when the time comes. You have to trust me on this." Bill shook his head no and crossed his arms. Dell said, "It will help Fatima."

Taking a deep breath and holding it until he felt himself calming, Bill handed his weapon to Dell. "Don't let anything happen to Fatima."

"You cover my back and I'll take care of the rest." Dell said. He knew when he returned Bill's gun and unleashed him no one could or would stand in his way. But he had to wait for the right time to turn him and Maddog Teasdale loose. Dell smiled at the thought.

Chapter 37

The team took up a position on the second floor of the CAR building. It was the weekend and the building was empty. There were five Fire Teams hidden just across the street and two teams that only answered to William were in the CAR building with them. There were no lights or sirens as they prepared for the assault. One team of techs was in the operations room set up in the CAR building.

The techs had their scanners set up and the agent in charge of reconnaissance, Agent Kilmore said, "Loretta, there are only twelve people in the building. Four on the twenty-eighth floor in the northwest corner, two in the lobby, and one underground, but I can't get an exact fix on that one. The other five are on the top floor on the south side of the building."

Loretta looked at William and he said, "The plans show new construction. Three more levels have been added below the basement. According to the records, they have added a vault area for the Zenton International Bank. The bank is an Israeli company but that's top secret info. Its headquarters is in Vienna. Public records show it's owned by a consortium out of Liechtenstein.

"The only access to the lower basement area, for now, is a maintenance elevator. The vault is installed but not operational. The floor won't be ready for use for at least three more weeks."

Commissioner O'Hara asked, "Why would only one person be in the basement? Do you think they will set the bomb off there?"

William said, "It would be quite foolish to detonate the bomb there. It would be all but contained except for possible minor leakage. Perhaps it is someone monitoring the surrounding area. We have jammed all external transmissions. They can communicate inside the building so they shouldn't suspect anything."

Bill had been pacing back and forth paying little attention to what was going on around him. He knew that there was a massive team ready to storm the building and secure the dirty bomb, but his only concern was for Fatima. Was she in the building? Were Sami and Haji with her? Was she hurt? He finally exploded, "Who gives a flying fuck about some asshole in the basement? Where is Fatima?"

Captain Teasdale yelled, "And where is Haji? Somebody's going to die if they hurt that dog!" He turned to O'Hara and said, "Give me my damn gun back!"

"Not yet, Phil. Soon, very soon." Pat said patting him on the back.

Dell knew his time had come and he welcomed it, but he had to make sure Sami would be looked after. His dark aura kept everyone but Bill away. He gathered Bill, Captain Teasdale and Commissioner O'Hara and led them into an adjacent room.

"We're going to get those kids and Haji back, but I need your help." He looked from one to the other.

Bill exhaled and said, "I'm sorry, Dell. You know when I say Fatima I mean Sami too."

"Yeah, I know, buddy. I..."

"If they hurt Haji I'm going to cut somebody's balls off!" Captain Teasdale had a wild look in his eyes. He was almost out of control.

Dell slapped him across the face and said, "Teasdale! Get your shit together. I need you in on this."

Captain Teasdale's eyes cleared and he looked around. "Who... who just hit me? Sharpton! You're under arrest!" Then he looked at Dell and said, "I... I mean... Oh shit, Dell. I'm sorry. That dog is like a son to me... Okay. What do you need?"

"Here's the thing. I need some time to see what's going on—we've got to have a plan. Keep everyone away from me for a few minutes. It's the only way we're going to save those kids and Haji if they're up there. Otherwise, the Feds are going to rush in and kill anything they see. So help me. Will you do that?" He handed Bill's pistol back to him and O'Hara handed Teasdale a rifle and his pistol.

Bill and the captain charged into the operations room. Bill yelled, "Nobody leaves this place until we say so!"

Captain Teasdale said, "I'll bust a cap in the first person that tries to interfere. We're not going anywhere until Lieutenant Anders gives the word." He hefted his assault rifle to show he was serious.

Bill looked at him and asked, "Lieutenant...? I'm only a sergeant."

"Not any more. I just promoted you." Teasdale looked over at Commissioner O'Hara and said, "You got a problem with that, Pat?"

"You crazy fucks. Hell, no, I don't have a problem." O'Hara pulled his pistol and moved to the exit. "Nobody leaves until the lieutenant says so."

William lifted his rifle, gave Bill a brilliant smile and said, "My most heartfelt congratulations, Lieutenant!" He leaned over to Loretta and whispered, "If you want your children back in one piece I would suggest you go along with this."

She turned to him and said, "How long have you known? Why are you doing this?"

"The NSA and Homeland Security teams have orders to kill everyone found in this building. Secrets, ma'am. You know about secrets, don't you?"

Loretta said, "Everyone stand down. Kilmore, continue monitoring." She picked up the microphone and said, "We're on hold for..." She looked at Bill and he flashed his hand twice. "We're on hold for ten minutes."

Through her earpiece Loretta heard, "Who is giving this command?"

"Team Leader, Commander Smithe."

"Aye aye, Commander."

Dell had tucked himself in the far corner of the room and heard none of what went on. His visions in the mist had returned when he learned that Sami and Fatima had been taken and that the officers trying to rescue them had been killed. Now it leaped at him and he was deep in the darkness.

The wraiths sped to him, swirling the mist in their wake. Raised arms with jagged spiked fingertips were poised to rip Dell to shreds. Dell turned his eyes on them and they froze while the mist enveloped the scene. Death and torment had come to the undead. They fled.

Dell looked out over the expanse of the desert and it called him home. He wanted so badly to rush to it, but something held him back. A new scene came to him. Four people strapped to chairs were poised at a broken pane of glass. Dell could only see sky beyond the opening. Three armed men stood behind the subdued group. For the first time, Dell could hear their voices.

"Why are we to kill these children?"

"Our leader has said it will be so. Why do you worry? We will all die when the bomb goes off. We will not throw them out unless we have to delay the attack from the Americans."

"But to push them out the window...? I want no part of that. I do not wish to see the faces of dead children before I enter Paradise."

A man standing behind the terrorist who raised the objection brought his rifle up and fired a burst into the one complaining. He said, "Very well. No need to watch. These infidels and the Arab whore die in ten minutes and then the bomb will detonate ten minutes after."

The mist swirled and Dell was looking at Aisha. She was standing in a large room with a bank vault opened behind her. Haji was chained to a small table beside her. She looked around as if someone was watching her, then the mist boiled and she was gone from Dell's vision.

Dell shook his head and stood up. He rushed to Bill and said, "Com'on, Bill. Let's get our family back!" He yelled out, "William! A Fire Team of five on me now! Teasdale, Pat. Haji is in the basement but wait ten minutes before you go in. The leader of the cell is there with Haji. Kill her!"

In Dell's earpiece Loretta said, "Where are my children?"

"With mine. I'll get them. Hold everyone back. The bomb is set to detonate in twenty minutes. That will give us time to get the kids. Have a *bus* ready to get them out of the area."

"Be careful, Dell."

"It's been nice knowing you, Loretta." Dell tore the earpiece off and threw it to the floor.

At the lobby, Dell killed both terrorists with two shots and never slowed.

As they ran up the stairs he pulled Bill to him and said, "No matter what happens, I want you to promise to take care of Sami and tell him I... Tell him I love him."

"Fuck that! You tell him yourself!"

"Tell him, Bill."

"You've got nothing to worry about. I'll do it."

Dell said, "William. Fire Team to the twenty-eighth floor. Four bad guys—one down. Four hostages. They're going to throw the hostages out the window. Don't let that happen.

"When we hit the sixteenth floor have someone start an elevator to the top floor. I'll be going alone to the top."

Dell looked over at William and said, "Get the kids out of here. Don't approach the top floor. I'll take care of that alone."

William gave him a thumbs up.

"Like hell you will," said Bill. "You don't go anywhere without me." Bill looked at William and said, "Don't you let anything happen to my family!"

"On my life, Bill!"

As they ran up the stairs and passed the sixteenth floor William gave the order to start the elevator.

Dell slowed at the twenty-seventh floor and walked up to the final floor. He allowed William and the Fire Team to move ahead. He said, "Go with them, Bill. Make sure our family is safe."

"I trust William. I'm with you."

"Bill. There's no way to live through this. One of us needs to be here for Fatima and Sami. Besides, you have a marriage to attend."

"Whoes?"

"Yours, dumbass!"

"Oh... Well, I ain't going without my Best Man. I'll get us out of this alive. I always do."

Dell and Bill followed the Fire Team in just as they opened up on the terrorists. It was over in three seconds. Bill searched the room and saw Fatima twist in her restraints and look at him. He gave her a small wave but was gone the next instant, following Dell to the top floor.

Chapter 38

Dell went through the stairway door first and a burst of automatic fire took him in the leg and upper right chest. He went down but continued firing at the muzzle flashes.

Bill opened up with his automatic rifle, spraying anything moving. When the smoke and the dust cleared, five men were down. One of the terrorists was crawling towards a large object by a bank of windows. Bill walked over, grabbed the man by the collar and said, "How do you disarm that thing?"

The man reached for his shirt pocket and said in a blood-bubbling voice, "Allah Akbar."

Bill blew the front of his face off and took the device from the man's shirt pocket. "I bet this won't do it." He looked around for Dell and saw him lying on the floor.

"Dell? Get up, Dell. It's all over." Dell's leg twitched and Bill ran to him.

Dell was lying in a pool of blood and coughing weakly.

"Oh, crap. You're not supposed to get shot."

Dell rolled over and whispered, "Defuse the bomb. Green wire."

"Defuse the bomb? Who, me? I can't do this alone!" Bill grabbed Dell by the collar and dragged him to the large device that reminded Bill of the Leaning Tower of Pisa. He dropped Dell who let out a groan.

Bill looked at the thing and all he could think was, "It's all Greek to me... It's all Greek to me." One of his dad's favorite sayings when things went wrong. He was pretty sure it meant "Oh, shit!"

A steel ball about the size of a basketball sat on top of a metal lattice tower. The whole structure was leaning towards the window. There were wires all over the thing except on the steel ball at the top. He saw at least ten green wires and they all ran to a timer that was counting down. He had about eight minutes to figure out how to disarm the thing.

Bill squatted down in front of the bomb and looked at the structure. He knew he couldn't figure out the wires but he was good at mechanical things. A large square container sat on the floor with a latticework of steel rising up at an angle three feet in the air supporting a steel ball on top. In the center of the steel supports there was a gleaming steel rod about one inch in diameter. The sharpened end of the rod was pointed up at a small depression in the steel ball. The ball was two halves bolted together with a crescent moon and morning star painted in green on it.

Bill looked at the timer—seven minutes and ten seconds was displayed. He said, "Oh, shit." Bill looked back at Dell, hoping he might be of some assistance, but Dell was bleeding and unconscious. "You're never around when I need you." Bill stood, wrapped his arms around the steel ball and lifted. It came off the stand and hit the floor with a loud clank. "Oh, shit!

That thing must weigh three hundred pounds. What do I do, Dell?"

Bill could see that the tower structure along with a small metal container came off with the ball. When it hit the floor, another LED attached to the tower lit up. It read five minutes in the indicator but it wasn't counting down. There was one green wire attached to it so Bill yanked it out of the small box. The timer started counting down. "This is not good."

Bill looked around with a wild gaze thinking he might roll it out the window but the large window panes were all sealed. His eyes landed on the elevator in the southwest corner. The door stood open. Without thinking, because thinking wouldn't do him any good, he began to roll the ball towards the elevator. The good news was the ball was perfectly weighted so the extended tower stayed parallel to the floor and it rolled easily. The bad news was it wouldn't fit through the elevator door.

He quickly had it at the door but then remembered Dell. Bill ran, grabbed Dell by the shirt collar and pulled him into the elevator. He then tilted the ball until the tower fit inside and he pulled the heavy object into the elevator with them. He pushed the BASEMENT button and the doors closed.

"William, can hear me? The damn bomb is going off in about five minutes. I've got the steel ball with me heading for the basement."

In his ear, William said, "What steel ball?"

Bill yelled, "The fucking dirty part of the bomb! I think it's got its own damn bomb. Get everyone out of the building—especially Fatima!"

"Your beautiful lady and the others are on their way out of the area. I have a full squad guarding them. Do you need any help? And Bill, do you know what you are doing?"

"Just get everyone out of the building. I've got this under control!" Bill thought, *I've got this under control. What a fucking joke! At least Fatima and Sami are safe.*

Kilmore said, "Uh, Willy. That elevator doesn't go to the bottom level. It only goes to the first level of the basement.

He has to get off in the lobby and go to the east end of the alcove to the maintenance elevator. I can stop the elevator he's in and open the maintenance elevator doors and send him down to B4, but that's where the terrorist leader, Captain Teasdale and Commissioner O'Hara are. Do you think that's a good idea?"

"Have you heard from O'Hara or Teasdale?"

"No. When they went down I heard Captain Teasdale yelling about too much noise in his bad ear. I think they both took off their earpieces."

"Bloody idiots! Do it. Stop the lift at the lobby. I'll bring Bill up to speed."

William said, "Bill, we have a minor setback. The lift you're in doesn't go to the lower basement..."

"Lift...? What the fuck is a lift?"

"Bill... mate. The elevator doesn't go to the lower basement. We're going to stop you in the lobby, actually. You'll have to transport the device to the east side of the alcove and enter the maintenance elevator. We'll send you down as soon as you're aboard."

"Speak fucking American!"

William said, "Listen, dipshit. When the elevator stops, take the fucking bomb out and turn..."

He looked and Kilmore said, "Left! Tell him to go left for twenty yards!"

"Go to your left and get on the elevator with the doors open. You got that, butthead?"

"That's better."

William asked Kilmore, "When will he be in the lobby?"

"About twenty more seconds."

"Bill, does the bomb have a timer?"

"I wish you'd quit calling this fucking steel ball a bomb."

"Does the fucking steel ball have a timer on it?"

"Yes. It's counting down."

"Bill. Stop fucking about! How much time?"

"One minute forty-five seconds. And listen, William. Sorry about being rude. I'm a little stressed right now."

"No problem, dear. Just move as quick as you can."

"Oh. One other thing. I've got Dell with me and he's been shot a couple of times and bleeding."

"You stupid twit! Why didn't you say so? We can send EMS. Just leave him in the... Hold one."

Kilmore said, "Sir, we pulled everyone back five minutes ago. We can't get EMS in there for at least fifteen minutes."

"Bloody, hell! Bill, you're going to have to take Dell with you. If the bomb goes off on the top floor the ceiling in the lobby will most certainly fall."

"Don't worry, William. Dell wouldn't want to miss the excitement."

"Hurry, Bill, and God Speed."

Five seconds later the elevator doors opened in the lobby. Bill tossed Dell out and he skidded across the floor with another groan. Bill lifted the tower, dragged the bomb out into the lobby, looked around and gave it a big heave towards the open elevator door at the end of the alcove. He then grabbed Dell and raced after the ball. Dell left a blood smear in his wake.

Bill threw Dell into the elevator, dragged the ball inside and the doors closed.

Dell groaned, "Why don't you just shoot me instead of beating the crap out of me?"

"Bite me. You're the one that got me into this! And I pulled the fucking green wire and guess what! It started the damn timer thingy. The one time in your life you needed to be right and you blew it!"

Dell looked at the steel ball with the time counting down. It read one minute, fifteen seconds. "Sorry, buddy. Why didn't you leave me on the top floor?"

"Because there's a bigger fucking bomb up there and it's counting down too. Ah, shit, Dell. Don't mind me. I'm a little flustered right now."

"What's the plan?"

Bill started laughing and had to take a big breath to stop. "Plan...? You tell me."

Dell said, "Oh, shit."

"You got that right, buddy!"

Just before the elevator reached the fourth level of the basement Bill glanced at the timer. Thirty-five seconds. "This is gonna be ugly. I'm not sure if this was such a good idea."

The doors opened. Bill tossed Dell out again. As he pulled the bomb out, Bill took a round in the left shoulder. He went to his knees, pulled his pistol, turned and saw Phil Teasdale holding a rifle aimed at him."

"You shot me... you dumb fuck!"

"Oh shit. I'm sorry, Bill... Ow!" Haji had taken a bite out of Teasdale's leg. "I didn't mean to shoot him, Haji. Honest."

As Bill looked around for an answer he muttered, "Everybody wants to shoot ole Bill." He saw the opened vault door and gave the ball a heavy shove and then he yelled, "Help me shut that fucking door!"

Commissioner O'Hara had been sitting in a chair nursing a bullet wound to his right leg during all of this. He had taken the round when Teasdale and he had burst out of the elevator. Aisha opened up on them but Haji had leaped, ran under her long dress and took a bite out of her crotch. Her screams were cut off as Phil and Pat opened up on her. She was dead before she hit the floor and Haji was barking with excitement.

Pat leaped up, limped towards the vault door and said, "Move your ass, Colin," Phil Teasdale's secret first name.

Dell and Bill said, "Colin...?"

Bill's shove had been perfect. The steel ball with the tower attached wobbled slightly but rolled neatly into the vault room.

As Bill, Pat and *Colin* pushed the door closed, Teasdale said, "Repeat my first name and I'll kill you."

Bill said, "I believe you, Phil. You've already shot me just for coming in the room."

The door whispered closed. Bill spun the wheel and he could hear electrical whirling as the mechanics inside the door finished the locking sequence.

There was a soft thud and a slight vibration in the floor, then silence. Bill said, "That's it? A little thud? I busted my ass and got shot," he looked over at Phil Teasdale with a withering glare, "all for a little thud. Fuck me."

Dell sat up and said, "That little thud would have killed a lot of people and Peoria would have become a dead zone for the next thousand years. You did it, Bill!"

The entire building shook as the bomb on the top floor went off. Small debris and dust rained down on the four men and the lights went out. About twenty seconds later the emergency lights turned on. Bill smiled and said, "Now that's more like it. That was a bomb!"

Dell smiled and said, "Buddy. You are amazing."

"Yes, I am."

Commissioner O'Hara had the good sense to strap on a first aid kit before he left the Command Center. He used scissors to cut away Dell's shirt. Dell's vest had taken most of the energy from the bullet that went into his chest but his leg had a nasty through-and-through.

While Pat attended to Dell, Bill cut away Pat's pants leg where he had been shot by Aisha. The bullet didn't exit but it hadn't hit an artery.

Captain Teasdale was busy releasing Haji and trying to explain to him that shooting Bill had been a complete accident. Haji raced to Bill and then Dell, excitedly licking them, and then he ran back to Phil and leaped into his arms.

Bill's shoulder wound was minor and Pat patched him up while they waited for help.

An hour later they heard banging and cutting on top of the elevator. They all took positions and readied for another fight. The building didn't collapse but was heavily damaged.

William yelled out, "I'll ask you not to shoot your rescuers. All of the antagonists are deceased and only the authorities are interposing themselves into the situation."

Bill looked over at Dell who said, "The bad guys are dead and the good guys are here to help."

"I should shoot that idiot for not speaking American. Com'on in, William, and talk so I can understand you."

A Fire Team with William in the lead rushed into the room and took up positions. William walked over to the armed group and smiled. "Where is the nuclear device?" He saw the angry look on Bill's face and then said, "Where's the bomb, Bill?"

Bill pointed at the closed vault.

"Did it go off?"

Dell said, "Inside the vault. I guess the bank's going to have to figure something else out. They won't be using that vault any time soon."

"Jolly good! I believe our friends in Mossad will be most happy to let us handle all the details."

Dell asked, "What about my family?"

"They are completely safe. I had a team of my men whisk them away to a secure location."

Bill asked, "What do you mean your men?"

"That will be a discussion for another time. Your family and Loretta's children are out of reach of anyone who might wish them harm. Loretta is now with them as well. She sends her heartfelt thanks to you both. Now, we must get you four out of here and attended to.

Assessing Bill's new wound William asked, "My poor Bill. Who shot you this time?"

"It doesn't really matter. Just get me, Dell and Pat fixed up and on our way." Bill gave Teasdale another withering look and then smiled. "Give me a hand, Phil."

As he helped Bill to a gurney Teasdale said, "You know you'll still have to call me Captain when we're on the job."

William said, "These men will take it from here. You're on your way home."

Bill said, "Home? Don't you need us to make a statement or maybe pick up a medal or something?"

"Believe me, Bill. It would be much too hard to explain why New Jersey's finest are in Peoria, Illinois. You would be kept here for days explaining. Never fear. You will all receive the recognition you so rightly deserve in the coming days." He took Bill's hand and said, "Fatima awaits your return."

Chapter 39

On the flight back to Trenton Bill hardly slept. He was keyed up about all the events that had taken place but even more at seeing Fatima and telling her his true feelings and asking her to marry him. He still couldn't understand why she had chosen him, but he knew she had and that she loved him.

Dell received medical attention on the flight but refused to go to the hospital. He wasn't going to miss reuniting with his family. While Bill threw him around the building, he decided that if he got out alive, he would put all his efforts into making Sami and Fatima happy. He chuckled softly as he watched that crazy Bill talking to himself about how he would ask Fatima to marry him. He started to ask one of the medics to give Bill a tranquilizer but changed his mind. He wanted Bill alert.

Dell and Bill looked like walking wounded as they moved down the hallway that led to the room where Fatima, Sami, Loretta and her children waited. Dell glanced over at Bill and smiled. Bill's face was as red as a tomato, his breath shallow and his steps jerky. "What's the matter, Bill?"

"I think I'm having a heart attack. I can't breathe and I can feel my heart trying to jump outta my chest. It must be the painkillers they gave me. I need to throw up."

"After all we've just been through you're having a panic attack about seeing Fatima?"

"Panic attack...? I ain't having no fucking panic attack! This is real."

Dell could see the wild look in Bill's eyes and laughed. He opened the door and shoved Bill inside and quickly closed the door behind him.

Bill stumbled into the room and stared back at all the people looking at him. Fatima was there with deep concern masking her features. Bill spun and ran straight into the closed door with a bam! He fell back to the floor, jumped up, spun to the facing crowd and stuttered, "What the fuck? Fuck me! What about me getting married?" Then he fainted.

Dell opened the door just as Fatima and Sami rushed to Bill's side. "Oh, crap."

Sami saw Dell and flew into his arms. Fatima said in Arabic, "What have you done to Hakim? I have never heard him speak these crude words before. What did he mean he's getting married?"

Loretta was laughing so hard she had to sit down. Her children huddled around her wondering what was happening. She looked at Dell and said, "Oh, Lucy. You got some *splaining* to do."

Fatima spun on her and said, "Who is Lucy? Is that the woman that will marry my Bill? I shall kill her!"

Loretta came to Fatima, wrapped her arms around her, and as she pulled her to the corner of the room she whispered in her ear and smoothed her hair.

Dell kicked Bill and he sat up holding his head. "What happened?"

Dell said, "Get up... and don't say a word."

"What did I just say to Fatima?" Dell told him and Bill looked at him wild-eyed and said, "I did not...! Did I?" Dell just nodded his head and Bill said, "Oh, shit."

Dell said, "Not another word, dipstick. Loretta is fixing it for you. Sit down."

After a few minutes, Fatima walked over and stood in front of Bill. "Is it true you wish to marry this Lucy?"

"Who the f..."

Fatima slapped his face and said, "I will hear no more of these terrible words from your mouth."

Bill shook his head as if coming out of a daze. "I'm sorry, Fatima. I don't know anyone named Lucy and I want to..." Bill sat Fatima down in the chair. He kneeled down and looked her directly in the eyes and said, "I want to marry you, Fatima Al Zayed. I have loved you since the first time I met you. I didn't know it then, but I've known it for a while and when you were kidnapped I almost went crazy. I love you, Fatima. Will you be my wife? And I promise never to talk like that again."

Fatima said, "I know now that you did love me, even when I was forced to disguise myself. I don't understand how you could love an ugly girl like me, but I know you do. I love you, Bill Anders." She switched to Arabic. "You are the heat of the desert to my body and cool waters to my soul. I am yours and will always be so." And in English she said, "Yes. I will marry you, Bill Anders." She kissed him softly and then remembered all the people watching. She turned her head in embarrassment.

Bill stood and turned to Sami and Dell.

He said, "I am late in asking, my brothers, but I hope you will understand the love I have for your sister. I ask both of you for permission to have Fatima as my wife."

Dell put his hand on Sami's shoulder and said, "You tell him, Son."

Sami said, "I am no longer Mr. Dell's brother and nor is Fatima his sister." Bill looked from one to the other, not understanding. Sami continued, "I want to introduce Fatima's and my father. Father has adopted us and we are now his children."

Bill said, "That's great! Congratulations..."

Sami held up his hand and said, "My Father has agreed that I should make judgment over your request." Sami smiled up at Bill. "From this day forward I shall call you Brother, because you will be the husband to my sister. My father and I are very pleased. We shall speak of the bride-price later."

Something had snapped in Dell's mind. He knew it when he held Fatima and Sami in his arms. The mist was gone and he would never again enter it. He felt the pull of responsibility, family and deep down the desert. He wondered if he could have all three, but no matter his choices, Sami was his and he would do everything in his power to help his son become a great man. Dell looked over at Fatima and Bill and knew their lives were set.

Dell spent several hours with Loretta and her children, Sam and Kiri. They were wonderful children and he knew Loretta had kept them hidden to protect them. Her love was plain to see.

Loretta took him to a private room and leaped into his arms, kissing him hard. "As soon as this is over I'm quitting the Agency. I'm through hiding my children. I've seen the change in you just by having those two kids around you. I think it's something I need."

Loretta asked, "Do you remember the promise I made to you after we first met?"

"You mean the one about banging me silly after the job was done?"

Loretta laughed and pressed her body to him. "That's the one. Will you still let me try?"

"I thought we already did that."

"Honey, that was just the tip of the volcano." She kissed him again and then pulled back to look at Dell. "I do want to see more of you and I'd like my children to get to know you and your new family. How about it?"

"I'd like that... but the banging silly part might have to wait 'til I recuperate. This is the first time I've been shot and it hurts."

"Gentle is my middle name."

"That'll be a side I'd like to see. Say, do you like the desert?"

Loretta said, "I've spent a lot of time in the heat. Where do you think I learned to speak the language so well? At night school? If you're asking us to take a trip, the answer is yes!"

"Us?"

"My children and yours go with us. Hell, we can even take Bill if we can unwrap him from that beauty he's going to marry."

Dell said with a laugh, "Hey, that's my daughter you're talking about. I don't think it will be a problem getting Bill to the desert again... except we have to keep him away from Israel. He's a popular guy over there."

"You must tell me what went on while you were there."

"All in good time, sweetheart."

Chapter 40

William and Loretta went after all the Americans involved in the conspiracy. Derik Bartholomew's body was never recovered but he was given a State burial. All the conspirators were dead—either by the terrorists or Executive Order. All but Senator Ottilie Weber. She had been the joker in the deck of cards. Ottilie had supplied enough information to keep anything but depleted uranium from reaching the terrorists. The yellow-cake Uranium 238 was the wildcard that no one could control.

The cleanup would take several years after the CAR building was taken down a piece at a time. Life in Peoria would go on without the general public suspecting anything.

Commissioner O'Hara petitioned the great state of New Jersey to make Haji an honorary State Trooper. Captain Phil Teasdale changed Haji's name to Snapper—in honor of his perfect bite out of terrorism. Snapper goes everywhere with Phil.

Fatima fell back on the rumpled, sweat covered sheets and said with an excited wiggle, "Let's do that again, *White Snake!*"

The End

Other Books by author Dannie C Hill:

Tyler Hill's Decision
In Search of a Soul
Outer World Prairie

COMING SOON

Desperate Straits

I would like to thank you for reading Death's Door. I hope you enjoyed this story.

Readers are the life blood of a writer and I strive in all I write to bring you good, well written, well edited tales.

Please tell me what you think of my writing at my website, http://danniehill.wordpress.com and be sure to write a review at the site where you purchased this book.

Your words are so important to me and they inspire me to continue writing!

Thank you,

Dannie C Hill